PEACH

'Ah Natasha. Did Monsieur Fauçon prove less enthusiastic in the cold light of morning then?'

'No,' I admitted, 'far from it. He's crazy about me. He wants me to move in.' Percy's eyebrows rose.

'I see very well,' he answered. 'So, what is to be done with you?' I shrugged. He stepped towards me, reaching out to take me firmly by the ear.

'Ow! Percy! Okay, but no bruises, please . . . he's really jealous. He said I was to tell you that you can't spank me anymore.'

'Oh he did, did he?'

It was hopeless. He was really hurting my ear and I didn't even try to get away as he pulled me towards some bushes. I was still begging him not to beat me, but I wasn't going to stop him if he did.

Why not visit Penny's website at
www.pennybirch.com

By the same author:

THE INDIGNITIES OF ISABELLE
(writing as Cruella)
PENNY IN HARNESS
A TASTE OF AMBER
BAD PENNY
BRAT
IN FOR A PENNY
PLAYTHING
TIGHT WHITE COTTON
TIE AND TEASE
PENNY PIECES
TEMPER TANTRUMS
REGIME
DIRTY LAUNDRY
UNIFORM DOLL
NURSE'S ORDERS

PEACH

Penny Birch

Nexus

This book is a work of fiction.
In real life, make sure you practise safe sex.

First published in 2003 by
Nexus
Thames Wharf Studios
Rainville Road
London W6 9HA

Copyright © Penny Birch 2003

The right of Penny Birch to be identified as the Author of
this Work has been asserted by her in accordance with the
Copyright, Designs and Patents Act 1988.

www.nexus-books.co.uk

Typeset by TW Typesetting, Plymouth, Devon

Printed and bound by
Clays Ltd, St Ives PLC

ISBN 0 352 33790 7

*All characters in this publication are fictitious and any
resemblance to real persons, living or dead, is purely
coincidental.*

This book is sold subject to the condition that it shall not,
by way of trade or otherwise, be lent, resold, hired out or
otherwise circulated without the publisher's prior written
consent in any form of binding or cover other than that in
which it is published and without a similar condition
including this condition being imposed on the subsequent
purchaser.

One

I had to have it, or I was going to pop.

'Oh come on, Percy, just a spanking. Please?'

'There will be ample time in the hotel this evening, Natasha my dear, and it will be a great deal more comfortable, or in your case perhaps I should say, less uncomfortable.'

'Very funny. Oh right, in the hotel, with half a dozen Frenchmen earwigging through the walls?'

He just chuckled, wobbling slightly, and changed gear. Clearly the idea of making sure other people heard me getting my spanking amused him immensely. It turned me on too, making me more resentful than ever, and more urgent.

I'd been that way since leaving the ferry at St Malo, an urge triggered by the tiniest thing. A girl on the quay had been waving as we drove out, jumping up and down in her excitement at greeting some friend or relative on the boat. She'd been in a short, light skirt, and just for an instant it had ridden up, providing a brief glimpse of white panties stretched taut over a muscular little bottom. We'd both seen, and Percy had given his dirty little chuckle. I knew what he'd wanted to do to her. What he did to me on a regular basis, tip her over, lift her skirt, pull down her little white panties and smack her bare bottom for her.

By the time we'd got to Rennes I'd been itching for a spanking. I didn't want to have to ask, and I wanted to deserve it, otherwise it wouldn't have felt right. So I'd started to tease him, about his weight. He'd just laughed, so I'd switched to his ridiculous car, a huge old three-and-a-half litre Rover from before I was born, which needed to have the oil and water checked every hundred miles or so. He had failed to react.

The trouble was, he knew me too well, and that the longer he held off the better it would be, for him. He was right too, adding still further to my consternation. I sulked for a bit, then gave up as we came onto the quieter roads south of Châteaubriant. The remark about the hotel really was the final straw. I could just imagine it, the quiet, country hotel, the couple who ran it, who were sure to have that rather formal and old fashioned propriety so common in rural France.

Eyebrows would be raised and knowing looks exchanged at the disparity between Percy's age and mine. That I could cope with, and nothing would be said. What I wasn't at all sure I could cope with was getting a spanking later, a spanking that was sure to be overheard. I'd howl, I always do, and even if Percy stuffed my panties in my mouth there would be the slap of his hand on my flesh. Again, nothing would be said, but they'd know.

That was the problem. They'd know, and that was what would bring my pleasure up to a whole new level. When I came it would be truly glorious, but that would not dilute my embarrassment and resentment one little bit, they'd be real, very real.

In the back of the car, parked by the road, it wouldn't be so bad. I'd still get that delicious shame, from having my bum laid bare for spanking where some stranger might see me, if only a glimpse as they

2

sped past. A glimpse would be enough, just the knowledge that not only was I submitting to a bare bottom spanking across a dirty old man's knee, but that somebody else had seen me getting it.

The difference was that in the car that would be that. I'd get the orgasm I so badly needed, and there would be no repercussions. Well, unless by some hideous piece of bad luck the police came past or we got reported. In the hotel it would be different. I'd have to spend two whole weeks among people who knew I got regular spankings. In fact, that was more or less sure to happen anyway. The chances of me not getting one in the hotel room across that period were close to zero.

It was impossible not to think about it. The looks of tight-lipped disapproval or little smirks from the hotelier and his wife, and from the other guests, the sidelong glances, the whispered comments, my bottom, nude and rosy over Percy's lap as I was spanked up to ecstasy. They might not even know I enjoyed it. They might think it was real discipline, me nothing more than a snivelling little brat being given a well-deserved punishment by her sugar daddy, kicking and squalling across his lap with my bare bum stuck in the air. That way it didn't matter who heard. Why should the brat's feelings matter? She was being punished, spanked, kept in line the way she deserved, the way I deserved . . .

'Percy Ottershaw, if you don't stop the car and spank me in the next minute, I shall . . . I shall . . .'

'We happen to be going through a village, my dear.'

'Well, after the bloody village then!'

He just chuckled, that same infuriating little noise. I closed my eyes and let my breath out, trying to fight down my anger and frustration. It was no good

3

begging. He wasn't going to do it. He would make me wait, and the more I begged, the more he'd enjoy it. There was no use in flirting either. A young man would have lost control, stopped, and at the very least given me a good, hard fucking across the seat. Not Percy.

My eyes came open as we began to accelerate once more. The road stretched ahead, arrow straight, bordered by dense wood. We passed a sign, showing 11 K to what was presumably the next village. I had to do it, or I'd burst.

My white summer dress came up, providing easy access to my panties. They were soaking, the cotton plastered tight over my pussy, my lips bulging out, eager to be touched. Percy likes me in plain white panties, a size or two too small. I usually oblige, and I've come to like it, to think of them as spanking panties. I began to stroke, teasing myself as I focussed on the awful humiliation of taking punishment, of being stripped for it . . .

'Natasha, what are you doing?'

'Masturbating, shut up.'

'My dear girl . . .'

'What are you going to do about it? Spank my bottom? Good. Do it by the road. Let everyone see . . . take my panties down for me . . . spread me open behind . . . show them all my pussy . . .'

'Natasha, I am driving a motor car.'

'Then stop, and give me what I need.'

'Natasha, I . . .'

'No? Then keep your dirty eyes on the road while I come.'

I felt our speed pick up a little more and realised he wasn't going to stop. Possibly he was even a bit cross with me, but I didn't care. It never lasts, at least not beyond the point I start to cry. So I ignored him,

4

concentrating on my fantasy as I slid my hand down the front of my panties to seek out the moist, eager flesh of my pussy. I felt very sensitive, my clitty a hot point, close to pain. I began to dab, gently, sure I had enough time.

I was really going to get it now, with a vengeance. It would be more than just an erotic spanking. There would be real provocation behind the slaps. Maybe he'd use a hairbrush, or his belt, to really make me kick, to really make me howl. Maybe he'd reduce me to tears, to a snivelling, squalling mess across his knee, my dress high, my panties at half-mast ...

No, my panties pulled off and stuffed in my mouth to shut me up, half hanging out, my face red and streaked with tears ... my hair flying as my head jerked in my helpless response to the smacks ... my boobs swinging free in my loose dress ... my bottom bouncing crazily ... my bumhole on show, winking to my pain ...

I came, with a little cry as my body went tight in orgasm. It had been so quick. I hadn't even reached the point of imagining the people listening in on my punishment, which was what I had expected to come over. It didn't matter. I'd done it, taken the edge off my need and provided Percy with a prime excuse to give me a really good walloping once we reached the Loire Valley and Rochefort.

It took another hour, Percy driving embarrassingly slowly as always, and stopping in Challones to check the oil and water, again. Beyond there it was a brief and very beautiful drive, along an escarpment over-looking the great, wide plain of the Loire and past vineyards with the leaves already rich with colour and the grapes golden and heavy with *Botrytis*.

Percy had cheered up, and was absolutely beaming by the time we reached the hotel in Rochefort. The idea of the trip was to watch the late vintage come in and write reports back to our respective magazines. My editor had suggested I actually help with the picking and *triage*, but that was going to have to be faked. Anything so strenuous was well beyond the call of duty. Tasting was a different matter.

Percy, as always, had all the contacts we needed, and had agreed to meet a grower, M. Moreau, at the hotel. I'd imagined a man of Percy's generation, sixty plus, probably with a nicotine-stained moustache and half a Gauloise hanging from his lip. He had the Gauloise, but was no more than thirty-five, smart, intense and an inch shorter than me. It didn't surprise me when Percy enquired after his father.

If M. Moreau was not as I'd expected him, then the hoteliers, the Sinsons, fitted my preconceptions to a T. Both were small, he plump and moustached, she thin and severe. Both had exactly that air of propriety I had expected, her in spades.

Fantasy is all very well, but actually meeting people and knowing that Percy really would spank me and really would enjoy it if they knew was something else again. I found myself blushing with each new person I was introduced to, and by the time we'd settled down to dinner I was feeling very nervous indeed. The other guests were all French, a couple of businessmen, a tiny round woman who obviously knew the Sinsons, and an old man whose eyes began to follow me around the room as soon as we entered.

It was all so proper, so much that typically French blend of formality and friendliness, that the idea of them hearing me spanked seemed not just embarrassing and incongruous, but outrageous. I was even wondering whether to beg off and take a sterner punishment at a more appropriate time, when Alain

Moreau provided something to take my mind off it. With a discreet nod he indicated the old man who had been eyeing me up, and whispered a single word.

'Fauçon.'

Percy responded.

'The artist?'

Alain nodded. I took another glance at the man, now astonished. It was a bit like being told I was in the same room as Adolf Hitler. Well, maybe not Hitler, but somebody associated with an age long before I was born. I'd done a term of History of Art alongside my degree, and could remember Fauçon as the *enfant terrible* of 'fifties Paris. It made sense though, on reflection. If he'd been in his twenties then, he'd only be in his seventies now, so it wasn't really so astonishing at all. It still seemed strange, and I couldn't help glancing over towards him as we ate.

He was tall, or at least moderately so, and slim, with a somewhat military character that seemed out of keeping with his reputation for Bohemian excess. Even his features failed to hint at dissipation, although the wispy grey beard beneath his chin was all I might have imagined. There was a severity about him too, suggesting a man very much aware of himself as above the common ruck, regardless of the opinion of others. Okay, so he had been ogling me, and my boobs in particular, but men do. Most are guilty about it. He wasn't. He would have made a great spanker.

Alain Moreau was a good host, ordering wines from his own estate and others as if cost were irrelevant, and repeatedly stressing that we were to make free with his land and facilities while we were there. It made sense, as he doubtless wanted good write-ups, and he nevertheless seemed entirely genuine. He was also more than a little deferential towards

7

Percy, presumably as an old friend of his father's. That left me free to concentrate on the wine and food, my surroundings, and my feelings, which had begun to mellow with alcohol.

The whole journey seemed to have gone by in a flash. It seemed only moments ago that Percy had been puffing his way to orgasm as I knelt for him in my flat. The drive to Portsmouth, the ferry, the longer drive south through France, might have taken minutes rather than hours. It still seemed a long way, oddly, and my surroundings very different, also my situation.

Here there were none of the social problems of London. I could admit to going out with a man old enough to be my father, my grandfather almost. There might be the odd disapproving glance, the occasional whispered comment, but it didn't matter. It didn't even matter if they knew I got spanked, not really. In fact it was for the best. It would keep me on edge, keep up that delicious feeling of naughtiness I've come to love so well.

I knew it was the drink making me bold, but that didn't stop it happening. By the time we were sipping glasses of Calvados I was feeling very rude indeed, and also submissive. My attitude to the other people had changed. Madame Sinson, who had seemed so off-putting, now seemed the perfect disapproving matron. It was easy to imaging her thinking it was a real punishment as the slaps of Percy's hand rang out around the hotel. I could just see her nodding to herself in self-righteous approval as she listened to my squeals and pathetic entreaties for it to stop.

Her husband would be different, assuming that I was naïve but that Percy knew exactly what he was doing. In his mind, as I snivelled and kicked my way through what he fondly imagined was discipline,

Percy would be enjoying my body. It would end with a stiff cock being pushed at my tear-streaked face for sucking, to my shock and bewilderment. By then M. Sinson would have come in his hand.

So would the two French businessmen, each in his room, masturbating in gloating approval of my humiliating fate. Even the little fat woman would enjoy it, listening in complacent satisfaction to what I was getting, and wishing it was her dishing it out. Then there was Fauçon. He would love it.

I glanced towards him, hoping to catch him admiring my boobs. He wasn't, but he was staring at me, and to my astonishment I realised that he had a tear glistening in one eye. I looked away, puzzled and embarrassed by what seemed a very peculiar reaction indeed. He had caught my glance, and my emotions grew sharply stronger as I realised he was rising from his chair.

He came towards us, slowly, but without hesitation. Obviously he was going to introduce himself, and all I could do was look up and smile as he reached our table. His first action was to acknowledge Alain Moreau with a formal nod, then Percy. He turned to me.

'You must excuse me, M'selle. I must see . . .'

He had taken hold of my chin, firmly, between finger and thumb, which even drunk seemed a liberty. I managed an inarticulate grunt of protest as my head was tilted up, quite sharply, then to the side, but he had let go before I could do anything more definite. Only then did I speak, as surprised as angry.

'Do you mind?'

He ignored me, and Percy, who had half stood from his chair, and shook his head.

'*Extraordinaire.*'

He took a seat, not awaiting for an invitation, and began to speak again.

'You will excuse my behaviour, M'selle, gentlemen. I am not myself. I shall explain. I am a neighbour of Monsieur Moreau, Phillippe Fauçon. Perhaps you know something of me?'

He had turned to Percy, who responded cautiously.

'Yes. You have something of a reputation as an artist, although I confess that I am not particularly familiar with your work.'

'Nor should you be, unless you were a man of exceptional taste and an utter indifference to the dictates of fashion.'

Percy coloured slightly and was going to say something, but Fauçon went on.

'No, little attention is paid to my work, nor was I ever celebrated, save for the wrong reasons. But what do critics know? They are as plastic as wax, never one with an original idea in his head. No, for renown, I am a man out of my time. But this is to the side.'

He reached out for a glass, one of those I'd been using, and filled it with Calvados. For a moment he admired the rich green-brown colour, before taking a reflective sip, which gave Alain Moreau a chance to speak.

'Monsieur Fauçon . . .'

Fauçon raised a hand and Alain stopped, then made a gesture of helpless apology to Percy and I. Percy responded with a nod of understanding, apparently now amused by the behaviour of the elderly and obvious drunken artist. Fauçon continued.

'It was my misfortunate to be born to a golden age, and to study in one of brutal and cowardly chauvinism. I refer to the art establishment of wartime Paris, a sorry thing indeed, save for we few . . .'

Again he trailed off to take a swallow of Calvados. This time nobody interrupted.

'I,' he went on, 'would not paint to suit the concepts of our conquerors, nor seek to capture the

10

stark misery of the time. No, I had no wish to be a mere child of the moment, but to seek beauty, as an absolute. This I did, for all their accusations of escapism and of indifference to the plight of France. Even my lover, my Helene, did not fully understand. She was beautiful, Helene, so full of life, of passion, her face never still. Never have I met a woman to surpass her. As a model, and as a lover, she was perfection . . . *La Pêche* they used to call her, on the stair.'

He stopped, took a huge swallow of Calvados and turned to me.

'You, M'selle, are Helene, reborn.'

Well, I've been fed some bullshit lines in my time, but this took the biscuit. It was in front of Percy too, which took amazing nerve, although he might well have thought Percy was my dad. It was quite amusing, nonetheless, and from the little mischievous smile on Percy's plump red features I could see he agreed. I was going to make some suitably arch remark when Fauçon went on.

'When I saw you, I thought the drink had taken me at last and that she had come to carry me to heaven.'

Again he took a gulp of Calvados, and as he did so, the tear broke free from the corner of his eye, to roll slowly down across his cheek. The way he drank, the idea that he was going to die of alcoholism seemed entirely reasonable, but his words still sparked a touch of sympathy in me. It was hard to know what to say, or to be sure if he wasn't just stringing me along, but he supplied the answer to the question in my head.

'She was too proud to live, Helene. She fought. The Germans took her.'

It was either the truth or the most callous of lies. Suddenly I felt a bitch for wanting to tease him. He

11

swallowed the last of the Calvados and started to rise, excusing himself. Before I really knew what I was doing I had lifted my hand, to gently push down on his arm.

'No, don't go. Join us. Do have another Calvados.'

He made a wry face and sat back down, immediately taking the bottle to pour himself a shot yet more generous than the first. Percy filled his own glass immediately, and shot me a questioning look even as he poured. There was a moment of awkward silence before I managed to frame a question.

'Do you still work?'

'*Bien sûr*,' he answered, suddenly cheerful. 'The day I cease to work is the day I die.'

'Do you exhibit much?' Percy put in.

'No. Although there is now a certain fashion for my work. Ironic, is it not, when I have been ignored for close on sixty years?'

'I suppose it is.'

'When I die, that is when my work, so long condemned, will miraculously become worthy of attention. Who will benefit? The dealers. My daughter, my grandsons, perhaps, as I have much that is left unsold. Not I. I will be dead. It will be soon.'

The idea didn't seem to trouble him very much, and I was still wondering if he was lying, and if so, whether the play for sympathy was intended to get into my knickers. He went on, his tone suddenly serious.

'As you may know, I rejected the premise that the advent of the camera renders realism in art obsolete. It is a narrow philosophy, a failure of understanding. As the great Emile Zola knew, art alone can capture the true essence of human reality, and that by observing and recording human behaviour, as it is, in reality. And yet it is the artist's task to seek deeper, to interpret for his lesser fellows that which they see. Photography is not art. Always I sought to capture that beyond the mere reflection of light, yet without losing the beauty of human perception. For me, no bizarre angles or impossible perspectives. Such things are nonsense, the product of frustration at the incompetence of those who think themselves artists but are not, can never be. We must reflect, record, reveal all, conceal nothing. For this I was called naïve, a romantic, a simpleton. After the war, with the focus of the world shifting from Paris to New York, my ideas became yet more unfashionable, to reach a nadir in the 'sixties and 'seventies, while those such as Warhol and Pollock, who have done more to trivialise art than advance it, were extolled as paragons. Now my star rises once more, and so the circle is complete. Thus is fate, and my last model is as my first, you, M'selle, who must be my Helene, *ma Pêche*.'

I seemed to have missed the section of the conversation in which I'd agreed to model for him, or even introduced myself for that matter. Okay, so the idea was intriguing, and his whole attitude played straight to the submissive in me, but it was really a bit much. At the very least I needed time to think, and to discuss it with Percy.

Fauçon stood, drained his Calvados and delved into his jacket. I was given a card, dog-eared and yellow with age, Percy and Alain were dismissed with a curt nod and he left. Alain immediately went into a babbled apology, but Percy simply laughed.

'Quite a character, old Fauçon! Well, my dear, do you intend to disrobe for the attentions of his brush?'

'I don't know. I might.'

'You should. Why not?'

'Don't you mind?'

13

'Not at all. I can see you want to, and I think it's fair to say that I have never tried to restrict you.'

'Well, no. Still, I'm not sure . . .'

'Just your sort, I'd have imagined.'

He winked and I felt the blood rise to my cheeks. He knew, of course, more or less what I'd been thinking, but perhaps not all of it. I smiled and lifted my glass to my lips, my imagination running at full tilt.

Fauçon had that severity, that confidence, which I adore. He would expect me to yield, and I would, revelling in my own submission. Yet there would be no ties, no consequences. When I wanted to go I would leave. Percy knew he could trust me, and he knew he could punish me.

It was all wonderfully intriguing, and as we said our goodbyes to Alain Moreau and made our way upstairs I was growing ever more excited. As we reached the landing I saw one of the businessmen go into the room beside ours. He was younger than Percy, but just about as meaty, and balding, with a patch of shiny skin reflecting the landing light at the centre of a circle of black, slicked down hair. He saw us, and bade us goodnight, his eyes glinting with lust and jealousy even as he smiled.

His door closed with a bang as Percy opened ours. The room was perfect, suiting my mood, dark, with a high ceiling and a yellow shade on the light, throwing the corners into gloomy shadow. It was also typically old-fashioned French, with a long bolster in place of pillows and a bidet plumbed in against the wall without so much as a screen for privacy.

As I lay back on the bed, all sorts of punishment fantasies were jostling for attention in my head. I wanted to be spanked, and I wanted the man next door to hear. I wanted worse too, to be thoroughly

14

humiliated. I knew I was drunk, but I didn't care anyway. I wanted them all to hear, all to know, as I was put through my paces. In fact I wanted them to join in, to take turns with me, each to take full advantage of my body. They could spank me, even take a cane to me. Once well beaten, they could use me, pushing their cocks into my mouth and up my pussy, up my bottom too, dragging my head in to make me lick pussy or suck on fat, salty balls.

Fortunately I had Percy, or I might have done something really stupid. He calmly locked the door and turned to look down on me, his fat red face beaming with delight. My thighs came up and open, offering myself in case he just wanted to pull off my panties and fuck me. The dress had ridden up, and I lifted my bottom to tug it higher, showing off my tummy and panty crotch, with the damp cotton tight to my sex. My thumbs went into my waistband, at either thigh, ready to pull down my knickers at a word.

Percy chuckled and shook his head, extending one podgy finger to indicate the bidet. I nodded and stood up from the bed, dizzy with drink, arousal and the most delicious sense of humiliation as I peeled my dress high over my head. I was bare underneath, something Fauçon and others had not missed during dinner, my boobs too large and my nipples too prominent to make concealment easy. Percy's tongue flicked out to wet his lips as his little piggy eyes travelled down over my chest and belly, to the soft bulge of my sex within the panties. Again I pushed my thumbs into the waistband, at once dreading and deeply expectant of what I might get.

I got it, a slow shake of his head. I nodded and swallowed. My hands had started to shake as I turned, to squat down over the bidet, stretching the panties tighter still across my bottom. Percy gave a complacent nod and sat down on the bed. I waited, watching as he tugged down his fly and pulled out his cock and balls. He was already half-stiff, his little pale cock rising above the fat bulge of his scrotum, and as I wiggled my bottom down onto the bidet, he began to masturbate. I knew what he wanted, but I waited for the order. It came.

'Wet your panties, properly.'

I understood, and I knew how much it would turn him on to watch me humiliate myself. I also knew he would not waste his orgasm. This was Percy, not some over-eager youngster. He would handle me as I needed to be handled.

My bladder was full, but I still had to concentrate, just because I had my panties on, just to break my toilet training. Not that it took long, and I sighed as the pee began to trickle out through my gusset, and spread my thighs wide to give Percy the best possible view. He began to tug harder, his eyes fixing to the little stream of pale yellow fluid running out through my panty crotch.

I knew exactly what he meant by wetting my panties properly, and let it out slowly, so that it would soak in at front and back. That way I got my bum soaked, and made the cotton see-through where it clung to my wet flesh. It was best that way, leaving me with thoroughly wet panties, and no question of what I'd done in them.

As I wet myself I focussed on Percy's cock, imagining how I would be made to suck on it and have it poked into my body, maybe even up my bottom hole. My mouth came open in the hope of having it filled, but he ignored me, tugging on his now stiff little shaft until the last dribble of pee had run out through my panties. At last he spoke.

16

'You may bend down now, my dear. Stick your bottom well up, if you would.'

I could only nod in dumb acquiescence as I began to get into the obscene position he had ordered. It meant going down on all fours, my lower body still over the bidet, my sodden panty seat stuck high in the air, my boobs swinging bare under my chest. Percy chuckled to see me in such a ridiculous position, and rose.

Still tugging at his erect cock, he walked over to our luggage. I swallowed hard, knowing that it meant I was to be beaten, not by hand, but with an implement. Two sharp clicks and the lid of his case was open, revealing the neatly stacked clothes within. I could only stare, wondering if it would be a belt, a hairbrush, or if he had packed something specifically for my discipline.

What came out was his clothes brush, a long flat oval of wood that might have been designed to be applied to naughty girls' bottoms. Certainly that was why Percy had chosen it, and I was no stranger to it. It stung like crazy, and on the seat of my wet panties, or the wet skin once they had been peeled down, it would be worse than ever.

As I hung my head in submission I groaned aloud, all my fantasies flooding back. The smacks would be noisy, and as I hadn't been gagged I was sure to howl. They would all know, every one of them, know that I was being spanked, being beaten, being punished. They would think they knew why too, that it was for flirting with Fauçon. Maybe they'd even tell him.

Fear and confusion filled my head as Percy came up beside me. It was sure to happen. He was going to beat me and they'd tell Phillippe Fauçon. Then if I did model for him it would be with my freshly bruised bum on show, as I was sure to be nude, beyond

17

question. He'd see, and he'd know, know that I got my bottom spanked.

I cried out in an ecstasy of shame even as Percy's hand settled on the small of my back, forcing me to lift my bottom and spread my cheeks inside my pee-soaked panties. My fear grew sharper still, and a muscle in one thigh began to twitch as the hard, flat surface of the brush tapped my bottom, full across my cheeks. It lifted away. Percy chuckled, and it came down again, hard.

My cry of pain and shock rang out in my ears even as I heard the smack of wood on bottom flesh, my own bottom flesh. It hurt so much, the pain at once sharp and dull, stinging and bruising. He didn't give me a chance to recover either, but laid in, sending me into a kicking, wriggling dance as smack after landed across my bottom and drops of my pee spattered out across my flesh and the floor. I howled too, and even in my pain the image of the businessman next door came into my head, listening in mingled jealousy and satisfaction to the unmistakable sound of a snotty little brat getting her bottom attended to.

It was too much for Percy. He stopped. I wasn't ready, and looked up, pleading with my eyes. He nodded and swung his leg around, to squat down and push his cock at my mouth. I took it in as he went back to his task, smacking the brush down across my bottom, one cheek at a time.

I didn't feel grateful or resentful for being gagged, but I was utterly humiliated by being made to suck the cock of the man who was beating me. It was perfect, a wonderful touch to my punishment. I was going to have to come, and was wondering if he'd find the energy to take his own orgasm in my mouth as he beat me and I masturbated, or whether I'd be subjected to some further humiliation first.

I'd begun to warm, and was lifting my bottom, wanting what had hurt so much just moments before. Percy paused, his thumb found the waistband of my panties and they were being peeled down, off my wet bottom, not all the way, but far enough to leave my rude little bottom hole peeping out from between my cheeks. Again the smacks started, and I began to suck harder, eager now for my mouthful of sperm, before I came myself.

My hand went back, to find the tangle of pee-soaked cotton around my pussy, then the wet, eager lips of my sex. It was awkward, the hard china digging into my arm, but I was determined to get there, and began to rub, and to fantasise. Percy realised, and began to spank me harder, puffing now as he belaboured my bottom and pushed his little hard cock in and out of my mouth.

They knew, they had to, that I was being spanked. The businessman would know, and Madame Sinson. Fauçon would find out, and he would make me show my smacked bottom when I stripped for him. He'd laugh at my perversion, and after that he'd have no compunction whatever of making full use of me. He'd make me suck cock, he'd fuck me, he'd have me up my bottom. Maybe he was dirtier still. Maybe he'd pee on me . . .

That was too much. The thought of being put on my knees, nude, with my smacked bottom stuck out behind and piddled over just took me over the edge. As I sucked furiously on Percy's cock I was wishing he'd do it then and there, in my mouth as he beat me, forcing me to swallow as the brush smacked merci-lessly down on my naked bottom, over and over.

It was so good, the smacks pure pleasure as my bottom bounced to their rhythm, my whole body tight in ecstasy, my mouth filled with my tormentor's penis as I came over my own utter degradation. Getting my mouth filled would have been the perfect finalé, but it was just too much for him, and as I began to go slowly limp, the spanking stopped and his cock was eased from my mouth.

He sat down heavily, puffing with exertion, his face crimson. I smiled my thanks, kissed him and stood up, turning to show off my bum as I peeled down my soggy panties and kicked them off into the bidet. He wasn't ready, so I squatted again and turned the thing on, to wash my pussy and bum, with everything on show to him. That got to him quickly enough, and when I reached back to tickle my bottom hole he stood with a grunt.

I rose even as he sat down on the bed, leaning back to leave his cock sticking up out of his trousers. I climbed on board, straddling him, bum to face, so that he could admire my spanked cheeks as I rode him. He took hold of my bottom as I guided him into my ready pussy, kneading my flesh and spreading my cheeks. I began to bounce, letting him do as he pleased, even when the ball of his thumb found my anus.

As I rode his cock I had my rear hole opened, slowly, his thumb going to his mouth for spit several times before popping my ring and slipping inside. That was nice, and I began to buck with more energy, wondering if he'd take the time to bugger me. I was willing, a cock up my bum a small price to pay for the pleasure he'd given me, and maybe even a route to another orgasm.

It was not to be. Percy grunted and filled me with sperm even as his thumb burrowed deeper up my bumhole, and that was that. At least, that was that for him. For me, there was simply too much going on in my head. As Percy washed I masturbated, and again when he had fallen asleep, each time my mind awash with fantasies of punishment and submission at his hands, and those of Phillippe Fauçon. By the time I finally began to drift towards sleep, I had determined to be his peach.

Two

The chance of playing out erotic fantasies was not my only reason for wanting to accept Fauçon's offer. There was another, and it was not something I could admit to Percy.

Looked at in the cold light of reality, Phillippe Fauçon was an elderly drunk. He was also an artist with an international reputation, albeit a somewhat soiled one. From what little I could remember from university, he had been an embarrassment to the art world his entire life, and was doubtless still considered an embarrassment. I could remember that he had been ostracised, first in Paris and then in London's Soho. I could also remember that the reasons had been more due to scandal than the artistic differences he stressed. What that scandal had been my lecturer had not said, leading to speculation among the students that it must have been something pretty juicy to get him thrown out of Bohemian society.

Once dead, and no seventy-year-old who drinks Calvados like water can expect to last all that long, he would no longer be an embarrassment, he would be a legend. There's nothing quite like death to render somebody respectable, when his bad habits can either be overlooked or painted as colourful eccentricity. Think of van Gogh, or Dali, both lauded, but neither of who would make good guests at a polite artistic dinner party.

As he had himself pointed out, after his death the price of his paintings would rise. By his own admission he had a large stock of the things, and it would be very surprising indeed if I couldn't persuade him to part with a few. Failing that, I could simply pinch some. Then, once he'd swallowed his last bottle of spirits, I would become part of the legend. I would be the great artist's last model. I would also be portrayed as his lover, and scandalously young, a piece of romantic nonsense that with any luck would help prices on their way up and leave me with a tidy sum. The whole business with the unfortunate Helene would just add to the glamour.

The scandal was intriguing too, for personal reasons. It was almost certainly sexual, and had to be pretty perverse. He'd been in a social set where homosexuality was acceptable while not only a strong taboo but illegal in general society. It had also been at a time when spanking a girl was considered a perfectly reasonable thing to do. That left a range of interesting possibilities, and if it did prove to be more than I could take, well, he wasn't exactly going to be making me do anything against my will.

All in all, it was irresistible.

The problem was Percy. Not that he minded if I spent my time getting roundly abused by Fauçon, so long as he got his share and could punish me for my bad behaviour. What he would mind was my little artistic scam, which he was sure to be very old-fashioned about. Rather than think of the paintings as a fair trade for my sexual favours, he would see it as simple theft, or at best taking advantage of an old man.

That meant I would have to keep whatever I took, or was given, firmly out of his way. Even if I just took

23

rolled up canvases, paintings are not the easiest things to conceal, certainly not in any worthwhile number. The only thing I could think of, lying in the dim green light of the hotel room in the morning, was to post them back to London individually, but that was going to look pretty suspicious. In any case, the first thing to do was establish myself as *La Pêche*.

I wasn't even sure if he would remember, let alone stick to his offer. For all I knew my resemblance to the long-dead Helene had been entirely a figment of his alcohol-fuelled imagination. I had the card though, and if I couldn't charm my way in, then I'd lost my touch.

Despite his comments on vivacity and passion, I was sure he was an old chauvinist at heart. So it seemed likely that he would appreciate innocence, naïvety, simplicity and that sort of thing in a woman, basically wanting a soppy moppet who would do as she was told and not make a fuss about stripping off or a little light sexual relief after the session. A touch of melancholy would add interest, and he would be hooked. I was sure I could keep up the act for as long as it would take.

So I went for girlish simplicity as my look, sandals and my lightest dress over plain white panties, also no bra. It looked right, although only a complete fool was going to think I was unaware of how much I was showing. Certainly Percy wasn't, and by the time I had finished dressing he was watching me with one eyebrow raised and a little quizzical smile. I had some bargaining to do.

'Quite beautiful, my dear,' he stated as I adjusted my hair in the mirror, 'but I somehow suspect that it is not entirely for my benefit.'

'No,' I admitted. 'I thought I'd take old Fauçon up on his offer. After all, it's not every day I get a chance to model for a living legend.'

'I am not sure that I would go quite so far as "living legend",' he answered, 'but yes, I see your point, and doubtless you appreciate his air of authority. Still, what of your work?'

'Well, I won't be modelling all the time, and anyway, you could make notes for me.'

He did the trick with his eyebrows again, only this time both of them.

'Pretty please, Percy? You can spank me as much as you like, even give me the cane.'

'No doubt.'

'Or anything else you like, anything.'

'Thank you, yet we both know that I would never dream of pushing you beyond your limits. Yours is the ultimate satisfaction, Natasha, either way.'

'Oh, come on, Percy, that's not playing fair. You know perfectly well that doesn't mean it hurts any less, or humiliates me any less!'

For a moment he continued to look serious, and I really thought I was pushing it too far. Then his face broke into smiles once more and he chuckled.

'Run along then, enjoy yourself. Meanwhile, I shall be thinking of something appropriate for your disgraceful behaviour.'

'Thanks, Percy, you're a sweetie.'

I kissed his nose and gave his cock and balls a squeeze through his trousers, but pulled away when his hand closed on my bottom. I wanted to arrive at Fauçon's fresh, and dry. If he got me bare he would see my bruises, inevitably, as my morning inspection of my bottom showed both cheeks blotchy with marks. That was fine. I was already considering how best to turn the fact that I got spanked to full advantage.

Breakfast was the inevitable combination of dry sections of baguette and sticky preserves in little

25

plastic pots, so I let Percy have mine and stuck to coffee. After a quick check of the ailing engine, we set off, back along the ridge road, the *Corniche Angevine*, as Alain Moreau had called it. Phillippe Fauçon's house was up a track, at the bottom of which Percy dropped me off.

The house was already in view, a great sprawling thing of crumbling yellow-grey stone, with white shutters, mostly closed. It was already warm, and very still, sultry, which suited my mood. Fauçon, I hoped, would be sensitive to such things, and I want my arrival to be something special. The track led between vineyards of mature, gnarled Chenin Blanc, each row with a rose bush at the end, deep, blood red at one side, white at the other. Ignoring the very unromantic fact that they were planted to attract aphids away from the vines, I made a selection, one of each colour, artlessly, all the while hoping I was being observed. I was, a movement in an upstairs window betraying a watcher, presumably Fauçon.

I walked on, unhurried, as if I didn't have a care in the world, making sure my dress floated nicely and caught across my breasts as I moved. The track ended at a pair of high stone posts, with the rusting remains of a gate pushed wide between them. I tripped gaily through, extending my hand even as the door swung open, with beautiful timing, so that he found himself faced with me, the two roses offered, blood red and virgin white.

'Choose,' I demanded.

Percy would have turned me over his knee, stripped my bum, stuck one rose stem up each of my holes and given me a thorough spanking for being an over-dramatic little flirt. Phillippe Fauçon fell for it completely.

His gaze lifted to mine, absolutely serious. I looked into his eyes, doing my all to project the emotions I had chosen to show for him. His hand came out, he hesitated, then took the red rose. I smiled.

'I will be your Peach, Monsieur Fauçon.'

He nodded wisely, although I was sure he had no idea of what my little piece of drama was supposed to represent. Nor did I for that matter.

It was a good entrance though, and had him absolutely bubbling with enthusiasm as he ushered me inside. I resisted the temptation of asking him to explain his choice, and followed him inside, into a great airy room, with furnishings even more old-fashioned than those in the hotel.

He called out, shouting for somebody called Madame Vaucopin to bring wine. A companion was not something I'd figured on, but from her name she evidently wasn't his wife, while his tone suggested she wasn't his daughter either. When she appeared he didn't bother to explain who I was or what I was doing, so it seemed likely that she was his house-keeper, but her presence still looked like being a bad thing. She was huge, not tall, but squat and solid, with massive red hands. I think she had been watching me approach, and the moment she saw me I was given a look of surly antagonism and serious disapproval, as if she'd caught me masturbating or something. I tried a girlish smile, but her look only hardened.

She didn't bother to speak, but she did leave a jug of wine on the table. Fauçon took two glasses down from a sideboard, fanciful things with green stems and a design of grapes and leaves, which Percy wouldn't have been seen dead using. He filled both, to the brim, evidently intent on starting his drinking early. I could hardly refuse, and took the one he offered me, sipping to find that it was the sweet, apple-scented Chenin for which the area is famous.

27

He indicated the stair and I followed, watching as he went up ahead of me. The night before he had seemed pretty decrepit, and at the least I'd expected him to be a bit hung over, but he was actually remarkably sprightly, certainly for his age. That didn't bode well for my wicked plan, which brought both disappointment and relief. It did bode well for the sexual possibilities, as did the length and apparent strength of his fingers as he gripped the banister. With hands like that it was going to be such a waste if I couldn't persuade him to smack my bottom for me.

We rose one flight, and a second, bringing us out into what was obviously his studio. It was huge, a converted attic cleverly designed to let the north light flood the central space, striking down on a dusty couch obviously intended for the model, for me.

The rest of the room was in shadow, but I could see enough to set my pulse racing. Barring the area set aside for paints and so forth, a sink, and the door itself, every single piece of wall was stacked with paintings. Most were still on their original frames, a few in display frames, a good many just rolled and tied. There was no order, smaller and larger works stacked any old how, sometimes several deep.

There had to be a couple of hundred, maybe more. All were either oils or pencil sketches, or all that I could see, most nudes or portraits, some landscapes, and painted with an attention to detail and realism out of vogue for well over a hundred years. He was good, that was plain at a glance, capturing not just form, but feeling, be it the sense of close heat in a Provençal street scene, or the cautious warmth of a young girl's smile as she began to disrobe.

The realisation that he was a genuinely skilled artist put a catch in my throat, of guilt. Allowing an elderly man a few moments of lust in exchange for rather more than he anticipated was one thing, but this was quite another. I could see now that his remarks in the hotel restaurant had been more than simple bombast. I'd assumed he was exaggerating, that he would be no more than a footnote in art history. If anything, it seemed likely that he had been understating the truth.

It might have made me guilty, but there was a great deal of avarice warring with that guilt. I'd been imagining examples of his work as selling for a few hundred, maybe a few thousand pounds. Now I could see that it might be a great deal more, and there were hundreds of them. If I could get away with ten or twelve I could not only make a serious sum, but carve myself a place as a celebrated artistic *demimondaine*, that, or end up in jail.

If he parted with them willingly it would be better still.

He'd been talking as we climbed the stairs, in rapid French full of colloquialisms I hadn't really been able to take in, so had ignored. On opening the door he had gone silent, waiting for my reaction.

I'd been play-acting before, trying to establish myself as the capricious innocent no more than half aware of her effect on men, and had been displaying emotion only by choice. Now my reactions were genuine, and as I managed to get control of myself I was hoping he'd mistaken them for simple awe, which certainly played a part.

Silence was best. Words of praise would simply sound hollow, and could never do justice to his work or the atmosphere of the place. To have started making technical remarks would have been worse. There was only one thing I could think of to do.

I swallowed my wine and put the glass to one side. I was still holding the white rose, and I let it drop from my fingers, to the floor, where I crushed it beneath my sandal. He smiled, clearly delighted and amused by my little girlish drama, and his smile grew broader still as I kicked off first one sandal, then the other.

Now it was his turn to stare. My dress was loose at the neck, so loose that it could be shrugged off with a simple, elegant motion, one reason I had chosen it. I let it fall, watching him all the while. He tried to play it cool, studying me with the detached, mild pleasure of the experienced man watching a woman strip for the thousandth time. It didn't work. As the dress slipped down over my breasts his Adam's apple bobbed in his throat, and when it reached the floor his hands had begun to shake.

I stepped clear of the dress, leaving it a puddle of white cloth on the floor. A quick push, a wriggle, and my panties were down, then off, kicked back to join the dress. I stood, nude, placing my hands behind my head to stretch and accent my breasts. He watched, his eyes full of lust, maybe hoping, maybe certain that my display was for more than just his artistic appreciation. At last he spoke.

'Stay just so.'

He went to where his easels and paints were, walking with surprisingly quick, nervous steps, and begun to prepare. It was not what I'd expected, far from it. I thought I'd made it pretty clear that I was open for sex. I had been ready for anything from being gently teased and cajoled up to readiness to being ordered onto my knees and having his cock stuck in my mouth. What I hadn't expected was for him to start painting me, but it was obviously what he wanted to do, and I began to wonder how much of his excitement was erotic and how much artistic.

My excitement was purely erotic, or at least ninety-nine per cent erotic. I'd wanted him to take full advantage of me, to thoroughly indulge himself at the expense of my supposed innocence. Standing stock still for however long it took him to do whatever he had decided to do might have been submissive, in a sense, but not the right sense.

I stayed anyway, holding my pose because to do anything else was clearly going to shatter the rapport I had built up so carefully, and so well. He seemed to take my acquiescence for granted anyway, never once addressing me as he began to work. He didn't comment on my smacked bottom either, which I'd been expecting to make plenty of, and he hadn't even asked my name. I wondered if he cared, or simply expected me to be *La Pêche*.

So I stood there, not even able to see what he was doing, except that it involved pencils, as my muscles began to stiffen. Modelling as such is not sexy. It's boring, as I had discovered in my one brief foray into being a life class model. The frisson of being naked wears off pretty quickly, and while it may lead to advances, they're not necessarily wanted. I prefer to make my own choices, and if I love to show off, that doesn't mean staying stock still until every muscle in my body feels as if it's on fire.

Fauçon must have known how I felt, physically, but he either didn't care, or was taking pleasure in making me hold such an awkward pose so long. I hoped the later, as it at least allowed me to take a masochistic enjoyment in it, to feel it was something being done to me as deliberate cruelty. I suspected it was the former.

It seemed to go on forever. Certainly it was long enough for the light to change, north face or no north face. Twice he broke off to take a swallow from his glass. Never once did he ask how I felt or so much as intimate how much longer he expected me to stand there. I was desperate to retain my poise, and the spell, but my body was complaining, and I was on the point of giving in when he finally gave a satisfied nod and stood back.

I took the gesture as assent for me to move. That hurt more than standing still, and I sank down on the couch, all my efforts at maintaining my image forgotten in the pain of my body. He ignored me, admiring his pencil sketch with one hand pulling at his beard, then nodded once more, reached down, and quite casually pulled his cock out of his trousers.

Again, it was not what I'd expected. What I had expected was seduction, flattery, at least to be asked. My mind rebelled, for a moment, but it was just too much my thing, and I also knew that surrender was the only sensible course. So my mouth came open, and in went his cock.

He was already half stiff, and quite long, bigger and thicker than Percy. He was uncircumcised too, the fat, rounded head glossy with fluid even before he pushed it between my lips. It left my jaw wide, and he tasted strong, making me gag for an instant before I got enough spittle to his flesh. I'd have sucked willingly enough, but even that degree of control was to be denied me. He kept hold, his eyes rolled up, and he was mumbling to himself as he masturbated into my mouth.

I was basically being used as a toy for his masturbation, all my efforts at creating a sensitive, romantic image brushed aside in his need for orgasm. It was impossible not to feel resentful, but it had my sense of submission boiling up in my head so fast that in no time I was beginning to feel the need to masturbate myself, as I was used. It would be over being used too.

He didn't give me a chance. However detached he had seemed, my body had obviously been affecting him, because I'd no sooner begun to stroke my pussy than he began to groan. His masturbation became abruptly faster, his cock jerked, he grabbed hold of the back of my head, and my mouth was filled with salty, slimy sperm. I was forced to swallow, and gagged again, even as he finished himself off with a quick flurry of jerks, each one banging his hand against my nose and lips.

Out he came, leaving me gasping for air with a trickle of sperm and my own spittle running down my chin. Percy would have rubbed me off, or stuck a finger up my bottom to add to my humiliation while I masturbated, or something. Not Phillippe Fauçon. He waited until I'd swallowed what was in my mouth, then stuck his cock back in, holding me by the head until I'd sucked him clean. That would have been enough, and I kept on playing with myself as he did it, but he pulled away long before I could get there.

A lot of men hate it when a girl takes affairs into her own hands. I didn't care. If he found the fact that I could come without relying on his cock demeaning, then that was his problem. I needed it too badly. It was in character anyway, the innocent, too naïve to do other than respond to her body's needs. If it wasn't, that was just tough.

His face did show a flicker of surprise as I spread my thighs open and pushed a finger up into my pussy, but that was all. Then he settled back to watch, his arms folded across his chest, his cock still hanging from his fly. I closed my eyes, content in the knowledge that I was being watched. For a moment I fingered myself, deep in the wet, ready cavity of my pussy, then applied myself to my clitty as I focussed on what he'd done.

It was so abusive, the way he'd just pulled out his cock and stuck it in my mouth, not asking, not giving so much as a questioning glance, but just assuming I'd be willing. He'd basically fucked my head, no, wanked in it, using me as a pretty toy to aid his masturbation, nothing more. It was right, the way to handle me, to make me feel not just horny, but dirty. Not many men can do it, almost no young men. Fauçon could, and it wasn't even as role-play. It was just the way he was.

I didn't want to hold back. I wanted to be natural, to be dirty, to show him what he'd done to me. My legs came further up, showing off my bumhole. My spare hand went down, and I was tickling the tiny, wrinkled ring, a blissful sensation, and so rude, with a man watching me do it. I was wet, with my own pussy juice, and as I pushed my finger slid in, the little firm muscle giving way, opening, to let me into the hot, slimy interior.

The man who had just used me was watching me finger my bottom as I masturbated. My mouth still tasted of his sperm, most of which was in my stomach, or dribbling down over my chin and between my boobs. That was enough, more than enough, and as my back arched in orgasm I was thinking of how it had felt to have that fat, round cock head just pushed crudely into my open mouth.

I wriggled about as I came, holding it to get the sensation of my bumhole pulsing on the finger inside as my thoughts slipped to how it would have felt to have his fat cock shoved up my bottom with the same lack of ceremony. I knew he would more likely have fucked me, and that would have been good too, but up my bum was dirtier, and dirty was how I felt.

Only when I'd come right down did I open my eyes. Fauçon was standing as before, just putting his cock away. As he saw that I was watching he gave a thoughtful nod, as if confirming to himself something he had already suspected.

34

'You are Helene indeed,' he said. 'Wine?'

'She liked to play with herself then?'

'Yes. She had the same passion, the same need to answer to her body, when and how that need came. Watching you then, you might have been her, nearly sixty years gone.'

That was a happy coincidence, although I wondered how big a part nostalgia played in his memory. Then again, if the memory was accurate, it had some interesting implications. I had to know.

'Helene then . . . she liked to touch her bottom?'

'No,' he admitted, to my immediate disappointment. 'Her attention was always to *la chat*.'

I went to the sink as he poured wine, to wash and splash water into my face. I still felt a little stiff, and took a moment to stretch and touch my toes. That also gave him a prime display of my smacked bottom, although he could hardly have failed to notice while I was posing. I'd wanted to make an issue of it, either to make it clear that I was up for being spanked, or to draw some sympathy for supposed severe treatment from Percy, as circumstances dictated. I still wanted it noticed, so I stayed nude, collecting my glass and walking over to look at the pencil sketch he had made of me.

It was certainly skilled, and if my pose was pretty pornographic I was sure he would be vigorous in his defence of capturing reality and in denouncing any prudish restrictions on his art. There was no question of it being a simple, contrived pose either. He had captured the way I was making an erotic display of myself perfectly, although I couldn't pretend to understand how. I even thought to detect a hint of deliberate artfulness in my pose, but told myself that was merely my guilty conscience.

He was watching me, with an open admiration that was more than sexual, and by which it was impossible not to be flattered. A part of it, no doubt, was simple appreciation of life, and another in my resemblance to the long gone Helene. Yet it was still good to be appreciated, and I made no effort whatever at concealment as I crossed to him and settled myself on the arm of the couch. He reached out his hand, to trace the curve of my waist and hip, his fingers momentarily touching a bruise.

'In you,' he stated, 'there is no dissemblance, no artificiality, your emotion is raw for the world to see.'

I wondered if he really thought that was true, or was simply playing to my character. He had undoubtedly seen a lot of life, but then, older, confident men often prefer to take their assessment of things as clear truth, without troubling to look deeper. As they say, there is no fool like an old fool. I smiled at his remark but said nothing, sipping my wine.

His hand went back to my skin, this time moving gently across the bulge of my bottom where I was sat down, full on bruised flesh. It was impossible to imagine him being indifferent to the fact that I'd been beaten, and he didn't seem the sort not to mention it for the sake of tact either. When the comment finally came, it was not what I had expected at all, and a light laugh preceded it.

'You English girls. Always with your *derrières* uppermost.'

He had me down pat on that one, although it was hardly fair to suggest that all English girls get spanked, or like it. It had taken me ages to get what I wanted. It showed a fair bit of understanding too, as he'd obviously worked out at least something of what went on between Percy and I, and why. It was clearly useless to pretend I got it against my will, so it seemed like the time for a straight question, or at least, moderately straight.

'Will you spank me?'

'Yes, I think so.'

It was impossible not to let my mouth curve up into a satisfied smile. He'd said it so well, as if it were entirely his choice, something he might or might not impose on me, at his will. He was still stroking my bottom, and I would have been more than happy to be taken down across his knee and given another roasting, bruises or no bruises. He didn't, but went on.

'But you are to be mine, and mine alone. Understand this. The fat man, what is he to you?'

So he was jealous. I hate jealous men, but it was only to be expected. After all, stern and kinky and liberal about other partners is a pretty rare combination. It was time to lie.

'Percy? He is a colleague . . . well, a little more. We are both wine writers, and he spanks me yes, but no more. It is something we share, a mutual need, just that.'

'From now on, I will take care of your needs. You must tell him this.'

I nodded, accepting what was a pretty extraordinary piece of arrogance, or at least pretending to. There was no way I was giving up playing with Percy, even for a couple of weeks. Besides that, it had occurred to me that I might need longer. He stood, still talking as he walked over to the easel.

'Bring what you have up this afternoon. The rest you must have sent, what you need.'

It was as simple as that. I was moving in with him. Obviously I didn't get much say in the matter, while the rest of my life could go to Hell on the grounds of being totally unimportant next to his needs. For a moment I considered putting up a bit of a fight, perhaps showing a little temper, only to abandon the idea. I may get into tantrums occasionally, but artificial ones are just too much like hard work, unless I get spanked at the end. I wasn't at all sure if that would be his response.

So I accepted, abandoning everything for him with a single nod of my head. If he thought that strange he didn't show it, and continued to inspect his work as I dressed. He didn't seem to expect anything else, or be about to offer me lunch, so I left, getting another scowl from Madame Vaucopin as I went.

It had been pleasantly cool in the studio. Outside it was baking. I wanted to get to the hotel for some sunblock and my Raybans, but I was pretty sure he would be watching me, and made my way down the track slowly, pausing occasionally to look back at the house.

I had no intention of going back to him immediately. Everything looked good, but I needed time to think. It was a bit much to take in so quickly as well, for all that he seemed to regard my coming to him as some sort of natural phenomenon. For a start Percy had been assuming I'd just be modelling occasionally, and was not going to be happy about our relationship changing abruptly from an open partnership to occasional moments of secretive and hurried sex. It was bad enough in London, and I knew he got pretty fed up with my keeping him a secret from almost all my friends. Our trips to France were the only opportunity of being open about our relationship, and he valued them a great deal. So did I, but I'd made my decision about Fauçon and was going to go through with it.

I couldn't tell Percy the truth. He was just too honest. He had already guessed I wanted sex and discipline from Fauçon as well, which was after all pretty obvious. So I'd have to lie and do my best to make it up to Percy when I could. I had to speak to him anyway, and the sooner the better. He would be at the Moreaus', hopefully having lunch rather than out in the vineyards, so I made a brief visit to the hotel to pick up what I needed and the address, and set off.

The house proved to be in the Layon Valley itself, less than a mile down the hillside from Fauçon's, by the river in a grove of mature poplars. The first person I saw was Percy, his ample backside showing beneath the hem of the jacket he wore despite the heat as he bent into the boot of the car. Nobody else was visible, and I steeled myself for the confrontation.

'Hi, Percy.'

He extracted himself from the boot, coming up holding the baby Stilton he had bought as a present for the Moreaus.

'Ah Natasha. Did Monsieur Fauçon prove less enthusiastic in the cold light of morning then?'

'No,' I admitted, 'far from it. He's crazy about me. He wants me to move in.'

Percy's eyebrows rose.

'I'm going to. For a bit. Not long. You see . . .'

'I see very well,' he answered. 'So, what is to be done with you?'

I shrugged. He put the Stilton down and stepped towards me, reaching out to take me firmly by the ear.

'Ow! Percy! No, not here! Someone will see!'

'Unlikely. All are at the winery, save Madame Moreau, who is preparing lunch.'

'Yes, but . . . Ow! Percy! Okay, but no bruises, please . . . he's really jealous. He said I was to tell you that you can't spank me anymore.'

'Oh he did, did he?'

It was hopeless. He was really hurting my ear as he pulled me towards some bushes, but I knew I deserved it. I didn't even try to get away, and let myself be dragged in and out of sight of the house. I was still begging him not to beat me, but I wasn't going to stop him if he did.

He let go of my ear as we reached a little bare patch beneath one of the trees. We were concealed, just about, but it was open enough to get me seriously nervous as I was taken by the scruff of my neck and bent down. Realising I was going to do as I was told, he stood back. I took hold of my ankles, shivering as I waited for exposure and punishment. My dress was going to be pulled up, my panties dropped and a stick applied to my bottom, hard. Worse, somebody might see it being done.

Nothing happened. I look round, to meet his eyes. He was staring thoughtfully at me, his mouth pursed, then moving into a wicked half-smile. He was tormenting me, making me wait with my fear and shame raging in my head. I was surprised he hadn't pulled my knickers down first, but it was more than I wanted to take anyway.

'Just do it, you bastard!'

'Very well.'

He squatted down, to push his hand into the damp black soil beneath the carpet of leaves we were standing on. As he lifted his handful, I realised what he was going to do. I was to be made to eat dirt.

'No, Percy! That's not fair. No, not that . . . Don't you dare, I . . .'

My little speech broke off in a muffled grunt as my mouth filled with wet, black soil and decaying leaves. I'd kept it open, my guilt and my sexuality betraying me, and he'd taken full advantage.

It tasted revolting, rotten and acrid. It was gritty too. I tried to spit it out, but he was ready for that, and had taken me firmly by the scruff of my neck, while his hand stayed pressed to my mouth. All I could do was make pathetic noises of entreaty and shake my head, not prepared to really fight, but praying he wouldn't make me go through with it. No such luck.

'Swallow,' he demanded.

I shook my head harder still, a desperate plea for mercy.

'Swallow, Natasha.'

Again I shook my head, with frantic urgency. His grip tightened on my neck. His hand moved a little, his finger and thumb pinched together across my nose, hard. I heard my own despairing grunt as my airways were shut off. The pressure in my head started to build, immediately, and then I was doing it, swallowing down some of my foul mouthful. He chuckled and let go of my nose. Immediately I began to retch, and to sob as the utter humiliation of what was being done to me became overwhelming. He kept his hand in place, forcing me to swallow it down, a good, big handful of soil, of dirt.

I was near to panic, sure the muck was full of worms and woodlice and all sorts of horrible things. I took it down though, all of it, Percy holding me firmly until he was sure I'd eaten the lot. As he finally let go he chuckled.

'I always wanted to do that, but until now the opportunity has never presented itself.'

I couldn't speak, still bent double, and trying to spit bits of soil and leaf-mould out of my mouth. He passed me a handkerchief.

'Here we are. There is some on the tip of your nose and your left cheek. There, almost. Yes, that's it.'

I gave him a dirty look as I stood up, but that was all. I couldn't bring myself to be angry, despite what

41

he'd done. I'd deserved it, and even if I hadn't, we both knew full well the effect it had had on me. I couldn't do it then, not with my mouth still dirty inside, but I knew full well that before long I'd be masturbating over it.

Percy was smiling, thoroughly pleased with himself.

'Time for lunch then, I think. Nothing like disciplining one's brat to work up an appetite. Alain makes an excellent marc, by the way, which should take care of any bugs you might have swallowed.'

I followed him as he set off towards the house, struggling not to pout.

I felt I had been genuinely punished by Percy, and with punishment comes absolution. So I was feeling a great deal happier about what I was doing as we ate lunch with the Moreaus. Percy was also in a good mood, and there seem no point in dissembling, so we told the Moreaus that I was to be Phillippe Fauçon's model, and that I would be staying with him. Alain was impressed, and obviously considered it a great honour for me. His wife, Monique, took a more down to earth view, and made a of point of extending an open invitation to their house and the use of the woods behind Fauçon's house, which were their land.

Old Moreau was also there, a wizened man in stained *bleu de travail*, who alone seemed to have no respect for Fauçon. He was like him though, both in his indifference to social niceties and unashamed admiration of my chest. More interesting was Alain's younger sister, Marie-Armelle, a lively, plump girl with a blonde bob and a constant smile.

It was a good lunch too. There was a generous spread of salads, meats and pâtés, along with their own wines, all of it excellent. Marie-Armelle was particularly good fun, to the point where I was wondering if she was ripe for seduction. Alain seemed determined to impress Percy, and to a lesser extent me, and opened bottle after bottle. I got fairly drunk, and was enjoying myself far too much to worry about getting back to Fauçon's. After all, it wasn't as if he'd invited me to dinner or even asked me to come back at any specific time, and the worst he could do was spank me, which was just fine.

So I drank and talked and nibbled at the food and cautiously flirted with Marie-Armelle for most of the afternoon before retiring for black coffee. Alain wanted to show Percy a section of ancient walled vineyard with one-hundred-year-old Chenin vines, the Clos St Aubin. It was more or less on my way, so I went along with them, to admire the stubby black trunks, which were as thick as Percy's calves, and taste the rich, apple-sweet grapes from them.

We parted at the top of the vineyard where the ancient wall met their woods. It was late afternoon by them, still warm, the air absolutely still, with no sound but the drone of insects and the occasional bird call. I was drowsy with drink, hot, and very, very horny. Alain had carried my bags up the hill, but when I picked them up they seemed to weigh a ton. It was only about a quarter mile through the wood to Fauçon's house, but I really couldn't face it, or the effort it took associating with him.

I got about fifty yards into the wood before I sat down on one of my bags. It was a great place, huge oaks and chestnuts rising high above to create spaces of cool green light, with copses of lesser trees and areas of tangled undergrowth shielding them from view. The others had gone back down the hill, there was not the slightest sign of human presence, and I could think of no reason whatever not to treat myself to a long, slow rub of my pussy.

43

It was what I wanted, what I needed, and I was going to do it. So I chose an area of thin grass well concealed on all sides, just in case, and lay down, closing my eyes as I let my thoughts drift. Fauçon had handled me well, and it looked like he was going to handle me better still, spanking my bottom if and when he thought it appropriate. That's the best way to treat a spankable girl, and if I wanted it I could always play the brat, while if I didn't I only had to be good.

The idea filled me with a delicious sense of apprehension, and would have deserved an orgasm, only Percy had handled me better still, and done something I'd never had done to me before. I couldn't feel it, and it had left no marks, as requested, but I knew that the handful of dirt he'd made me eat was still in my tummy, and that knowledge was enough.

Then there was Marie-Armelle, with her rounded, cheeky bottom and fat breasts, so pretty, and just a little unsure of herself, which made her all the more appealing. It would be fun to think about playing together, although it was hard to imagine her dominating me, more the other way around. She was lovely, but she could wait. After what Percy had done to me I was firmly in a submissive mood. It would be the dirt eating I came over.

I sat up and took a last moment to listen. There was nothing, and I decided to add to my pleasure by going completely nude. A moment later and my dress was up over my head, my panties and sandals kicked aside and I'd done it. It felt wonderful, to be stark naked in the woods, stronger than it had done in front of Fauçon. He expected nudity. This was different, this was naughty.

My thighs were coming up and open even as I lay back. The grass tickled a little, but the ground was dry, unlike the ground down by the river, unlike the ground from which Percy had scooped a handful of soil to push into my reluctant mouth. It had been the perfect punishment for the occasion, painless, yet utterly humiliating. It brought back memories too, of awful threats at school, threats that had never been carried out, yet which had left their mark – threats of being made to eat dirt.

I took my breasts in hand, to squeeze them gently and run my fingers over the already hard nipples. It felt lovely, and I paused to play with them, just teasing myself to bring the need for orgasm to a still more urgent state. I'd arched my back too, to push my bottom against the ground, so that bits of grass and leaf were tickling in my bottom crease. A sigh escaped my lips as I gave a little, delighted wiggle. It felt so rude, so nice, and before long I was going to bring myself to the most wonderful orgasm, just as soon as I got the fantasy exactly right.

When he'd done it the whole experience had been too disgusting to be sexual. The memory was a very different matter, both vivid and intensely erotic. I could remember the mouldy, bitter taste of the soil, and the horrible texture, slimy and gritty at the same time. I could remember the shock of fear as it was pushed at my mouth, and the sharp stab of humiliation and disgust as it went in. Worst of all, best of all, I could remember the awful, overwhelming gush of emotions as my nose was held and I was forced to swallow.

I was writhing on the ground, gasping and shaking my head in an ecstasy too strong to be dealt with by simply playing with my boobs. My hands went lower, to my pussy, and I was masturbating urgently, all thoughts of taking my time forgotten. With my clitty burning beneath one finger and another pushed well up my pussy I played that awful feeling over and over in my head, thinking of myself eating dirt, swallowing dirt . . .

It was only a shame Percy hadn't done more, forcing me to my knees, stuffing handful after handful into my mouth, forcing me to swallow each, ignoring my pleas for mercy between mouthfuls and my gagging and retching as I struggled to swallow. He should have done. He should have made me eat until I could eat no more, until my stomach was packed with soil, until I was choking on it. Then he should have fucked me . . . no, buggered me, pushing his cock deep up the dirty little hole between my rear cheeks as I gagged and coughed on the dirt in my mouth.

I had to do it. My hand came out, grasping at the woodland floor to scoop up a handful of leaves and earth. The hand went to my mouth, held over it as I frigged harder and faster, feeling my orgasm rise, higher and tighter. My back arched tighter, my pussy began to spasm under my finger. I was coming, and as it hit me I packed my mouth with dirt, inflicting that same, awful humiliation on myself right at the moment of orgasm.

For one long, glorious moment it was exactly right, pure perfect ecstasy, with my mouth soiled and my whole body tight in climax. Then I was choking, unable to breathe for an instant, and coughing and spluttering as I jerked my head around to spit out my filthy mouthful, with my fingers still pushed firmly in between my pussy lips.

I rolled over to let it out, onto all fours, spitting and gasping, with dirty mucus running from my nose. It had been a stupid thing to do, when I had no way of cleaning up properly, but I'd needed it so I'd done it. Even as I wiped my mouth I was smiling.

It took a while to make myself presentable, and even then I badly needed water. Being on top of a hill, there wasn't going to be a stream or anything, so I made straight for Fauçon's house, hoping I could find an outside tap. I did, directly outside the kitchen, but as I was washing my face Madame Vaucopin appeared through a rear door. She didn't bother to speak, but made a single curt gesture to indicate that I should come inside. I might be prepared to put up with Fauçon, but I was damned if she was ordering me around, so I finished washing my mouth out before going in.

Fauçon was in the hallway, looking drunk and belligerent. For a moment I thought he wanted to punish me, and was wondering if I could take it, but he simply growled a question, demanding to know where I'd been. I resisted the temptation to tell him to fuck off, shrugged and followed Madame Vaucopin upstairs with my bags.

Three

I have no idea what time it was when Fauçon finally came upstairs. It was dark, and I'd been asleep for hours, in the huge four-poster bed Madame Vaucopin had told me I was sleeping in. It was his, of course, but the first thing I knew of his presence was waking to the slam of the door.

He climbed in beside me, and a moment later his hand had closed on my bottom, fumbling at my cheeks, then between, and muttering in French. It was hot, and I'd expected to be molested when he came to bed, so I'd pulled on a loose top and nothing more. I hadn't expected it to be in the middle of the night, but I was sleepy and in no mood to argue. So I let him fumble and listened to the fleshy tugging sounds of him bringing himself up to erection as he fondled my bottom.

Pretty soon he had slipped a finger into me, and he chuckled to himself as he found that I was sloppy and easy. He had been tickling my bumhole too, and with the finger still in me I pushed my bottom out, half in docile acceptance, half in need. He chuckled again and came closer, his erection sliding up into the groove between my bottom cheeks. I sighed but reached down, to pull my cheeks wide and put my pussy on offer. He was big, and if he wanted me up

48

my bottom he was going to have to open me up with something first, but I needn't have worried. He simply took hold of his cock, put it to my hole and pushed it up. It felt nice being filled, and this time my sigh was of pleasure rather than resignation.

So I was fucked, in rather a perfunctory manner, with his hand up my top to grope my boobs as he pushed himself up me from the rear. He mumbled as he did it, and called me Helene when he came, and that was that. Minutes later he was asleep, and not long after, so was I.

It was only a vague memory in the morning, so much so that for a while I wasn't sure if it hadn't been a dream. The damp patch where his sperm had dribbled out of my pussy gave the lie to that, but he didn't mention it, despite it being our first fuck. That seemed typical enough. Sex to him seemed to be something that happened, that he took, not something to discuss.

Breakfast was large bowls of *café-au-lait*, bread and blackcurrant jam, grudgingly prepared by Madame Vaucopin, whose attitude to life seemed to be uncompromisingly bleak. She was deferential enough to Fauçon though, and I began to wonder if her attitude to me came from wanting him for herself. It seemed at least possible, either that or she was hoping to benefit in his will and regarded me as a threat on that score.

What I hadn't expected was further company. Fauçon hadn't mentioned anybody, but we were halfway through breakfast when there was a clatter of shoes on the stair and a man came in, then a second. Both were young, late teens, and roughly similar in build, above average height and lean, not unlike Fauçon himself. There the resemblance ended. One, the elder, was strikingly handsome in the classical

French manner, dark, muscular, with a face that hinted at both strength at arrogance. The other was a bit of a sorry specimen, weedy rather than slim, and with a face that could never have been called handsome for the expression of benign idiocy.

If I was surprised by them, they obviously knew about me. The older greeted me with a friendly '*ça va?*', while the younger contented himself with a knowing leer at my chest. Evidently they were Fauçon's grandsons, and when the older introduced himself as Patrice and his brother as René-Claude, I finally managed to assert my own identity.

Patrice seemed keen to talk, and I had no objection whatever to responding. He was very good looking indeed, and I was already wondering if he might not provide an occasional alternative to his grandfather. I could tell he was thinking the same thing, but unfortunately so could old man Fauçon, and as soon as I'd finished my coffee I was ushered upstairs with a proprietorial pat on my bottom from Phillippe and a knowing grunt from Madame Vaucopin. René-Claude hadn't said a word, and had made no effort at all to conceal his admiration of my chest. He had even taken two oranges from a fruit bowl and made an odd hooting noise as he hefted them meaningfully in his hands. Nobody had said anything, so he was presumably a half-wit, and possibly dumb into the bargain.

Fauçon was in a bit of a surly mood, but keen to get on with the painting. I adopted my pose again, wishing to God I'd shown off by stretching languorously on the couch instead of pushing my boobs out. He made me move twice before he was satisfied, and got down to work, this time with paint. As before, it was dull and quickly became painful, but I put up with it, waiting until he called a pause before moving.

I got the same treatment as before. Out came his cock, into my mouth, and he finished himself off down my throat with a few quick jerks. It was really too early in the day for being turned into a fuck-dolly, but I took it, telling myself it would be worthwhile in the long run and that I'd remember the experience as horny in due course.

He barely gave me time to clean up before he was bellowing for Madame Vaucopin to bring up a jug of wine. He then ordered me back into my pose, without so much as a thought for whether I minded being seen stark naked by the housekeeper. As it was, she barely deigned to notice me, contenting herself with a single disdainful look and a muttered word as she put the wine and a single glass down on a table.

Fauçon began to drink and paint, silent as always, with his dark eyes flicking between me and the canvas. I was quickly growing stiff again, and had soon began to wonder it my entire plan wasn't misconceived. For one thing he wasn't an alcoholic, or at least not in the sense I recognised it. Sure, he hit the wine in late morning and seemed to consider about a third of a bottle of Calvados a reasonable *digestif*, but I'd met people in the wine trade who drank more. I'd expected him to be taking a bottle of spirits down with his breakfast.

The other thing was his age. All I could remember for sure was that he had enjoyed a reputation as a firebrand in 'fifties Paris, been unfashionable, and left after committing some unmentionable outrage. I wasn't even sure of my dates, but even if the whole thing had happened in 'fifty-nine and he'd been nineteen at the time he would now be in his early sixties. He'd looked older in the restaurant, but he'd managed to use my mouth with one leg on the couch and one on the floor, and I've known Percy to be unable to get there like that. Also, from the intensity of his gaze as he studied my body and the speed of his movements as he painted, early sixties looked about right.

That was a complete contradiction with what he'd said about Helene. She'd been his first model, and it was easy to see him as precocious. Still, precocious or not, it was hard to imagine him working as a serious painter in wartime Paris at less than eighteen, while if the unfortunate girl had been shot by the German's it couldn't have been later than 'forty-four. That made him seventy-seven at an absolute minimum, more likely eighty-odd. He did not look eighty.

I wanted to know, because if he had been stringing me a line from the start, it was going to make it a lot easier to pinch a few of his paintings. I could hardly accuse him of lying, and it was not going to be easy to burrow around the house for documents, not with Madame Vaucopin around. He was well enough known for his details to be on the internet though, certainly his dates, maybe even the full facts of his outrageous behaviour.

It seemed likely that Patrice would have a computer, and if not, there was sure to be an internet facility in Challones, or at the very least Angers. Getting there on my own might not be easy, but it could hardly be impossible. I needed to do it, for my own satisfaction.

I was really beginning to ache, especially the muscles under my arms, and my boobs felt like a pair of lead balloons. Finally I had to move, just a tiny bit, but it must have altered the pattern of light or something, because Fauçon immediately threw his hands up in a gesture of despair and stalked over to pour himself another glass from the wine jug. That was it for me, and I dropped my arms, then stretched to get my circulation going again. He took a swallow and looked round at me.

'This morning,' he said, 'and last night, when we made love, you did not touch yourself.'

If he thought the swift and pre-emptory fuck he'd given me the night before was making love, then he was even more egocentric than I'd imagined. I tried not to laugh and managed a sulky, Helenesque reply.

'I was tired.'

He nodded, put his glass down and beckoned to me. I came, expecting him to do something to prove himself and his ability to turn me on. Sure enough, as I approached he sat down on the couch. I thought he was going to make me suck him again, as he evidently supposed that the penis, and his penis in particular, was a the source of all sexual pleasure. It meant me going down on my knees between his legs, but as I dipped he reached out to take me by the wrist.

The knowledge that I was to be spanked came at the same instant I was turned across his knee. I squeaked in surprise and protest, but my arm was already being twisted up into the small of my back, and all it took was a lifted knee to stick my bare bottom up in the air. The next instant a heavy swat landed across my cheeks. I squeaked again, this time to the stinging pain.

He never gave me a chance to catch my breath, just laying in, smack after smack, to set my bottom flesh bouncing and leave me squealing and breathless. I never gave a thought to my dignity, there was no time, it was just too sudden. I was kicking my legs apart immediately, making the full rude show of pussy and bumhole that is inevitable for a properly spanked girl.

It hurt like anything, delivered on my cold flesh, with the pain and shock and humiliation bubbling up inside me, raw and sudden. I felt my anger flare and tried to wrench myself away, only to find I couldn't, and be rewarded with a truly agonising jolt of frustration and despair. I managed to call him a bastard, between two pained gasps as the slaps jammed into my bottom. I meant it, but it came as much from what I knew was going to happen to me as from what he done.

Sure enough, I couldn't fight it. Even as I kicked and swore and tried to scratch, even as my bare bottom danced and wobbled under the slaps, my feelings kicked in, heat in my bottom and pussy, arousal in my head, an arousal I could no more resist than I could stop him spanking me.

I gave in with a sob, burying my face in the couch to fight down the still burning sense of consternation at what he'd done to me, even as I stuck up my bottom for more. I got it, his slaps raining down on my jiggling buttocks, sending the heat straight to my sex. My legs came wide, open across his knee, splaying my pussy wide and showing off my bumhole in detail, a display deliberately rude and utterly submissive.

It stopped, suddenly. I was gripped by my pussy, his thumb pushing up into the wet interior of my hole, his hand cupping me, one long finger slipping down between my lips. He still had my arm twisted up behind my back, painfully hard, and he held me still as me masturbated me, sending me straight into a helpless ecstasy as I squirmed my sex and my hot bottom against his hand.

I could have come, so easily, and he took me right to the edge, only to let go, suddenly. It was completely unexpected, and I squeaked in surprise as I slid off his lap, to sit down hard on my well-smacked bottom. I was panting, my head spinning with emotions, not all good. I was going to do it anyway. I knew he wanted me to masturbate in front of him, and I didn't need to fake it.

I squatted back, thighs spread, in blatant sexual display. Supporting myself on one hand, I put the other to my sex, dipping a finger up into my pussy before I began to rub. He could see everything, my boobs flaunted, my tummy pushed out, taut and sleek, my spread sex, my bumhole already twitching between my open cheeks. I was going to come, in moments, and as the orgasm started to rise I turned my mind to the way he'd spanked me, just tugging me down across his knee and slapping me up to a rosy glow, indifferent to my feelings . . .

My mouth came open in a gasp and I was coming. I had closed my eyes, the knowledge that he was watching me enough as I revelled in my punishment and the lewd display I was making of myself. My clitty was burning beneath my finger, so hot, and I could hear the slopping noise I was making as I rubbed.

I never heard the door. I never realised we weren't alone, not until I had sat my hot bottom on the floor and opened my eyes, my mouth twitching up into a satisfied smile as the orgasm faded. The smile didn't last long. Madame Vaucopin was standing in the doorway, staring right at me. She announced lunch with a single, clipped phrase, addressing him, then turned, with a final word as she left the room.

'*Salope.*'

It sent the blood straight to my cheeks. I accept that I'm a slut, or at least that a prude would think of me as one, but it was just the way she said it, as if I was completely and utterly beneath contempt, nothing. I found myself hastily covering my pussy and boobs, which was ridiculous when she had already left the room, and I dressed in a flurry of embarrassment, not even stopping to attend to my bottom.

Fauçon appeared indifferent to the incident, to my annoyance, and before I could decide what to say, he had ambled off down the stairs. I followed, my face just about as red and hot as my bottom, an embarrassment made worse by wondering if other people in the house had heard my spanking, Patrice in particular. Older men I don't mind so much, or women, but to have an attractive young man know I got spanked, especially by his grandfather, was hideously embarrassing.

He knew something had been going on, because he gave me a sly wink as I came to the table. Not that he said anything, any more than René-Claude, who was leching over me as openly as before. There was nothing I could do, and I began to serve myself to cover my embarrassment.

Fauçon had cheered up, although I wasn't sure if it was because he had dealt with me so effectively, or at the prospect of lunch. The food was simple but good, bread and goat's cheese washed down with the same delicate white wine as before. Between that and Fauçon's cheerful conversation, my embarrassment quickly began to fade. It was still a bit irritating with René-Claude staring at me and making rude gestures as he nudged his brother, but as he obviously was half-witted I tried to make allowances.

I was hoping not to send the afternoon modelling, and so was extremely glad when Fauçon retired to a comfortable chair with a glass of marc large enough to ensure that he would completely unable to paint within minutes. It was the same one the Moreaus made, and which Percy had given me after making me eat dirt, an evil brew tasting of pickled dogfish and containing a good fifty per cent alcohol.

If he was going to actually pass out, that was just fine by me. There was a definite twinkle in Patrice's eye, and if he hadn't been flirting openly, I'd caught more than one suggestive look. It was risky, in the face of his grandfather's jealousy, but it was also tempting. I might have to play Helene for Phillippe Fauçon, and I was well up for being used and spanked. Variety is nice though, and Patrice was going to be a lot more energetic, while he could hardly be less considerate of my needs.

I played it cool, going to sit on the arm of Phillippe's chair and stroking his hair while I all but ignored Patrice. Phillippe put his arm around my waist, and I could sense his ego swelling as I made up to him. Patrice didn't respond at all, which I hoped meant he'd got the message. René-Claude on the other hand, was anything but reserved, with jealousy in his eyes and an erection in his trousers. He had even begun to stroke himself, only to stop as he caught a gesture from his brother.

That was more than I'd expected, especially considering I was in jeans and a crop top, hardly blatant. Obviously the boy was seriously frustrated, and when he left the table to go upstairs, I was pretty certain it was to masturbate over me. That was a little embarrassing, but amusing too, in a way, just to think of him up in his room tugging frantically at his cock as rude images of me ran through his head.

His brother was going to get more than images. Phillippe had slumped down, and his fingers had stopped working on the flesh of my hip. He was asleep. I gently prised the glass from his fingers and stood up. Madame Vaucopin was in the kitchen, washing up. One glance to Patrice was all it needed.

We both knew what we wanted, but it was going to have to be quick. I left the room first, making my way unhurriedly upstairs to the master bedroom. A few minutes later Patrice followed. Unfortunately, so did Madame Vaucopin, to peer suspiciously in a me from the door. I was on the bed, curled up and pretending to read a leather-bound *La Terre* I'd taken from Phillippe's bookcase.

She disappeared, and I listened as her footsteps retreated, across the landing and down the stairs. There were butterflies in my tummy, and I felt very ready, nearly as much from the thrill of doing something illicit as at the prospect of sex. There was silence, then the gentle creak of a door and a stealthy footstep. My heart gave a little jump as Patrice slipped sideways into the room.

There was no time for preliminaries, or reluctance. I was pulling up my top as he crossed the room, my bra with it, to spill out my boobs, right into his eager hands. He fondled for a moment, stroking my nipples with his thumbs until they were stiff and urgent, even as I tugged the button of my jeans open. He was still feeling me as I hastily pushed my jeans and panties down together, to my knees. His hands went to his fly. I rolled over, kneeling, bum up for entry. He grinned, his eyes glittering as he pulled out a fine fat cock, the head already pushing out from his foreskin. I was taken by the hair and fed it, sucking greedily as his fingers went down between my bottom cheeks, brushing my bumhole before slipping up into my pussy. For a moment he fingered me, opening my sex for his cock. Then he was out, scrambling up behind me, to slide his full, gorgeous length up into my body.

My mouth came wide in pleasure as I filled, and I was gripping the bed cover as he began to fuck me. It was wonderful, bum high, with his hands on my hips as he pushed into me, fucking away with so much energy and passion. He had me gasping in moments, and I was forced to bite onto the bed cover to stop myself from screaming.

I wanted him to do me properly, and to masturbate while he was in me, maybe even make him go up my bottom. There was no time. He knew it too, hammering furiously into my pussy, until he suddenly whipped his cock free, to jerk it over my bottom and spray my cheeks with sperm, the same cheeks his grandfather had so recently spanked.

As he sank back I heard the creak of the stair. He scrambled away, even as I jerked my top down, not bothering to adjust my bra. My panties came up, his sperm squashing up into my crease and over my bottom as I pulled them high, then my jeans. He had disappeared behind a curtain, and even as I opened my Zola the head of Madame Vaucopin appeared around the door. She threw me a glance yet more suspicious than before and sniffed the air. I returned a bland look, praying that the smell of sex wasn't too obvious. Again she sniffed, then turned away with a grunt.

Patrice emerged from behind the curtain, put his finger to his lips, gestured to the door and shook his head. I nodded my understanding and he disappeared again. Sure enough, it was some time before another creak signalled Madame Vaucopin's descent of the stairs. Once more Patrice came out of hiding, this time to slip across the landing to his room.

I was finding it hard not to giggle. Our fuck had been quick, and hardly satisfying for me, but deliciously naughty. I felt seriously uncomfortable, the crease of my bottom slimy with sperm and my panties sticky over my cheeks, but I didn't mind. It was rude, keeping me in mind of what I'd done. The temptation was to masturbate, just with a hand popped down the front of my panties, but before I could turn thought into action I heard the stair creak one more time. I turned back to my book, expecting Madame Vaucopin on yet another of her visits. It wasn't. It was Fauçon himself.

He looked a bit bleary-eyed, but seriously randy, his hand going to his crotch to squeeze a conspicuous bulge as he let his eyes wander slowly down my body. I gave him a lazy smile and shut the book, wondering how I was going to conceal the mess Patrice had made of my bottom. He was nodding as he came forward, and mumbling to himself, something about me being his English Helene. I quickly pulled up my top, exposing my breasts to make sure he didn't discover my dishevelled bra. He chuckled and took hold of one as he came to sit on the bed, squeezing me.

'So eager, ever eager, *toujours la même,*' he mumbled.

His other hand was on his cock, squeezing at it through the material of his trousers. I took my boobs in hand, cupping them to make them as round and inviting as possible.

'Sit on the bed, Phillippe. I have a treat for you.'

He hesitated, for a second, then moved to lean back against the bolster, making himself thoroughly comfortable. I sat up and cocked my leg across his body, bouncing my boobs in my hands to keep his attention firmly on them. His response was to peel down his fly and pull out an already stiff cock. I imagined he'd woken, the way so many men do, erect and eager to do something with it.

What he was going to do was my boobs, something I hoped would keep his attention from my lower half. He certainly didn't seem to mind, but as I bent down to fold his erection between them, I was wishing he was just a bit more considerate.

It was a comfortable position for him, but a seriously awkward one for me, with my bum stuck up in the air and one leg off the bed. I could feel his grandson's sperm moving between my bum cheeks, sticky and wet, as I began to rub his cock in my cleavage, sparking a fantasy of being shared by them, with Patrice up me from behind as I entertained Phillippe with my boobs and mouth. There was no way it could happen, but it was a nice thought, and I settled on it as I worked the big penis between my boobs, alternately wanking it and nibbling at the straining tip.

He soon started to get urgent, pushing himself up and down in my cleavage, with the fat read helmet of his penis appearing from between my boobs with each push. I squeezed them tighter, letting him get more friction. I realised that I should have taken my top and bra right off an instant too late, as he came over them and into the fleshy tube I'd made for him. I finished him off slowly, rubbing his cock in the now slippery valley between my breasts until he had stopped grunting.

It felt deliciously mischievous, to be slimy top and bottom with two different men's sperm, and neither know what the other had done. I love that, especially when they think they're in control, or I'm hooked on them. I sat up, still holding my boobs, to show Phillippe what he'd done. He'd want me to mastur-bate, or I thought he would, but his eyes had already closed, despite the display I was making of myself.

I called him a pig under my breath and climbed off. Between them they had me badly in need of climax, and I was not going to miss out. Nor did I want to take a sneaky frig in the bathroom, although it was the obvious and sensible thing to do.

My top was soiled anyway, so I pulled it down over my boobs and went to the door, poking my head around. Nobody was visible, and the silence was absolute save for the regular sound of Phillippe's breathing from behind me. I stole forward, across the landing to Patrice's door, and pushed it quickly open.

He wasn't there. I cursed, doubly disappointed, as not only had he gone off somewhere, but the room was obviously a guest room, meaning he didn't actually live there. So it looked like the bathroom after all. I was about to move back when I heard a click from the landing. I turned, expecting Madame Vaucopin, only to find René-Claude standing in the doorway of another room. He was grinning like the imbecile he was, and staring fixedly at my top. I was bare underneath, my nipples were hard and there was a smudge of semen right in the middle, all of which added to the immediate rush of blood to my face. He made an obscene gesture, evidently suggesting I should do him a favour.

I wasn't having it, not with René-Claude. It was just too demeaning. I put on my sternest face and gave him a firm '*non*', then slipped across to the bathroom. There was no lock on the door.

For a moment I just stood there, seething. I couldn't play with myself, not with René-Claude likely to come in at any moment, and I wasn't even sure if I wanted to shower. I had to though. The mess between my bottom cheeks was starting to itch and my panties were already glued to my cheeks. Soon my top half would be as bad.

With a resigned sigh I began to strip. The shower was some ancient thing, all enamel and brass taps, poised over a trough that would have made an adequate bath, but with no curtain. By the time I was nude there was still no sign of René-Claude, but he didn't seem to have any inhibitions at all, and it was hard to imagine him resisting taking a peek at me showering.

The thought of him looking at him kept me on edge as I put my soiled clothes in the sink to soak, and as I struggled to adjust the wretched shower so that it wouldn't either scald me or freeze me to death. It was not good, and made worse by the nagging voice of my desire for submission and humiliation telling me that what I ought to do was go next door and let the dirty little bastard have his fun with me.

I didn't, and by the time I'd managed to get the temperature right he still hadn't made an appearance. Obviously my stern look had had the right effect, and with just the tiniest trace of regret I began to wash, hurriedly soaping myself and all the time watching the door. My heart still jumped when it started to swing open, and I yelled out, telling him to fuck off and calling him a pervert.

He took no notice whatever, but stepped calmly into the bathroom, to stand staring at me as I did my best to cover myself. I told him to fuck off again, putting real anger into my voice. His response was to pull his cock out of his trousers. I threw the soap at him, sacrificing a flash of my boobs for the pleasure, but he just dodged, and began to wank.

I opened my mouth to scream at him, but stopped. I'd wake Phillippe, or attract Madame Vaucopin, and I knew what they'd think. It was hopeless, while my dignity was fighting a losing battle with my arousal, so much so that I was sure that if he didn't come soon I was going to really disgrace myself.

So I let my hands go to my hips, showing myself, but in an attitude of disapproval mirrored by the expression on my face. The effort was lost on him. He just began to wank faster, his eyes flicking between my boobs and my pubic bush, until his cock jerked suddenly, to send a great stream of sperm high in the air, so far out that some of it caught my leg. I let him finish, then told him to get out in no uncertain terms. He went, leaving the evidence of his dirty behaviour on the floor for me to clean up.

I did it, my frustration absolutely boiling inside me as I used my hand to scrape up the sperm. That really got to me, having to go down on my knees to clean up the come of some filthy little bastard of a Peeping Tom. By the time I'd finished I was seething and dizzy with arousal. Three men had come over me, each taking his pleasure in my body, and I hadn't done it once. Next it would probably be Madame Vaucopin, coming up to sit on my face. It was enough to make me want to bang my head on the wall.

It was too much, far too much. I retrieved the soap bar, deliberately crawling just to enjoy the sensation of being on my knees. Back in the shower, I slumped down, into the hot water of the trough, with more cascading down on me as I pushed the soap to my sex. I was rubbing immediately, lathering up my pussy and pressing the firm bar to my clit. It stung, but I didn't care. In fact it was nice, suiting my mood as I sought for the right fantasy to come over.

I did not want it to be Phillippe Fauçon and his wretched grandchildren, but I knew it was going to be. All I could manage was to try and spare myself the ignominy of thinking about René-Claude. I focussed on Patrice instead, on the sheer erotic joy of our frantic fuck. I'd gone doggy, by choice, a deliciously rude position, and better still after a smacked bum, to show it off to the man inside me, whether or not he's the one who gave me my punishment.

That was good, and I closed my eyes, forcing myself to ignore the possibility of further intrusion. My whole pussy was stinging from the soap, and the froth was running down between my bum cheeks, the bubbles tickling my anus. My spare hand went down, one soapy fingertip tickled the little wrinkly hole for a second before popping inside. The sting of the soap came immediately, making the sensitive little ring burn, enough to draw a gasp from my lips.

I was quickly juicy and open, enough for a cock, and I could all too easily imagine the stinging pain of being buggered with soap for a lubricant. It would hurt like anything, as would my pussy, with Patrice's cock put to one, then the other, enjoying both well lubricated holes without thought for my pained cries. Better, his grandfather could join in, underneath me, his big cock pushed well up my bottom hole as Patrice mounted me and fucked me.

The soap would be squishing in my twin holes, just as it was in reality. I'd be crying, gasping and crying, tears rolling down my face even as I came up to orgasm. They'd spunk in me, both of them, deep in my body, adding their sperm to the mess between my legs, to dribble out as I masturbated in it, just as I was, a finger up each hole, another dabbing at my clitty.

I was going to come at any moment. My feet were braced against the edge of the trough, my bottom was bucking up and down, splashing in the water, my boobs were bouncing on my chest, the nipples so stiff they ached. I began to make little mewling noises, quite out of control as I let the fantasy run one more time, being caught in the shower, told off, maybe spanked with Patrice watching, bare bottomed as I kicked helplessly over his grandfather's lap. It would turn them on. They'd agree to have me. Phillippe would go up my bottom, right up, but only after he squashed half a bar of soap up my bumhole, to leave me shivering with pain. The other half would go up my poor pussy, and Patrice would fuck me. I'd be rocking on their cock, thrashing in the stinging pain of the soap, when René-Claude would come in, whip out his cock, smear it with soap and stuff it into my open mouth . . .

My scream of ecstasy came out as a strange bubbling sound as I tried desperately to hold it back. For a long moment I rode the climax, my whole body tight in orgasm, but already cursing myself for letting the wretched René-Claude come into my fantasy. I'd needed it though, and as I finally slipped down into the water I let out a long sigh of pure contentment.

Four

Sex wise, I was getting most of what I had imagined from Phillippe Fauçon, if not all. It also left me with some thoroughly confusing emotions. He was an egocentric pig, who in five of more decades of his sex life had never bothered to learn how to stimulate a woman. Yet he did stimulate me, mentally, exactly because he was such a pig. He wasn't the first man to make me feel that way, and I could cope.

Patrice was a bonus, René-Claude an irritation, Madame Vaucopin another. All together they made for a situation that was going to wear out my patience within days. Fortunately, that was all I needed. The more I thought about it, the more I was sure that old Fauçon had been lying to me from the start. He could not possibly be eighty, and the whole thing about Helene's execution and my resemblance to her was a play for my sympathy, and a pretty sick one at that. I still wanted to be sure, but after my first full day with him I had very little compunction indeed about taking a few pictures. It was fun to plot too, and to enjoy my affair with Patrice behind his back. Okay, I'm a little brat. So spank me.

I needed internet access, and I also needed to be sure he didn't have the entire collection of pictures beautifully catalogued. It didn't seem likely when they were in such a jumble, but I had to be sure. As with his age, asking questions was clearly not a good idea. So I kept my eyes open, and waited my chance.

It was going to take a while, with Madame Vaucopin around. She was horribly suspicious, so much so that I began to wonder if she could see right through me. It seemed unlikely, when it was Fauçon who had made a play for me and not the other way around, but there was no question that she both disliked and distrusted me.

Nothing much happened on the evening of the first day. That night Fauçon gave me a fucking if anything more perfunctory than the one before, only this time on top of me with my legs rolled high to let him get in as deep as possible. I was game for more, and fortunately he wanted me to masturbate, but it was hardly satisfying.

I was hoping for better in the morning, but I didn't get it, only the normal head fucking, the pleasure of which was beginning to wear a bit thin. From his reputation and the mysterious scandal, I'd been hoping for something considerably kinkier than simple callous abuse. I didn't get spanked either, and the bruises Percy had given me with his clothes brush were already beginning to change colour.

So by lunchtime, after another long stint of modelling, I was hoping to get away for a while, either to Challones or to see what Percy was up to. Unfortunately Phillippe declined to get properly drunk and insisted on another session, only to change his mind after half-an-hour. Instead he said he would show me some of the places he wanted to paint me, and decide which would be best. I had little choice but to tag along, and to listen as he explained about light and form and his concepts of realism.

I was taking it in, at least partially. There were other things to think about too. The Moreaus had pickers out in some of the vineyards, a pretty rough lot, including several swarthy-looking men who were working stripped to the waist. For all their lack of refinement, they seemed to know who Fauçon was, and to have good deal of respect for me. We were on what was mainly the Moreaus' land, and it seemed likely Percy would be around, but I couldn't see him, or Alain.

We had walked out along the top of the vineyards, which Phillippe seemed to consider unsuitable as a backdrop for some reason not immediately clear to me. From there we made our way down the wall of the Clos St Aubin and across the road to the flatter ground by the river. There was an abandoned mill which he wanted to consider, several crumbling, ivy-grown buildings and a great rotting water-wheel. By the time we'd pushed our way to it down an overgrown track I was getting pretty hot. There was a great stone-lined pond that looked tempting for a swim, but Phillippe was again dissatisfied and couldn't even be tempted by the idea of me stripping off to go into the water.

So we walked on to the village, which he finally decided was a suitable place. I could see his point, as almost nothing around the central square was modern, and it was clear that a great deal of nostalgia was involved with his choice of subject, even if the story about Helene *La Pêche* had been made up. So I spent an hour sitting on walls and projecting languor and innocence while he contemplated the light and complained about my choice of clothes and generally mumbled to himself. I could think of worse things to do, but I was getting hotter and stickier by the minute, and was extremely glad when he decided it was time for a beer.

We sat outside the tiny local bar, drinking *pressions* as he continued to expound his theories and damn his critics. I kept trying to turn the conversation to his scandal, but he was less than forthcoming, far preferring to curse the people he saw as his persecutors than explain the details. He kept going off at tangents too, until I gave up and switched off to watch the rough looking grape pickers coming in from their work.

They looked even rougher than before, but they repaid watching, their muscles hard beneath skin glistening with sweat, unshaved, unkempt. Some of the women were worth looking at too, muscular in their own way, and many heavy breasted. It had been a while since I'd had sex with a woman, and it didn't look like my brief interest in Marie-Armelle was likely to bear fruit. I prefer a woman to take charge of me anyway, and some of the older female pickers looked as if they would be able to dish out a fine brat spanking, while some of the younger looked as if they deserved it. Both ideas appealed, with me as victim and voyeur respectively.

It was a nice thought. Perhaps with one of the big, burly mothers pulling a recalcitrant daughter across her lap, one of eighteen or even twenty, old and proud enough to be truly outraged as her bottom was stripped nude and set dancing to heavy-handed slaps. It would be best in front of all the others, me as well, and with the girl's legs forced well open to show off her hairy pussy, her deep bottom crease, the dark flesh of her lips and anus. Maybe she would even have her boobs pulled out, just to add one more agonising detail to her humiliation, and left bouncing under her chest as she was spanked . . .

A cough from Phillippe broke into my fantasy and I realised I'd been staring a little too openly. He was looking stern as he spoke.

'You are a woman of passion, Natasha, my little one. This I understand. I am a man of passion too. You will not look at other men.'

'Sorry, I was . . .'

'I know. Do not.'

I gave him a sulky look, wondering how it would feel if I was the one who got the bare bottom spanking, right there in the street. It was a nice idea, but only as a fantasy. For all his machismo, I was sure he simply didn't have the guts to do it.

It is not easy to find the balance between play and reality for submissive sex. Maybe there is no balance. Percy came close, bringing me to the edge again and again, but ultimately it was play, always. Phillippe was the opposite, even the spankings he had agreed to give me entirely on his terms, and intended as genuine discipline for the sake of discipline. Percy likes me free. Phillippe wanted me cowed, and no man but no man does that to me. I could see why Helene had joined the resistance, to salvage her own pride, assuming she had existed at all.

He finished his beer and stood up, a deliberate gesture of authority, as I'd only drunk half of mine. I left it and followed him meekly up the street. He was loving it, and took me by the hand as we passed a cluster of pickers outside one of the wineries. Several glanced at us, and as we walked past I could feel their eyes on my back. Well, more likely my bottom.

The road snaked back through the vineyards, curling around the back of the hill, so we cut up through the Moreaus' wood. Back at his house Madame Vaucopin was already preparing dinner, or what passes for it in France. Both Patrice and René-Claude were around, one snatching a quick kiss and a grope of my bottom when nobody was looking, the other just leering.

There didn't even seem to be a television in the house, let alone a computer, and after dinner entertainment consisted of talking and getting drunk, or rather, of listening to Phillippe Fauçon pontificate and getting drunk. Some of his stories were well worth listening to, of Paris and London in the 'fifties and 'sixties, although once more he refused to be drawn on the scandal. Otherwise it was French art, French politics and French rustic philosophy, with constant references to Emile Zola and other long-dead men. Those alive he generally considered beneath contempt, and woman as ornamental but barely sentient. He hated to be criticised, and twice grew angry when Patrice dared to disagree, both times on utterly trivial points.

As most of the conversation was in French, and pretty colloquial at that, I paid less and less attention. With nothing else to do I drank steadily and let my imagination wander, all the while cursing the egotism and jealousy that prevented them sharing me. Without it, the evening could have been far more entertaining. I was well up for giving them a striptease, even a round of blow-jobs afterwards, excepting René-Claude. As it went it was clearly out of the question, especially with the looming presence of Madame Vaucopin eternally in the background.

So I stuck it out, making sure to keep Phillippe's glass full in the hope that he would pass out so deeply that I'd be able to sneak in with Patrice late at night. He was certainly going the right way, and from the looks Patrice had been giving at me I could see that I would be more than welcome.

When the great Phillippe Fauçon went to bed I had to go to bed, leaving Patrice attempting to play cards with his idiot brother. Phillippe was in a dirty mood, and was trying to grope me as I supported him up the stairs, his hands on my boobs and bum. He was mumbling out endearments too, pretty dirty ones, in

French, and was kissing me as soon as we were through the door.

I responded briefly, despite the beard and the stench of Gaulois and garlic, and was fumbling with his trousers as he tried to get my top up over my breasts. His cock came out, stiffening quickly in my grip, but I had to help him with my top, pulling it high to spill out my breasts into his eager hands. His mouth went to a nipple, suckling on me as I held up my top and bra for him. His beard was tickling my boobs, making me giggle, along with the almost demented urgency of the way he was wanking at his cock as he fed on me.

He was going to spunk in his hand if he didn't get on with it, so I popped my jeans open and eased myself back onto the bed, taking him with me. He came on top, still sucking as my legs came high and wide. I was trying to get my jeans and panties down, but his body was trapping them and I could only just get my bum out, leaving his cock prodding between my cheeks as struggled to fuck me.

I hadn't had a chance to get juicy, and it hurt a little as his big cock head found the still dry mouth of my sex. He must have felt it, but he didn't care, pushing again to make me wince. I snatched at myself, pulling my lips wide to let him get at the moist interior, and the next moment he was in, sighing in satisfaction as he forced his cock roughly up into my body.

The position was seriously awkward, with my legs rolled high and wide, my jeans and panties taut between my thighs and pressed down hard under his body. He didn't seem to care, fucking away merrily. I tried to get comfortable, but he'd caught me under the shoulders and crushed my body to his, kissing my neck and face as he did it. I tried to make the best of it, but I couldn't even get at my boobs, and had to be content with clinging onto him as he pounded into me, puffing and grunting desperately as he struggled for orgasm.

It happened, in maybe a minute. I felt the mouth of my pussy go sloppy and that was it. He come inside me. I hadn't had such clumsy, crude sex since I was a teenager, maybe not even then. The rudeness of it had barely begun to get to me, and if I was wet it was almost entirely with his come.

He lay on top of me for a while, his cock slowly deflating in my hole, mumbling about how beautiful I was and how much I turned him on. I finally got fed up and pushed him off when my right thigh began to cramp. Even then I'd have masturbated if he'd shown any interest, but he seemed to be too drunk to care.

So I put him to bed, undressing him and helping him into his night-shirt, which made me feel more like a geriatric nurse than the carefree young lover he pictured me as. He was asleep before I'd finished undressing.

I stood over him, his sperm trickling slowly out into the crotch of the panties that were my only garment. It wasn't fair. I'd been game, more or less for anything he wanted, certainly to do as I was told. He could have had me crawling naked on the floor, or stripping, showing off every rude detail of my body for him before he fucked me, or made me get down on my knees to suck his cock. He could have spanked me, taken his belt to me even, maybe buggered me, or made me wet my panties on the huge chamber pot being used to house some geraniums on the window sill, worse even.

For a moment I considered sneaking upstairs, pinching a couple of paintings and nipping out of the back. It was no good, and not just because Madame

Vaucopin was still up. I had nowhere to put them, not without Percy's help. Nor was I prepared to give up without something to show for it.

I peeled off my soggy panties and pulled on an outsize T-shirt. Phillippe was out for the count. A visit to Patrice was clearly on the cards, but so far as I knew he was still downstairs, presumably thinking his dear old grandfather needed a long time to be cajoled up to sex and would make the best of me once he'd got started. There was also Madame Vaucopin. I was in no mood to wait, but I'd have to. One o'clock or so would be sensible, so I crawled into bed beside the now snoring Phillippe and lay back in the semi-darkness, watching the ancient and ornate clock on his mantelpiece.

The next thing I knew it was morning. Phillippe was up, and had been sketching me as I lay asleep. My T-shirt had ridden up in the night, and the bedclothes were well down, exposing my bottom and hip as if in unintentional display. He was thoroughly pleased with himself, and none the worse the wear for the drink he'd put back, speaking volubly of how essential it was to capture what was natural. That was despite the fact that he'd obviously pulled the bedclothes off me to make the pose more erotic.

I agreed with him anyway, hiding my true feelings. Mornings should start with coffee, not artistic discussion with elderly perverts. Not that he seemed much of a pervert, for all his reputation. I'd missed out on Patrice too, who was now likely to throw a French paddy because I hadn't come in to him.

The rest of the morning was thoroughly predictable, *café-au-lait* and cock-sucking on either side of a barely tolerable period flaunting my boobs for Phillippe. I was sure René-Claude had been watching me through a crack in the studio door as well, although when I'd pointed this out to Phillippe he'd just laughed. Presumably he didn't think either of his grandchildren would dare cross him.

He was wrong there, as a brief and fiery exchange with Patrice had established that he'd waited up half the night for me to come in to him. I'd been in no mood to apologise, but had promised that I was his just as soon as the opportunity presented itself.

Unfortunately, the only way I was going to get rid of Phillippe was if he trusted me absolutely. That meant feigning indifference to Patrice, and even then I wasn't sure he'd buy it. Protestations of undying loyalty seemed more likely to do harm than good. He might be a complete pig sexually, but he had had a long life behind him and was sure to suspect my motives.

I pondered the problem over lunch, and came up with what I thought was rather a neat solution, or at least a start. All it was going to take was a moment alone with Patrice, then a little show of supposed anger, not in Phillippe's sight, but in his hearing.

All I wanted to do was slap Patrice's face, just hard enough to leave a mark. Then I would give him a bit of invective on the subject of me being his grand-father's woman and that he was not to touch me. I managed to speak to him, in the hall as lunch broke up, but he wouldn't go for it, or explain why, and got quite shirty when I pressed him. In the end he stalked off outside, leaving me feeling thoroughly fed up.

That was the moment René-Claude chose to come out of the dining room. He was grinning, and as he saw me he made a gesture with his hand, as if wanking off. I gave him a stern look, but he kept coming forward, reaching out as if to grab a tit, just as Phillippe stepped through the door behind him.

It was a split second decision, made with a great deal more emotion then logic. Phillippe was bad

enough, but I was not being his idiot grandson's
wank toy. That, far more than the sudden chance to
show my loyalty, dictated my actions as my hand
shot out, to catch René-Claude full across the face.

He staggered back immediately, clutching at his
cheek, his eyes full of shock and hurt. I stood my
ground, and was just about to go into my pre-
prepared little speech when it was cut off by a bellow
of anger from Phillippe. He came right at me, his face
suffused with anger. Surprised, I made to speak, but
it came out as a yelp as he snatched at my shoulder
and spun me round.

My ankle hit the bottom step of the stairs and I
went down, clutching at the banister to stop myself
falling. Before I could get my balance Phillippe had
got me by the hair. He was shouting at me as I was
dragged back. I stumbled, squealing in shock and
pain as I went down on my knees, calling him a
bastard and flailing at his hand. He took no notice,
forcing my head down, and then he other hand was
grappling at my dress.

I could have fought, I suppose. I didn't. Instead I
was whimpering apologies as my dress was hoisted
high over my bum, to leave my panties on plain show.
His hand found my waistband on the instant, and I
screamed out, imploring him not to pull them down,
even as he did it, jerking them hard to spill out my
bare bottom. His hand came down and I was getting
it, a bare bottom spanking, just as I'd wanted, just as
I'd asked for.

Only I hadn't asked for it like that, not in the hall,
not in front of the appalling René-Claude. It was
what I was getting though, whether I liked it or not,
with my bum cheeks dancing and jiggling to a furious
crescendo of slaps as I was beaten. I screamed,
writhed, kicked, and tried desperately to get my

panties back up. He was having none of it, snatching my hand away, twisting my hair until I screamed afresh, and finally yelling for René-Claude to hold me still as he belaboured my bottom.

René-Claude took no notice, but Madame Vaucopin did. I'd got my panties halfway back up and the first I knew about it was when she took a firm grip on them and wrenched them back down. I realised who it was, crying out in fresh consternation as I tried to get them back up. She just grabbed my wrists, wrenching them back with a strength far beyond my own, to trap my arms behind my knees with the disputed panties left in a tangle, right down, and also gripped in her powerful fingers.

It was an awful position, trapped, bum-up, showing everything, and helpless to prevent it, or my spanking. Fauçon had stopped yelling at me, but only because he was spanking me so hard he had to fight for breath. I was the same, gasping and yelling as my stinging buttocks bounced and spread behind me. My dress had come up so far my boobs showed, and they were slapping on the floor to the rhythm of the spanking, making the utter humiliation of my position even worse.

I just burst into tears, not just from the pain, but in utter frustration at my helplessness and the way I was being held. It was so unfair too, when the little idiot had been about to touch me up. He was the one who deserved punishment. Not that that mattered. I was not the one who made judgements. I was the one having her bare bottom turned red in front of the little pervert whose fault it all was, with her fanny on show and her bumhole winking behind her.

He stopped, finally, to leave me shaking with sobs and whimpering brokenly into the curtain of brown curls around my face. My bottom was on fire, and even when Madame Vaucopin let go all I could do was slump down on the floor. For a moment I just lay there, with my poor red bum still on show, before I could get it together to reach back for my panties. Not that it mattered. They'd seen everything I had to show. As I covered myself I looked up, to find Phillippe staring down at me.

'*Jamais* . . . never, do that again!' he spat. 'He is simple. He does not understand. Have you no heart, no feelings?'

It was so unjust, and all I could manage was a sob and a miserable nod of my head. Yes, René-Claude was simple, but that did not give him the right to grope my breasts. Nor did my love of spanking give Phillippe the right to do it in front of inappropriate people.

I knew it was just self-pity. I'd asked for it and I'd got it. Maybe he'd have done it anyway. It didn't matter. It had been done. I'd been spanked, bare, in front of the hateful Madame Vaucopin and stupid René-Claude, who'd now seen everything, not just my boobs and bush, but the rear of my pussy lips and my bumhole, every little fold and wrinkle of me, and in the most ignominious position imaginable.

They were all looking at me as I climbed miserably to my feet. Phillippe was looking stern. Madame Vaucopin had her arms folded across her chest and looked thoroughly pleased with herself. René-Claude was sniggering in the corner, with an extremely conspicuous bulge in his trousers.

I just ran, upstairs, into my room, where I threw myself down on the bed, feeling utterly sorry for myself. My tears started again, rolling slowly down my face as what had been done to me went around and around in my head. It was too much, far, far too much. Before long I had taken my dress up and eased down my panties once more, to lie, red bottomed and snivelling on the bed, wishing I had just a bit more control over my feelings.

Fauçon would come, I knew, or I'd have to masturbate. I'd be crying with shame as I did it, I'd be confused, and angry with myself, but that wouldn't stop me. I'd been spanked. My bottom was hot and throbbing. My pussy was aching for attention. That's what spanking does to me, and I know I can cope, that the humiliation will turn to pleasure as my arousal grows.

It did, until by the time Fauçon came up I had my red bottom pushed up in invitation, my anus showing deliberately. I was hoping he'd bugger me, to inflict the final indignity and come up my smacked bottom. At the least I was hoping he'd make me go doggy, to admire his handiwork as he took his pleasure up my sex, or make me suck his cock until he came down my throat or in my face.

He didn't. He took one look at my exposed body and tear-streaked face and picked up the sketch pad he'd been using earlier. I stayed dead still as he began to draw, trying to bite down my need and make the added humiliation of having the aftermath of my punishment captured for posterity. Nothing was going to be left out either. He was at a fine angle to see my bottom hole and at least a glimpse of my pussy, and I knew he'd want to capture both, making my exposure as raw and powerful as my emotion.

I was shaking as he did it, and pouting, my lower lip stuck out, my eyes full of hurt and accusation, none of which was fake. He took his time too, always the perfectionist, but at last was satisfied and put down the pad. I was sure he knew. He could see the state of my pussy.

He came to me, but sat on the bed and began to stroke my hair.

'You are angry with me, my little peach?'

I shook my head. He wouldn't understand.

'I did not think so. In punishment you seek absolution, yes?'

No, the spanking had been completely unfair. I nodded anyway.

'And also pleasure.'

Again I nodded. This time I meant it.

He continued to stroke my hair. I was on blatant display. I could smell my own sex. He had to want me. Still he stroked, smiling down at me as if he was God with a repentant sinner. I had to do something.

'Let me suck you, Phillippe.'

He nodded complacently, as if he was granting me a privilege, but his hand went to his fly. I was not missing out this time. As he pulled out his cock I put a finger into my mouth, sucking in my cheeks to make saliva quickly as I moved up the bed to lay my head on his lap. His cock was swollen, the skin a little damp, making me wonder if he'd been erect while he spanked me. I took it in, even as I pushed out my bottom for my finger.

My bum cheeks felt warm and rough as I splayed them with my fingers, to find the tight dimple of my anus. I began to tease the little hole, tickling and running my nail over the tiny wrinkles. Phillippe was growing in my mouth, and I took his balls in hand even as my bumhole began to respond, opening a little. My ring was a little sweaty from the spanking, but there wasn't enough spit, and as I began to suck in earnest I was delving into my pussy, to pull out some cream and smear it to my anus. That worked, and I slid a finger in past the tight ring of muscle, and up.

I felt warm and sloppy inside, a deliciously rude sensation as I wiggled my finger in my bottom hole.

In my mouth, Phillippe's cock was rock solid, and he had begun to moan. I slowed my sucking, determined he wasn't going to spunk in my mouth and spoil the fun. His response was to take me by the hair and pull my head hard onto his cock. I burrowed deeper up my bottom, letting my ring go loose, to open myself, and prodded a second finger up my now slimy hole.

My pleasure was rising steeply as I readied my bottom hole for the penis in my mouth, and I was praying he would treat me properly and bugger me. It was obviously what I wanted, no question, with my two fingers working in and out of my straining anal hole, on full view to him. He was big though, and I needed to be properly loose to take him at all easily. I pushed in a third finger, to make my ring gape. He was grunting, but I was soon sloppy wet, and as loose as I get.

I tried to pull back. He resisted, but only for a moment, and his cock was standing proud in front of my face, glistening with my saliva, rock hard and ready for insertion into my bottom. My fingers came out of my hole and into my mouth, to be sucked on as I rolled over. I went face down, presenting myself for a comfortable rear entry. My hands went back, to pull my cheeks apart, presenting my dirty bumhole for his cock.

He said nothing, but came between my legs, holding his cock. I felt the hard shaft settled between my smacked cheeks and I closed my eyes in bliss, concentrating on what was being done to me as his fat, firm cock head pushed to my bumhole. I sighed as my anal ring stretched to the pressure of his penis. It felt so good, that dirtiest of acts, taking a man's cock up my bottom hole, and not just willingly, but by my own choice.

I kept my bum wide as he began to force himself up me. It wasn't easy, even with me as sloppy as I was, and I was soon grunting and hissing through my teeth as my rectum slowly filled with cock. He'd done it before though, pulling in and out to moisten his shaft in my bowel, and letting me pull myself wide to engulf his meat.

It seemed to take forever before it was all up and his balls had settled squashily against my vacant sex. I finally let go of my bottom cheeks and folded my hands under my chin, purring as he began to fuck my bottom. Finally he'd done something really right, and I just wanted to soak it up as I was buggered. Even the bad points of the way he had spanked me were forgotten as the breathless ecstasy of having a big penis moving about up my bottom hole took over.

He was going to come though, quite soon. He'd nearly done it in my mouth. Now he was starting to grunt again, and call me his peach, a sure sign he was getting there. With just a touch of regret I pulled up my knees, straining to lift his weight so that I could get a hand in under my belly. I managed it, to find my pussy puffy and moist, my clitty a hot point where my lips met, ready to be frigged off.

It was enough that I was being buggered, or it should have been. That didn't stop my dirty mind from working as I started to masturbate to the rude, squashy noises of my bottom hole being fucked. The terrible humiliation of my spanking came back, only now as a mental pleasure strong enough to match what was being done to be physically. I'd been taken by the hair and forced to the floor, for spanking. I'd had my bottom stripped in front of the idiot René-Claude, for spanking. I'd had by panties held down by some horrible old woman, for spanking.

Now I was red-bottomed and contrite, and the man who had punished me had his cock up my bottom, buggering me, by my own invitation. It was an act of utter, grovelling submission, to surrender my bottom hole to the man who had beaten me . . . to suck his cock for him . . . to open myself with a finger, in full view . . . to let him spunk up in my rectum with his belly slapping against my newly smacked bum cheeks . . .

That was what was going to happen, to, at any second. He was getting frantic, gasping and hissing obscenities as he buggered me. My bumhole had begun to contract, squeezing on the intruding cock, slowly, then faster, and faster, going into spasm as came under my fingers. I was screaming, then biting on the bed covers, and screaming again, knowing I could be heard, knowing René-Claude would be sniggering over what he would suppose to be an admonitory fucking from his angry grandfather, knowing that Madame Vaucopin would be thinking what a dirty slut I was.

She was right too. Just at the peak of my orgasm I felt Fauçon's cock jerk in my bowels. There was a final squashy noise as he jammed his cock in to the very hilt, and I knew he'd come, injecting his sperm into my gut, a truly filthy piece of knowledge that kept me rubbing and snatching at my sex even as he went limp on top of me.

All my shame and confusion came flooding back as I slowly came down from my orgasm. I knew that no other way would the orgasm have been quite so good, yet that did little to dull my emotions. He'd really dealt with me, and even knowing what the consequences would be, I promised myself to be better behaved in future, accepting my defeat and his right to punish me.

I was spent, and fortunately so was he, pulling himself slowly from my now aching bumhole as I once more spread my cheeks for him, and collapsing back on the bed. He was gasping for breath, and it was a long time before he could speak, so much so that I'd begun to get worried. Having him die on me as a result of sexual exertions was no part of my plan.

When he did speak, it was not even to thank me, but to demand I wash his cock and balls. I went, despite feeling pretty resentful, waddling badly with my panties still a bit down. In the bathroom I washed quickly, then filled a basin and took a sponge and some soap. Back in the bedroom I cleaned him up, grateful only that he hadn't made me suck his cock and balls instead.

He also demanded that I apologise to René-Claude, which really was a bit much, and left me feeling very much the spanked girl, too scared of another bum toasting to disobey. As I'd guessed, René-Claude had heard my screams, obviously, as when I came back downstairs he was grinning from ear to ear and there was a damp stain on the front of his trousers. I hung my head and said sorry, another humiliation despite his complete lack of response.

For all my muddled feelings, the experience perked me up considerable. I was no longer bored, with the knowledge that Fauçon was prepared to spank me in front of other people keeping me firmly on my toes. He also seemed to trust me more, or possible he had become more confident in his hold over me. It made sense, I suppose, if he could spank me without so much as a by-your-leave and instead of running for the police I got him to bugger me.

I didn't want to push my luck though, so I was very good all afternoon, quietly watching him finish off the two sketches he'd done of me and putting in the occasional compliment. They were good, and I had to admit he'd captured the serenity of sleep and the anguish of punishment beautifully.

He'd also included every tiny detail, right down to the wrinkles of my bumhole. I asked if it had to be quite so rude, and got a half-hour lecture on realism, freedom of expression and the art critics of the last fifty years or more. These he considered stupid, prudish, unprincipled, timid and much more. The artist, he said, should fear nothing, restrain nothing and conceal nothing.

I ignored the temptation to ask why the Germans hadn't shot him as well as Helene if he thought like that, and gave a respectful nod instead. I was already curled up at his feet, very much the adoring pupil worshipping at the shrine of her brilliant master. Adulation was obviously just what he wanted from me, and he grew more and more pleased with himself, reaching a peak of self-satisfaction after I'd got down between his knees to take a leisurely suck of his cock while I played with myself.

That left me firmly in favour, which was ironic as it derived from my bad behaviour, or supposedly bad behaviour. I still felt I'd had a perfect right to slap René-Claude's silly face, and if the incident had proved all to the good sexually, it had also removed my last trace of guilt at what I intended to do. So I plotted as we ate supper, and afterwards, with Phillippe expounding his theories on modern art to Patrice and myself.

For one thing, it seemed highly unlikely that there was a catalogue, and even if one did exist I couldn't see the subtraction of even a dozen paintings from the studio being noticed. As he had said himself, what mattered was the work of the moment, and not what had gone before. It existed, that was enough for him, or so he said. If that was true, all I had to do was make my selection from the darker recesses, and among the smaller canvasses, which was sensible anyway.

The next problem was getting the paintings out of the house. Phillippe spent a fair bit of his time asleep or thoroughly drunk, sometimes both. A heavy lunch, a good fuck and I could probably count on him to nap for as much time as I would need, or more. Unfortunately there was also Madame Vaucopin, with her beady little eyes constantly following me, even if I went to the loo or for a glass of water. Patrice and René-Claude were also a problem, both likely to be seeking me out while Phillippe was asleep, for a fuck or a leer respectively.

Even once I had my loot out of the house there was the problem of transport. It would be best if I didn't have to disappear at the same time as the paintings, but for that I really needed an accomplice. Percy was hopeless, and the only other people I knew at all where the Moreaus, who not only seemed thoroughly upright but obviously had a great deal of respect for Fauçon.

So I was on my own, in which case the best bet was to hide the paintings somewhere and come back to the Loire later in the year. Percy might be a bit miffed if I went without him, but otherwise it was easy. The question then became where to conceal the paintings. I'd have left Phillippe, and he was very clearly not the sort to let me stroll casually in and out of his life. When I left I was either going to have to run for it or make a big scene. Either way I was not going to be able to come back and retrieve my property . . . well, his property.

The old mill Phillippe had shown me had to be at least worth investigating. It was long disused, yet parts still had roofs. It was also big, so it was sure to have nooks and crannies in which the paintings could be concealed. Damp might be a problem, and it seemed just the sort of place local children might come to play, but for the time being I could think of no better option.

What I had to do was get out of the house, on my own, and not just for nefarious designs. I wanted some space, and to see Percy, and taste something other than young Coteaux du Layon from a jug. The cost was likely to be a thorough spanking, but that was fine so long as he kept Madame Vaucopin and René-Claude out of it. Even if he didn't I could handle it.

My best bet was to get up early and just go, while Phillippe was still asleep. He was a late riser anyway, and if Madame Vaucopin probably got up a fair bit earlier, it should not be too hard to evade her. Both the boys could be counted on to lie in. So I kept off the drink and did my best to ensure that Phillippe kept on it, keeping his glass full, and generally ministering to his needs.

What with the wine, my respectful attention and the ability to spout off without anyone opposing his views, he was in a pretty good mood by the end of the evening. I had to help him upstairs again, and again he used the contact as an excuse to explore my bottom.

In the bedroom I was told to do a striptease. Barely had my panties hit the floor than I'd been pulled down onto the erection he had been massaging as he watched me dance. I was made to suck, pulled up long enough for a Gauloise-flavoured kiss and put back down, to be held by the hair, trying to suck as he fucked my mouth. Before long he'd come, his grip locked in my hair as I gagged on spurt after spurt of salty sperm, to leave me gasping, with bubbles of it coming out of my mouth and nose.

I was eager by then, high on submission and the smell and taste of cock. He wasn't, and demanded that I tuck him into bed before telling me not to be too noisy if I had to frig off. By the time I'd got my T-shirt on he was asleep. I hadn't masturbated. I had other ideas.

He was sound asleep. Madame Vaucopin had long gone to bed. René-Claude had been in his room when we came up, making noises the origin of which I did not want to know. That left Patrice, who I might have been cross with earlier, but was young, virile, and there.

My tummy was fluttering as I nipped across the corridor, and the sensation of naughtiness was adding a lot to my excitement. He was expecting me, sitting up in bed with the side light on, trying to look cool. I climbed in, kissing him even as my hand went to his cock. He was nude, and already pretty stiff, presumably in anticipation of me. It was raw, teenage stuff, groping at each other's bodies as we snogged. He was an eager kisser, and tasted a lot better than Phillippe. I didn't point out that his grandfather had just come in my mouth.

His fingers were in my pussy in no time, opening me until I was aching for them to replaced by his cock. He obliged, mounting me and groaning in ecstasy as he slid himself up into my body. I lay back, legs wide, for once delighting in the feel of a good, old-fashioned fucking. He had stamina too, pumping away until I was dizzy with pleasure and whipping it out at the last second to come over my belly.

There was plenty of it, spattered across my tummy and pooled in my belly button. I just wanted to come, and even as he rolled off I was snatching at his mess, to rub it over my boobs and pussy before settling down to masturbate. He said nothing, just watching as I brought myself to a rapid, tight orgasm with my body smeared with his sperm.

It was plainly unsafe to stay, and I needed a wash, so I made for the bathroom. I'd just about finished when I heard a door close. A moment later Phillippe appeared, bleary-eyed and dishevelled, just in time to catch me industriously brushing my teeth. He didn't seem suspicious, as such, but led me back to the bedroom by the hand and sent me to bed with a smack on the bottom. There were no further demands on me, and as I settled towards sleep I was feeling well pleased with myself if less than entirely satisfied.

Five

As I'd hoped, I woke up before he did. Long before, in fact, with dawn just breaking outside and a distinctly autumnal chill in the air. Normally I'd have rolled over and gone back to sleep, but I was determined, and forced myself to get up. It was foggy outside, definitely the weather for jeans and a jumper, although it was likely to be baking hot by mid-morning.

By the time I was dressed I could hear Madame Vaucopin, opening the downstairs shutters. She was pretty noisy about it, and managed to seem irritable even doing something so mundane. It also meant I could tell where she was, and I managed to sneak out of the back door without being noticed.

Outside it was damp, the grass wet with dew and the sun struggling to break through the mist. I was going to get soaked in the woods, so I skirted the top of the vineyards and made my way down along the side of the Clos St Aubin. The first of the pickers were coming along the road as I crossed it, a trio of tough looking men who responded to my greeting with wolfish smiles and turned to watch as I walked away.

Not entirely sure if I was safe, I kept going until they were out of sight before pushing in among the bushes. I was wet to my knees by the time I reached the mill, and also nervous, wondering if they might have followed me. For a while I stood waiting, but heard nothing more sinister than the rustle of a bird in the foliage.

As I began to explore I quickly realised that the mill had been deserted for longer than I'd imagined. The great wheel was rusted onto its bearings, with the wooden paddles so decayed that orange and white fungi had begun to grow on them. Inside it was a death trap, the floor and stairs gone through in places, and obviously too rotten to take any weight at all. It was damp too, and even those areas where the roof remained were open to the wind. Storing the paintings there was out of the question.

That was disappointing, but the atmosphere of solitude was pleasant, and the more so for being under constant scrutiny at Phillippe's. For a while I stood by the mill pond, just for the joy of being absolutely alone. It was even tempting to strip off for a swim, but just a little too cold, while I had no intention of getting caught bathing nude by the pickers. There was something in the way they had looked at me that suggested they'd expect sex, and might well not be prepared to take no for an answer.

On another day I might have fantasised over it, imagining them catch me nude and putting me through a round of cock-sucking, fucking and buggery before sending me away naked, sore and with my bum red from beating. As it was the idea seemed just a little too close to reality for comfort.

I knew I was probably being silly, but just in case I left along the river path, away from the village and towards the Moreaus' winery. It occurred to me that Alain and Monique would be up, although Percy was unlikely to be around. I wasn't in the mood for modelling, and had already been away long enough to catch Phillippe's anger if it was coming. So I decided to call in and see how things were going, perhaps leave an apologetic message for Percy.

All the fine wines were handled in the older part of the winery, in a deliberately traditional manner. They also made basic table wines, a Cabernet and *Rosé d'Anjou*, in a modern facility, which was what I reached first. There was only a low fence separating it from the rough land along the side of the river, so I climbed over, into an open yard between high sheds. There was nobody about, but one of the shed doors was partially open and I could hear noises from within. I went across, hoping it would be Alain himself, and poked my head around the door.

It was Alain. He was standing by a press, poring the contents of a hod into the hopper, a perfectly reasonable thing to do for a wine maker at vintage time, except that the hod didn't contain grapes, but blackcurrants. I managed an awkward smile as he turned towards me.

Personally, I didn't give a damn if he was providing his *Cabernet d'Anjou* with a bit of extra fruit. It was harmless, and probably improved the stuff. Legally it was adulteration, and short of the local board of control, a wine journalist was the last person he would want to know. It was not good, but the only thing I could think of to do was play stupid.

'*Faites vous du Cassis*?'

His worried look immediately turned to a smile.

'*Mais oui.* It is new to our *tarif.*'

'I er . . . I was hoping to look round, but if you're busy . . .'

'No, no. *Pas du tout.*'

He was busy, obviously, but quickly tipped the rest of the blackcurrants into the hopper and climbed down. As the hustled me out and pulled the great sliding door to behind us I was already wondering if I might be able to turn the discovery to my advantage. He had plenty of space in which the pictures could be stored. It was a risk, but a small one when compared one considered the difficulty he'd get into if I reported him.

I didn't say anything, but ran the idea over in my mind as he escorted me to the older part of the winery. There he excused himself, giving me free rein to look round. There was plenty to see, ancient equipment mixed with modern, and storage tunnels leading over a hundred yards back into the hillside, every one lined with cobwebbed bottles. There were vintages going back to the 'twenties, which I determined to get at if it meant blackmail. Less appetising was the discovery that when they said 'bottled by hand', they really meant it. The 'bottling plant' consisted of an ageing and toothless peasant seated on a stool with a tube leading from a barrel. He started the flow by sucking on the tube and controlled it with a large and grubby thumb, making me extremely glad that the stuff had a decent percentage of alcohol.

They were attentive in typically French fashion, but unlike the pickers, completely unthreatening. It was all too easy to flirt, and a relief after the air of jealousy at Fauçon's, and I had soon decided to wait until Percy turned up and take my medicine when I got back to the house. So when I was offered samples from the casks I accepted, and was soon discussing the merits of the different vineyards. We'd got about halfway through the range when Percy turned up.

He was extremely pleased to see me, and the feeling was mutual. At the first opportunity he patted my bottom, and kept the attention up with an eagerness that wouldn't have been out of place in a man one third his age. He also managed to get a comment in to the effect that I was long overdue a spanking, which along with all the male attention and the wine had its inevitable effect on me.

I was not going to miss out, and I had a fair bit of guilt to assuage as well as simple lust. It would have been easy enough, either to drive back to the hotel or risk a quickie in among the bushes. Unfortunately I couldn't very well let my bum get reddened when Phillippe was sure to have my panties off, be it for a spanking or just modelling. So it had to be gentle, but when I told Percy nodded wisely and promised to make up for it with added humiliation.

We'd taken our glasses outside to talk, tasting as we discussed the best way to get me spanked. Percy was not in favour of the hotel, on the grounds that something might get back to Fauçon, despite the comfort it offered. What he wanted was somewhere quite he could take the car. I had the answer, the mill.

After a last glass each we made our excuses, saying we had to drive into Challones. I was tingling all over as we left, the anticipation so high it was as if I'd done without it for a month, not less than a day. It wasn't the same though. Phillippe turned me on but he made me feel small. With Percy it was just plain naughty.

Naughty is good, the best, spanking English style, with the girl's bum showing because it's rude. I have never had a hang-up about nudity, but it is still deliciously embarrassing when my panties come down for a spanking. That was what I wanted, and Percy was the man to give it.

I had to get out and move a fallen branch to let Percy get the Rover up the track to the mill, and once he'd parked in the shadow of one of the buildings the balance between safety and being outdoors was just right. I could hardly wait to get the seat down and into position, bottom up and completely vulnerable to him, with my jeans button popped to make it easy to bare me.

He took his time, first stroking the seat of my jeans, just firmly enough to keep me in mind of what he was doing. I shut my eyes, letting my feelings build as my bottom was molested. That was what he was doing, no question, molesting my bottom, exploring me through my jeans, to get off over the shape and feel of my flesh, making the most of me, as any dirty old man would want to do with a young girl's bottom.

Soon he'd begun to squeeze, cupping my bum cheeks and making them wobble, really enjoying what I had to offer. It became more intrusive too, his podgy fingers slipping down between my thighs to investigate the bulge of my pussy lips beneath the taught denim of my jeans. He began to smack, just pats really, and to pinch, tweaking my bum flesh and my pussy, until I began to squeak.

I was breathing hard, my head spinning with images of the way I was, my bottom lifted for his inspection, a bad girl, a naughty girl. It was going to get naughtier too, and just when I was about to break and beg to pull down my jeans, his hands found my waistband. He pulled, his plump fingers pressing into the flesh of my hips, the tightness of my jeans eased over the swell of my bottom, and down. The top of my panties came on show, the crests of my bum cheeks, and at last the whole, panty-clad globe of my bottom. He gave his dirty little chuckle as he settled my jeans down around my thighs, and went back to enjoying my bum.

Now I had only my panties to cover me. I was no longer proper, no longer showing what society deems reasonable in the street. I'd had my jeans pulled down. I'd let a dirty old man pull my jeans down. That made me a really bad girl, thoroughly improper. It was being done in the open too, in the back of a car, making it that little bit naughtier.

I was purring as he fondled me, stroking and tickling and patting and pinching, both on the seat of my panties and where my cheeks showed below the leg holes. After a while his fingers strayed down again, finding my now wet panty crotch to push a fold of cotton in between my sex lips and briefly rub at my clitty. I pushed up my bottom, eager for a finger in my hole, or to be frigged. He stopped, his palm settled on the top of my bottom and he had began to wobble my cheeks instead, chuckling to himself as he watched my bum flesh move in my panties.

If he didn't hurry up I was going to have to take matters into my own hands, but again he seemed to know when I needed more. After a last squeeze of my cheeks, he put his hands in my panty waistband. For a moment he just held them, sending my anticipation soaring. Only when my muscles had begun to twitch did he begin to pull, easing them down even more slowly than he'd done my jeans, so that I could feel my bum coming on view, inch my inch.

They came down, all the way, my last scrap of modesty removed as the damp gusset was jerked out from between my thighs. I felt cool air on the back of my pussy lips and I knew it was showing. So was my bottom hole, a little, then completely as his fingers locked in my flesh and my cheeks were hauled wide. I groaned at the rude treatment and stuck it up, putting myself on blatant display.

I was no longer just a naughty girl, letting her panties down for a dirty old man. I was a slut, eager for a cock in her pussy or even up her bottom, flaunting herself for the rude attentions of the man molesting her, without a thought for social approval, or anything but her dirty needs. A girl like that needs a spanking. She was going to get it too.

Percy went back to work, fondling and smacking at my now bare bum, ever so gently, and never enough to risk adding to the now fading bruises from the last beating he'd given me. I revelled in it, lifting my bottom to the slaps, wiggling it to encourage him, and wondering how he would take his pleasure of me.

I knew his cock was out. I'd heard his zip. He was wanking it, feeling and spanking my bum as he wanked his dirty little cock. Soon he would make me suck him, or mount me, his fat belly pushing me down into the car seat as he made use of my pussy, or buggered me, probably buggered me.

The slaps had begun to get harder, and I knew I'd be pinking up. I wanted it harder, a proper spanking, and Phillippe's reaction didn't seem so important any more. He could beat me, cane me for all I cared. He could have the horrible Madame Vaucopin hold me down by my lowered panties and take his belt to my bottom. I'd laugh at them, and masturbate on the floor to show what I thought of their punishment . . .

I was going to have to come. Percy chuckled as I cocked a leg up to get my hand to my pussy. He'd been wanking pretty furiously, and I didn't know if I wanted him to climb onto me or to frig freely with my bum on show as he molested me. Not that it mattered. It was his choice. He could use me as he pleased.

He was, too, his fingers slipping down between my bum cheeks to find the hole, and tickle. As he teased my anus he began to spank me again, just a little more firmly. It was all I needed to get there, the idea of a spanker touching up my bottom hole. He might

even be going to bugger me, to get me slimy and easy
with his finger, then push his cock up me.

Sure enough, his finger went in, slipping past my
ring and deep up, where he began to wiggle it about.
I was getting there, moaning and sighing in pleasure,
begging for the smacks to get harder. They didn't,
they stopped. The finger stayed in my bottom hole
though, deep up, and as I once more heard the
slapping noise of him pulling at his cock I knew he
could hold back no more.

Nor could I. I'd began to grunt and buck my
bottom up and down on his finger, behaving like the
wanton little slut I am, to get off on letting a
sixty-something man amuse himself with my bottom,
grope me, spank me, finger my hole . . .

The finger came out, with a rude pop as it left my
anus. I moaned in disappointment, my eyes coming
open, my head turning to protest. Percy was wanking
furiously, into the hand he'd just had between my
cheeks. I guessed what he was going to do, but I was
too high to stop myself and my mouth came open
even as the sperm erupted from his cock.

I watched it pool in his hand in dirty fascination,
my tongue hanging out like a dog's. He was going to
feed it to me, a handful of dirty spunk, and my mouth
was wide to receive it. My clitty was burning under
my finger. I was right on the edge, waiting. Then he
had wiped the last blob of come from the tip of his
cock and it was time. His hand came out. My tongue
pushed forward, and I was lapping it up, eating his
sperm as my rubbing grew faster once more.

My orgasm started even as the taste filled my
mouth. Then I had buried my face in his hand and
was licking at it, swallowing the sperm, sucking at the
finger he'd had up my bottom as I came in squirming,
writhing ecstasy. Right at the peak he reached down

his other hand between my cheeks and stuck one fat finger firmly up my bottom, pushing me still higher. A third peak came, and a fourth, but I wanted it to last forever, and was still wriggling on his finger long after the pleasure had begun to die, trying to bring myself off one more time.

It was only when Percy finally took his hands away that I really came down. He was well pleased with himself, as he always is when he has made me behave in some especially dirty way. I was thoroughly satisfied too, and very glad indeed I had waited. My only concern was that Percy might have felt hard done by.

'I'd thought you were going to have my bottom, at least?' I asked him as I struggled up my panties and jeans. 'Was that all right?'

He gave me a big smile.

'Splendid, thank you, my dear, and all the better for the wait, I dare say. Now, how about a bite of lunch?'

'Lunch? Isn't it a bit early, even for you?'

'One o'clock in the afternoon is, I have always been led to believe, a very civilised time for lunch.'

'One o'clock! You're joking!'

'I assure you . . .'

'No, I mean, is it really one o'clock . . . It is, shit!'

'You were expected back?'

'I never said I'd gone!'

'Then eat with me, and return afterwards to say you took a stroll and got lost.'

'How can I claim to have got lost when all I have to do is follow the river?'

'Say you went the other way.'

I gave in. I'd been gone ages, and I was either going to have to accept Phillippe's decision when I got back or have a row. Either way another hour or two would make no difference, and a lunch with Percy at a restaurant was sure to be superior to what Madame Vaucopin produced.

So I went with Percy. The morning mist had burnt off, leaving it clear and sunny but very still, ideal weather for a leisurely lunch, which we took at a restaurant he'd discovered on the opposite side of the valley. I told him everything that had happened, including how Phillippe Fauçon had spanked and buggered me, and about Patrice and René-Claude. What I held back was my wicked plan and Alain Moreau's little scam with the blackcurrants, both of which might have given him apoplexy.

He accepted my dirty behaviour with perfect equanimity, as he always did, and as I started back up the hill after being dropped off, it was an attitude I was wishing Phillippe shared. Unfortunately the reverse was true, and I was sure he was going to be furious, however realistic I made my protestations of having become lost. It was unfair, when I had a perfect right to go out as I pleased, but I knew full well that made no difference.

It was nearly three by the time I cautiously pushed open the door. Within, there was absolute silence. I awaited, expecting an angry shout at any moment, Phillippe demanding to know if it was me. Nothing happened. I shut the door, quiet nosily, not wanting to be accused to trying to sneak in and hide upstairs or something. Still there was no response.

I was sure somebody would be in, but a quick inspection of the kitchen revealed only the washing up, drying in a rack. So they'd had lunch, but Madame Vaucopin had obviously gone out, to the shops perhaps. I went upstairs, hoping to find the house deserted. It wasn't. Phillippe was there, fast asleep on the bed. That was it though, no Patrice, no René-Claude.

It was seriously tempting. All I had to do was nip up to the studio, make my selection, cover them with a rug or something and make my way down the hill to the Moreau's. I'd point out to Alain that I knew exactly what he was up to and promise to keep quiet in return for a little favour. It was simple.

Only it wasn't. There would be other people in the vineyards and at the winery. Alain might not be blackmailed so easily. Phillippe might wake up. Above all, thinking about it was one thing, but plucking up the courage to actually do it was something else again.I went up to the studio anyway, telling myself that it was perfectly reasonable to want to look at my lover's paintings.

The studio was warm and silent, the smell of oil paint and age more pronounced than ever. I began to search, my finger shaking even though I was knew I was doing nothing wrong, yet. The feeling grew worse as I lifted up canvas after canvas, until I was starting at every tiny noise. I'd imagined myself as a cool thief, quick, decisive and smooth. It was a lie.

I kept looking anyway, determined that at the least I would decide which I wanted and which I could afford to take. Small ones hidden behind larger ones were clearly the best choice, and in many ways the most appealing too. Most were sketches, or facial studies, as always capturing the emotions of the subject. Almost none were of males, something that clearly reflected the way Phillippe thought, men as creators, women as subjects. Of the girls, some seemed to be locals, including Monique Moreau as a teenager, and Marie-Armelle. One was well worth looking at, of Marie-Armelle, on a swing with her skirts flying up to show off a bare, chubby pussy, not unlike Fragonard's classic, only ruder. Another was interesting, showing Monique and Marie-Armelle together, cuddled close. Both were dressed, but Phillippe had managed to convey an intimacy between them that hinted of lesbianism, although it might just have been my dirty mind. There were also several of Madame Vaucopin, some painted recently, more when she had been much younger, perhaps in the late sixties or early seventies, when he had returned to settle in the Layon valley. Others were clearly models, of whom he seemed to have had a string stretching back over the years.

There had been fewer models recently, and several of those showing Madame Vaucopin as a young woman were nudes, so it seemed yet more likely that her resentment of me sprang from jealousy. That was interesting, but less so than the possibility of finding a picture of Helene, or not finding one.

If there were any, they would have to be at the back, while she would presumably be recognisable by her wartime clothes, if she had any on, and her resemblance to me. Looking for them meant moving those at the front, and disturbing the dust of years, but I persevered, telling myself that curiosity was only to be expected and that Phillippe would surely be flattered. If there weren't any, it seemed fair to assume that he made the whole story up to get me out of my knickers.

I had very soon realised that there was not going to be time to make a proper search. Even if I resisted the temptation to study the irrelevant paintings, it was going to take me hours. As it was, I for one found it very hard not to stare at least a little when I found an exquisitely rendered pencil sketch of a pretty hippichick in nothing but a flowery hat. Her face was buried between a much older woman's thighs. That was about as rude as it got, but there were plenty of other nudes, and all with every single detail made out exactly.

Finally I decided that I was pushing my luck and began to put the canvases back. I had not found a single one I could safely identify as Helene, and few if any showed clothing from before the early fifties. He had lied to me, I was sure of it. For that lie he had had me naked, as his lover, as his toy. A dozen paintings were a fair exchange.

Choice was another thing, and one I considered as I did my best to hide the evidence of my search. The blatantly pornographic ones had their appeal, but as Fauçon pointed out so frequently, the art establishment claims to be inherently liberal, but lacks the courage of its convictions when it comes down to young girls licking out elderly matrons. The portraits were probably best, and some of the less extreme nude studies. Even if I stuck to those and took ones well buried in the pile I had a broad choice.

I had finished tidying up and was studying my own painting when I heard a noise from downstairs. Evidently Phillippe had woken up, and it seemed sensible to go down immediately. After looking at all the nudes I knew a spanking would quickly warm me up, while if he wanted to punish me at least it wouldn't be in front of either Madame Vaucopin or the boys.

So I tripped gaily downstairs, calling out as I reached the landing, only to find Patrice coming up the stairs and Phillippe visible on his bed, as sound asleep as before. Patrice's eyes had lit up as he saw me, and before I could even speak he had taken me in his arms and was hustling me towards his bedroom. I resisted, briefly, but he already had one hand on my bottom and the other up my top, squeezing a boob.

He was whispering in my ear too, in between nibbles, telling me how gorgeous I was and how he was going to put me on my knees to fuck me. That was too much, the thought of presenting my bum for rear entry breaking down the last of my caution. I let him have me, pulled into his room and the door pushed carefully shut behind us.

I knew his style, quick, rough and energetic. That was just as well, with his grandfather asleep across the corridor, and I was sinking to my knees even as he turned from the door. He pulled his cock out. It went straight into my mouth, and I was sucking. It was nice, but it wasn't really necessary, his cock swelling extraordinarily quickly, until I was gaping on a full erection with my boobs in my hands.

He was thoroughly enjoying himself, and I think would have settled for him doing it in my mouth, but he responded quickly enough when I came off and tugged him towards the bed. In moments my jeans and panties were down and he had my thighs apart, his fingers pushing roughly up into my pussy as our mouths met. He was pulling at my top too, clearly keen to get me nude. I knew it was foolish but was in no mood to argue, and had soon been efficiently stripped as we rolled on the bed.

Even as my panties were tugged free of my ankles I was scrambling into doggy position, determined that he would be as good as his word and have me from behind. I needn't have worried, his hands closing on my hips to help me over and his helmet nudging between my bum cheeks an instant later. His cock pressed to my hole, pushed in and he was up, fucking me once more as my mouth came open to the delicious feel of a nice big cock inside my hole.

It started, and I was gasping immediately, and clutching at the bed, out of control under the sheer power and urgency of his thrusts. He told me to shut up, but it barely registered, and the next instant my panties had been thrust into my mouth. That was glorious, dirty, dominant, and just so me. I closed my mouth on the cotton, tasting my own sex as he went back to fucking me, harder still, hissing between his teeth as his lean, hard belly slapped over and over on my well lifted bottom.

He was going to come, long before I could get there myself, but the knowledge that I was going to end up frigging off on my back one more time just provided that extra kick of submissive pleasure. He'd spunk on my bottom and I could use to it to open my hole, fingering my anus in front of him, such a filthy, dirty thing to do . . . He stopped.

I'd heard it too, a door, undoubtedly Phillippe's. We froze. Phillippe's voice sounded, calling Patrice. I spat out my panties and we came apart, Patrice wrenching at his fly as I rolled off the bed, to find the space underneath packed solidly with boxes. Patrice hissed at me, pointing frantically, at the fireplace. He had to be mad, but Phillippe's voice sounded again, right outside the door, questioning, angry.

I dashed for the fireplace, pausing only to hurl my clothes under the bed. It was huge, a black tunnel disappearing upwards, with an iron bar across it and a ledge. I wrenched myself up even as I heard the door pushed wide, and was dragging myself onto the ledge as Phillippe spoke, asking Patrice if he'd seen me.

Patrice was good. The tone of his answer expressed absolute indifference, as if not just to whether I was in the house, but whether I existed at all. How he'd got his cock away with an erection like an iron bar I didn't know, and the room must have stunk of sex, but Phillippe accepted the statement.

That was a relief, but it was the only one. I had scrapped my leg as I pulled myself up onto the ledge, and I was bent double in a tiny space. Both my hips, my bottom and my shoulders were pressed to hard stone, while I could only keep myself in place by supporting myself on the iron bar. It was filthy too, my body soiled and my hair full of cobwebs, while the air was full of dust and it was a desperate struggle not to cough.

It got worse. Having accepted that I wasn't around and presumably therefore that he had nowhere to stick his erection, Phillippe began to chat with Patrice, discussing the alarming rise of the extreme right in French politics of all things. They agreed, wholeheartedly, lambasting Jean-Marie Le Pen and various people I'd never heard of, while I desperately wished they shut up.

They went on, becoming more and more vehement, as I became more and more uncomfortable. Before long I'd have cheered happily if a group of fascists had burst in and shot them, and that was before the spider started to walk down my back. It was big. It felt huge, and if it had only eight legs it was making full use of all of them. Just the touch of it sent shivers the length of my spine, and set my hands shaking, for all my desperate attempts to tell myself it was harmless. It was getting lower too, down my spine, then into the crease of my bottom, which tickled so much I had to grit my teeth to stop myself screaming. Outside, the topic of conversation switched to the EU, one of Phillippe's favourites.

The spider had stopped, about an inch from my bumhole, leaving me shaking my head in an agony of fear and consternation. I was praying it wouldn't decide that my pussy made a convenient hidey-hole, but I knew if it did I was going to scream and to Hell with the consequences. It didn't, but began to do a little dance between my cheeks, making the tickling worse than before.

I was going to scream. I had to. I was stuck up a chimney, covered in soot, a large spider was making a web between the cheeks of my bottom and Patrice wasn't even trying to get rid of his wretched grandfather . . .

Phillippe excused himself, saying he needed the loo. I risked moving, snatched at my bottom to brush the spider away, and nearly fell. The spider was gone, but it was behind me, and I could feel panic starting to well up. I had to come down.

The moment I put one foot down Patrice hissed for me to stop. I heard the loo door and realised he was right. Phillippe might well come back. As I pulled up my foot I just snapped. Tears of frustration burst from my eyes and I let out a broken sob. Patrice told me to shut up.

I'd have answered him back, only the loo door went again. Footsteps sounded outside, coming nearer, and past, down the stairs. Relief flooded through me. I started to shake, so hard I had to force myself to calm down before I could try and get off the ledge. As I got one foot onto the ground I heard Patrice's voice, urging me to hurry, from right outside the fireplace.

I dropped down, ducking, to find him standing directly in front of me, his erection in one hand. The next instant I'd been taken firmly by the hair and his cock was pressed to my lips. I hit out, furious at him, and opened my mouth to call him a bastard, only to break off in a muffled grunt as his cock was pushed in to the back of my throat. He groaned in pleasure as he began to fuck my head, holding me tight, and indifferent to my slaps as I struggled to get free.

It took me about ten seconds to decide to bite the bastard's cock, which was a second too long. He'd barely begun to fuck me when he pulled his cock free, to jerk frantically at the shaft even as my head was tugged back hard, by the hair. I screamed in pain, just in time to catch the first explosion of his come right in my mouth. I shut it, and my eyes, not a moment too soon as the second spurt caught me across the bridge of my nose and in both eyes. Again my mouth came open, this time in utter disgust. More spunk went in, and over my nose, then his cock had been wedged deep into my throat once more.

I actually felt his helmet squash into the spermy mess in the mouth of my windpipe, and then I was choking, my throat going into spasm after spasm on his meat as I struggled to get away. He gave a deep groan of ecstasy and just kept pulling on my hair, holding me until I finally managed to get my knee around and jam it into his shin. He jumped back, cursing and calling me a bitch.

There was no answer. I went into a coughing fit, sperm and saliva and mucus exploding from my mouth and nose, all over his legs and the floor. He cursed again, in disgust, and told me to stop it, but there was nothing I could do, only collapse down, doubled up as I struggled to cough up the muck that was choking me.

It came, most of it, down my front and onto the floor. By the time I'd finished coughing and pitting I could feel some on my boobs, and I knew my face was covered. Unable to see, I could only grope for the coverlet from his bed, using to wipe my eyes despite his angry protest. I told him to shut up as my eyes came open, and ran for the bathroom.

I was a fine state, my hair thick with dirty cobwebs, my face black with soot except where the sperm had begun to dribble down to make pinkish-white lines. My boobs and belly were only a little better, spotty with black smuts and blobs of bubbly sperm. More sperm was hanging out of my nose, mixed with mucus, and my mouth was still full of it.

As I stepped into the shower I was calling Patrice a bastard over and over. It had been completely uncalled for to expect me to suck him after I'd been up the chimney. Just because he'd still been horny didn't mean I was, but he'd actually been surprised when I resisted, and when I kicked him. He'd had his jollies anyway, all over my face, and then had the nerve to be cross because I spat it out on the floor. What did he expect me to do!?

The answer was simple. Swallow it. I had, quite a lot, but that was beside the point. I was furious, but my body still felt extra sensitive, and as I washed it was impossible to ignore that I was still turned on. It had been humiliating anyway, no question, but I was determined that Patrice would not get the benefit of my arousal.

Not that he needed it. He'd had his orgasm, and being a man, had more or less lost interest. He didn't bother to come in to the bathroom anyway, despite knowing I was showering. I had to get my clothes though, and found him bundling up his bed cover in obvious annoyance. He'd cleaned the floor.

I dressed in angry silence, cross not so much for what he'd done, but because he was angry with me for making a mess. It was just so arrogant of him, and completely unreasonable when he'd virtually forced himself on me. I could have said plenty, but I knew he'd have answered me back, and with Phillippe downstairs a shouting match was not a good idea.

Not that I cared all that much, going to the kitchen to make myself a badly needed coffee without bothering to make up a story for how I'd got downstairs. He was in the dining room, and looked up in surprise as I came in.

'Natasha, where have you been?'

I was in no mood for lectures, but trotted out the excuse Percy had suggested for want of a better one.

'I went for a walk. I got lost. Sorry.'

'All day?'

'Yes. I've been miles. I just had a shower. I was wondering where you where.'

'What of your modelling? Today we have done nothing.'

'Sorry . . .'

'Perhaps so, but you should not have gone . . .'

'Look, I just went for a walk, that's all! I . . .'

'No matter. We have wasted time. What of my work!'

'Well, it's not that urgent, is it?'

He threw his hands up in exasperation. I shrugged, not wanting to argue, not willing to accept that he was right. He rose, and stalked off towards the stairs, signalling that I should follow him. I did, sipping the big bowl of *café-au-lait* I'd made myself. I wasn't sure if he was making for the bedroom or the studio, but it turned out to be the latter. As he pushed in I was worrying that he might notice the evidence of my earlier visit, as it had been impossible to hide the marks in the dust properly.

I needn't have bothered. He walked straight to the easel, pointing to the chalk marks where I was supposed to stand with a click of his fingers. I swallowed my coffee down and began to undress, Phillippe waiting impatiently until I was nude, then once more indicating my position. I got into pose, feeling more than a little resentful as I put my hands behind my head and pushed out my boobs. For a moment he examined me with a critical eye, then made a gesture. I turned a trifle.

'Chin, Natasha. Up.'

I lifted my chin.

'No! Not so high, and where is your emotion, your pride! You look slack, tired.'

I struggled to regain the way I'd felt when I'd first struck the pose. It was not easy. After the way Patrice had treated me the last thing I felt was proud. There was humiliation, yes, and I knew it would be nice in retrospect, when I didn't feel stiff and exhausted. Pride was out, but I tried.

Fauçon greeted my effort with a surly grunt and started to paint. He seldom spoke while he was working, and I knew I wasn't supposed to. That was fine. He wouldn't interrogate me and I wouldn't have to lie.

Unfortunately he wouldn't let it be, or accept that I was doing my best. That, as he pointed out, was not enough. He, he said, was a perfectionist. I, he stressed, had to understand that for an artist to work he had to have unquestioning loyalty and commitment from his model.

That was fine, except that all I was getting out of it was the privilege of bathing in his reflected glory and of having my body used as a repository for his sperm. No, not a repository, he used me like a sink, a dustbin. Okay, so I was out to pinch as many of his paintings as I could carry. That was irrelevant. He didn't know.

He went on, each little aphorism making me that bit more rebellious. The pain was getting worse too, and it was more than just stiffness. I felt weak, and light headed, as if I hadn't eaten in ages. My bladder was beginning to hurt too, and I was wishing I hadn't drunk a whole bowl of *café-au-lait*. Phillippe obviously had no understanding of how I felt, or if he did, he didn't care, or expected me to put up with it. Certainly he seemed to think that being his model was a high honour.

As my aches and pains grew steadily worse, I tried to think about the paintings I'd seen. It didn't work. I could only make the decision at the last minute, and my choice was going to rely more on size and how deeply he'd buried them than any artistic considerations. So it was back to my aching boobs and the sharp tension in my bladder, all the while hoping Phillippe would decide to call it a day.

He had shut up, but he seemed to be on a roll, painting with intense concentration, his eyes flicking from me to the canvas and back, over and over. To judge by his stance he was painting the details of my chest and belly, which left me less than sympathetic. It was all very well him demanding absolute commitment, but a tiny change in the set of my muscles or breasts surely wouldn't matter? I had to speak.

'Phillippe?'

'*Silence! Ne bouge pas!*'

'No, seriously, Phillippe. I need to pee.'

The answer was an irritable grunt. Denial.

'Please?'

'*Silence!*'

He muttered something less than complimentary under his breath and went on painting. I struggled to hold my pose, telling myself it was what I had to do, to maintain my persona as *La Pêche*, to make it all work. A different voice screamed at me that he was being utterly unreasonable and that I should just move, that my body was my own, Natasha's. I had to do something, or burst. My bladder was worst, so I let my abdomen go as loose as possible.

Phillippe's reaction was immediate, a string of rapid, angry French, directed at my stupidity, base nature and lack of consideration. It was so unfair, so unreasonable, and it really hurt, after the effort I'd been making. I turned to answer him back, which was a big mistake.

The muscles of my abdomen cramped. It was totally unexpected, and agonising. I doubled up, and at the same instant I let go of my bladder. Pee erupted from my sex, to spray out, front and back, trickling down my legs and pattering on the floor. I cried out in shock and misery, but I couldn't stop it, piddling everywhere in helpless consternation, the spray of yellow fluid completely out of my control. The cramp began to die as the pressure reduced, but there was no way I could stop the flow. I just had to let it come, sobbing out my pain and emotion as I urinated down my own legs and over the floor, all the while cursing Phillippe.

It was only when I straightened up that I even realised he'd stopped painting. He was sketching instead, with frantic energy. The pee was still dripping from my pussy, but I could only stare. He gave an angry hiss as I moved. I'd wet myself, I was standing in a puddle of pee, the insides of my legs soaked, utterly dispirited, and he was cross with me!

He had no sympathy at all for me. All he wanted to do was capture my emotion as I wet myself, and it wasn't even as if I'd done it for fun. That was too much, and I ran from the room, leaving him still sketching and shaking his head in irritation, presumably at my inability to get my priorities straight.

It didn't even occur to me that I shouldn't be wandering around the house stark naked until I was halfway down the stairs. I'd grown so used to being in the nude, and after sex with both Phillippe and Patrice it shouldn't have mattered to me, except for René-Claude.

He was on the landing, just staring into space, or else he'd been peeping through the door to watch me modelling. His eyes went round as he saw me and his hand went straight to his cock. I told him to fuck off and stormed past, into the bathroom. He would

114

follow, I was sure of it, neither tact nor sensitivity to criticism being his strong points. He had to have noticed that I'd wet myself as well, which was sure to appeal to his filthy little mind. I was not having him wanking over me in the shower again, so I contented myself with splashing water over my pussy and down my legs and left, to find him right outside the door. His fingers closed on my bottom as I passed, a painful tweak, right under one cheek.

I managed to hold back from slapping him, in no mood to take another of Phillippe's very public spankings. That made me more resentful than ever as I hurried back up the stairs. It was bad enough having to let him get away with pinching my bum, but because of him, and his pig of a brother and his bigger pig of a grandfather, I was even scared of what normally gave me the most pleasure of all, having my bottom spanked. Worse, the arousal that came when I did get it was stronger still, a seriously humiliating fact, which in turn prompted more arousal, more humiliation and so on, a piece of positive feedback I could only bring to an end by masturbating.

It would happen. I know myself. I wasn't going to give in to it easily though, or set myself up for more. So when I reached the studio I apologised to Phillippe and complimented him on the skill with which he had captured the shame and stress in my face as my bladder burst. He still gave me another of his little lectures on the relationship between artist and model. From his point of view that meant my total subjugation to his will. He even stressed that it was important for me not to try and influence him, on the grounds that any such input could only serve to erode his talent, a statement of mind-boggling arrogance.

I accepted it meekly, playing *La Pêche* even as I promised myself that if my scheme ever came to fruition I would expose him as an absolute bastard to all and sundry. It was small consolation. I was still there, with my pride and dignity seriously eroded and my need for sex feeling not like a joy, but a betrayal. Maybe I would have to come, but I was determined not to let Phillippe get anything out of the state I'd got myself into, nor Patrice. I'd hold back until I could do it myself.

The opportunity came sooner than I'd expected. Fortunately Phillippe was too involved in making subtle additions to the sketch of me peeing to demand his customary after session blow-job. I'd managed to dress before he finished, and was going to go downstairs when the bang of the back door signalled the return of Madame Vaucopin.

Phillippe had obviously asked her to get something important to him, because he went downstairs immediately, leaving me to my own devices. I went down too, but paused on the landing outside our bedroom. I could hear Phillippe's voice, and Madame Vaucopin's. Then came Patrice's, asking if there was any wine in the jug. A moment later Madame Vaucopin told René-Claude not to sit on the table.

They were all downstairs, and if they'd begun to drink then they were unlikely to come up again. I had maybe ten or fifteen minutes before Phillippe began to wonder where I was. The chance was too good to miss.

I slipped into the bedroom, closed the door and threw myself down on the bed. Even knowing I was going to masturbate and so deny Philippe my submission felt good, but I knew it was pointless to try and focus on anything other that what was uppermost in my mind, the way he treated me. It made me angry and resentful, but I forced that down, surprisingly easily.

My hand went down the front of my jeans, onto the gentle swell of my pussy. One finger pushed the cotton down into my crease to find my clitty and I was doing it. The tension immediately started to drain away as I gently massaged myself through my panties and let my mind roam over the things he'd done. There was plenty, the head-fucking, the brief, pre-emptory fucks, my first spanking, my public spanking. The last had been the best, a classic, delivered hard to my bare bottom with some appalling harridan holding me down by my panties, the idiot René-Claude giggling over the lewd show of my pussy and bumhole, and my pain.

A shiver ran through me at the thought. For all the bad feelings it had brought, in the long run it was going to become one of my favourite memories, I was sure, something to masturbate over for years. It would also be something to think about during a session of less than successful sex, with some muscular ox pounding away on top of me and fondly imagining my pleasure coming solely from his cock.

There was every chance there might be a next time too. There would have been if I had slapped René-Claude's face for pinching my bum. Phillippe might have waited for Madame Vaucopin to come back and brought her upstairs to hold me down while I was spanked. He might have let the boys watch too, both of them, gloating over my exposure and pain and misery as my buttocks were slapped up to a burning heat. They'd have seen the state of my pussy too, the juice dribbling down to betray my excitement. That would have got their cocks hard, along with the sight of my bare, dancing bottom and the dirty little hole winking between my spread cheeks.

Phillippe would have fucked me afterwards, and left me on the bed with come dribbling out of my pussy as well as juice. He'd have gone away. I'd have started to masturbate, just as I was. The boys would have caught me. They'd have fucked me, Patrice up my pussy, René-Claude in my mouth as he groped my boobs. They'd have buggered me, Patrice laughing as he pushed his cock up into my straining anus. René-Claude would have thought it was hilarious, watching my anus pull in and out on his brother's cock. He'd have wanted it too, and once Patrice had finished in my bum, up he'd have gone, sniggering as my gaping, slimy bumhole took the head of his penis, dirty sperm squeezing out around it. He wouldn't have come up my bottom though. Patrice would have been egging him on to put his dirty cock in my mouth, the cock he'd just had wedged up my bumhole. He'd have done it too, and I'd have taken it, sucking eagerly on the taste of my own bottom and Patrice's sperm as they laughed at my utter degradation . . .

I came, unable to stop myself, the filthy fantasy just too much. Shame welled up inside me even as my spine arched in ecstasy and my legs began to twitch, but I held the fantasy, imagining the moment when I took René-Claude's dirty, steaming cock into my mouth over and over until I could bear it no more. At last I collapsed, gasping and sobbing, exhausted and confused, with all the resentment and anger I'd so carefully pushed down flooding back.

Six

The night's sleep went some way to restore my balance, if not all the way. Phillippe got so drunk at dinner that he passed out while I was still sucking his cock, and although I knew Patrice would be waiting for me I left him to stew, which was extremely satisfying. It worked too, because he was all sweetness and light in the morning, complimenting me on my hair and even fetching me a glass of orange juice from the fridge. With Phillippe around there was no opportunity either to flirt or play cold, but I was thinking more kindly of him as I went upstairs to the studio.

Phillippe was also in a better mood, full of compliments and wistful remarks, about my beauty, and Helene's, and how similar we were in every way. By the time I was naked and in position I was even beginning to think of my behaviour the day before as a bit of a tantrum. I determined to stay still, anyway, and not to disrupt his work, despite a lingering resentment.

I'd remembered to go to the loo, which made a big difference, and Phillippe was in a talkative mood for once. He was working on background and shadow, which took a lot less concentration, and I was settling in to my task when there was a creak from the door.

I stayed still, expecting Madame Vaucopin, which was irritating, but not really a problem.

Nobody came in, and I relaxed once more, only for the sound to come again. This time I began to wonder if it was René-Claude, peeping. I was sure he had before, and the thought made my skin creep. Phillippe took no notice and I held my pose, wishing I could see the door properly instead of just being able to glimpse it from the corner of my eye. There was a crack, and a big keyhole, which I was sure would give a prime view to anyone peering through.

It was all too easy to imagine René-Claude kneeling down outside, wanking as he stared at my naked body, just as he had done in the shower. I even began to imagine I could hear the fleshy slapping of his cock in his hand, although it was impossible to be sure. It was only when Phillippe made a remark that I broke my silence.

'You are nervous, suddenly, Natasha. There is a problem? You need to piss?'

'No. I . . . I thought I heard something outside the door.'

'It will be René-Claude.'

He didn't sound bothered at all, and just went on painting.

'Yes, I'd guessed it was René-Claude, but . . .'

'*Du calme.*'

'But . . .'

'Let him watch. Be sympathetic, Natasha. He is simple, yes, but underneath he is a normal boy, with normal needs. What harm is there to you?'

He shrugged and went back to work.

Put like that, it made me seem a real bitch. After all, René-Claude was only looking, and I go nude readily enough in other circumstances, outdoors where anyone might see, on the beach sometimes, even when I know there will be men around having a good stare. Circumstances matter, but by and large I'm okay about it.

There's a difference though, between being admired and being leched over, not a physical one, but an emotional one. To be honest, the real difference is in me, whether or not I enjoy the attention. The man's reactions are the same, a hard cock in his pants. Mine aren't, and can vary from a sodden panty gusset to stark fear. Realistically, though, it would be silly to expect the watcher to see himself in my terms.

René-Claude certainly didn't see himself in my terms, that was for sure. It was hard to know how he did see himself. His sexual reactions seemed to be pure instinct, animal, no more considered than those of a dog, yet there was something calculating about him, and he certainly knew how to be rude. He was always making suggestive signs and sniggering, as if my body was arousing, but also somehow comic. It was not an easy attitude to accept. I had to say something.

'He makes me nervous, Phillippe.'

'René-Claude? Nonsense.'

I was going to reply, but stopped, in horror. He had stopped painting, and was walking to the door.

'Phillippe, no!'

It was too late. He had opened it. Sure, enough, their was René-Claude, squatting down, his cock in his hand, grinning. Phillippe ruffled René-Claude's hair and walked back. René-Claude followed, crouched low, like a chimpanzee, still tugging at his erection. He began to make his weird hooting noises.

'Phillippe, look, I . . .'

'*Du calme, Natasha.* He will watch, what matter?'

'But he's wanking himself!'

'And so?'

'And everything! He's . . .'

'Don't be so *bourgeoise*, Natasha, it is not like you.'

'Bourgeois!'

'Yes. To object to him is foolish. Understand, Natasha, my Peach, he has no sense of morals, of what society deems right and wrong, he understands nothing of this. Yet he does no harm. He is a good boy. Yes, René-Claude?'

René-Claude nodded eagerly. I was left speechless, wanting to cover myself but knowing I'd only feel bad if I did. Phillippe made it seem perfectly reasonable to let René-Claude wank over me, and the act of a prude not to. So I swallowed my feelings, and my pride, telling myself it was an act of kindness to let the dirty little sod get his jollies over my body.

Phillippe went on painting, apparently oblivious to his grandson's behaviour, and my discomfort. I was also telling myself it was bound to be quick, at first. Unfortunately, René-Claude was in no hurry, his eyes feasting on me as he alternately stroked and tugged at his penis. Simple he might be, but he knew how to take his time, just nursing his erection long after most men would have come.

So I put up with it, all the while feeling put upon and more than a little humiliated. All the while I was wishing he would hurry up and come. I know myself, and I knew my sense of humiliation would become ever more erotic, growing slowly with time, until I was at risk of doing something dirty. Fortunately all I had to do was stay still, because before long I was letting my mind wander again, to thoughts of the two of them sharing me, using me . . .

Phillippe wasn't going to make me suck his cock in front of René-Claude, I was sure of that. Even for him it was too dirty, too depraved. At least I hoped it was, because the way I felt, if Phillippe made me get down on my knees and fucked my mouth, it was going to be very hard to stop René-Claude mounting me. Part of me would want it, for a start, but if Phillippe held me I certainly wouldn't have the willpower to stop it. Maybe I wouldn't be able to stop it, full-stop. Up would go René-Claude's cock, into my body, and I'd get fucked . . .

My dirty daydream broke as Phillippe put his brush aside. It had to be about the time he took his morning wine, and with luck that would put an end to René-Claude's dirty behaviour and spare me any further indignity. I moved, to stretch my aching muscles, then reach for my top. René-Claude stopped wanking, his face setting in comic disappointment.

'Sorry, show's over,' I managed.

His response was to make his odd hooting noise as he held out his cock, only louder and somehow questioning. I shook my head, trying to seem kindly yet firm, rather than just telling him to fuck off. He made the hooting noise again, pushing his cock out with greater urgency, then turning to Phillippe to make a series of urgent signs. Phillippe laughed.

'Go on, Natasha, be kind. Suck his cock.'

'Suck his cock! You have to be joking!'

'*Pas du tout. René-Claude, une pipe?*'

René-Claude understood, hooting urgently and bouncing up and down on the floor, more ape-like than ever.

'Phillippe!'

'Suck his cock, Natasha. Have some feeling, some pity!'

It was an order, and couched in terms that made me look the unreasonable one! That wasn't why I found myself wanting to do it, it was my own dirty mind. It was just such a humiliating thing to do, and in front of Phillippe. I'd come over the thought, and worse. Now I had the chance, a total surrender of my dignity, to go down, nude, to my knees, boobs hanging down, bum stuck out, and suck some subnormal boy's cock . . .

Phillippe wanted me to do it out of pity, and I was sure it would make him feel good to see me do it. I'm not strong on pity, but I do like to take my emotions to the limit, to the point where I'm writhing in an agony of self-inflicted humiliation, and I was going to do it.

René-Claude's ape-like hooting rose to a crescendo as I got down on my knees. My mouth came wide, for one terrible moment I held back, knowing that to take the big cock he was holding out for me in my mouth was one more social taboo broken, one more submission of my dignity to my sexuality, and then I was sucking penis. René-Claude grunted as my tongue found the underside of his cock, to lap at the meaty flesh of his rolled down foreskin. He tasted strong, of man and salt and sweat, no different from any other.

It was different, there was no denying it, no denying my feelings. I'd done it, and I was going to take it all the way, let him come in my mouth, maybe wank him off into my mouth on purpose, like the dirty little slut I am. Yes, that was it, I'd wank him, and masturbate as I did it. Phillippe could watch, could see that I wasn't just doing it out of pity, but because I liked it, because it turned me on. Maybe then he'd be jealous, as he was so jealous of Patrice. Maybe then he'd understand a tiny part of how I felt about him for making me do it.

I put my hand to René-Claude's cock, tugging at the thick shaft as I sucked and nibbled at the head. He gave an excited hoot, then moaned. Phillippe chuckled. My other hand went to my pussy, finding my clit in among the moist, puffy folds. I started to rub myself. This time there was no chuckle from Phillippe.

The sheer humiliation of what I was doing was burning in my head as I struggled to make René-Claude spunk in my mouth. I was going to come, at any moment, and I wanted my mouth filled at the same time. That would make it good, as I'd imagined it, only it would have been better still if he'd fucked me, buggered me, used me in every hole before sticking his filthy, slimy penis in my mouth for his orgasm . . .

I came, jamming my head down on René-Claude's cock as it hit me, to push his cock head into my windpipe. He came, instantly, right down my throat, and I was choking on sperm and cock flesh. My climax broke, but came back, stronger than before as I jerked back and his second gout of sperm caught me full in the face.

I broke free, to sink down on my knees, coughing and spluttering, one eye blind with sperm, the other hazy with tears. René-Claude finished himself off in my hair, chuckling obscenely as he squeezed out the last few blobs of thick, creamy sperm into my curls. I let him, too exhausted to care, or to do anything about the mess hanging from my open mouth. Only when Phillippe threw a rag down onto the floor below my face did I respond.

All my resentment had come back as my orgasm died. It grew worse as I mopped up. As if it wasn't bad enough to make me suck his idiot grandson off, he expected me to clean up the mess afterwards! I did it anyway, feeling thoroughly put upon as I began to wipe my face, only to be given the final insult and told to do René-Claude's cock first.

'He has no patience,' Phillippe explained. 'Sometimes you must put your own needs second.'

He was lecturing me again, trying to make me feel bad for not showing René-Claude enough consideration, as if cock-sucking sessions are a reasonable service for the disadvantaged to expect!

I ignored the order, wiping the mess from my eye first, then doing René-Claude. He was grinning, thoroughly pleased with himself, and making signs to Phillippe, conveying both triumph and delight in my behaviour and body. Phillippe responded with a benevolent smile, and came over, to tousle René-Claude's hair again as I mopped the spunk from the floor.

By the time I'd showered and dressed they were all downstairs. Phillippe hadn't even thanked me, and I could tell he was less than happy about me bringing myself off as I sucked René-Claude. That was satisfying, in a way, but irritating too, as it implied I had to dish out sexual favours to others on command but wasn't allowed to enjoy it. I started lunch in a sulky silence. It didn't seem to matter what happened, Phillippe had a knack of taking me right to my limits, while my revenge was not only trivial but pretty abstract.

The way he made me feel wasn't intentional either. If it had been I wouldn't have minded. It would have been a game, as it was with Percy. What really rankled was that he expected me to do it because he felt that my personality and my needs should be entirely subordinate to his. That was not good, and for all my efforts at telling myself I'd have the last laugh, it was extremely hard to pull myself out of the sulks.

What lifted me was a wink from Patrice. It was given when he was filling Phillippe's glass with wine for the umpteenth time, and the implication was clear. After lunch Phillippe was likely to doze off, and when he did, Patrice and I would be free to play.

I didn't return the wink, I was feeling too sullen, and his behaviour the day before still rankled. I'd meant to tease him, and so get my own back, but sex with him was good, if brief and simple. The real question was whether it was better to turn him down for the sake of denying him, or to accept him and soothe my resentment at Phillippe's treatment of me.

If it hadn't been for René-Claude I'd probably have resisted. As it was, just knowing what we'd done and having him leering at me across the table and making rude gestures with his hands was too much. Still I hesitated, but by the time I'd put back another couple of glasses of wine I'd decided that if Patrice made a move he would get what he wanted.

Phillippe had been hitting the wine jug with a vengeance, and he hadn't eaten a great deal either. When lunch finally finished he demanded that I help him upstairs, and was mumbling remarks about what he was going to do to me as we left the room. Madame Vaucopin heard and gave a disapproving sniff. René-Claude hooted and made an odd gurgling noise in his throat that still managed to seem lewd. Patrice held his peace.

He'd said he was going to fuck his peach, or possibly my peach, it was hard to tell. He meant me anyway, and possibly up my bum, which put the thought of buggery into my head. As usual I was in two minds, the pleasure of the idea warring with the thought of the rest of the household listening to the bumps from upstairs and knowing it was me getting one up my bottom from Phillippe. I also knew that was exactly what I would come over.

I was ready for it, but I never got it. It was too soon after he'd come before, and what with that and the drink, he just could manage it. That upset him, and the more upset he got the softer his cock became, despite the fact that I was down on the bed with my bum stuck in the air and my mouth around his genitals, balls and all. Finally he gave up. Ten minutes later he was asleep.

Patrice was on the landing. I had the taste of a man's cock and balls in my mouth. Madame Vaucopin was washing up. René-Claude was doing whatever he did with his afternoons. There was no question of what was going to happen. It was just a question of where. Patrice wanted to go upstairs, which seemed foolish after the mess the day before. I was not going up the chimney again.

'What about Phillippe?' I demanded. 'Wouldn't it be better to go out somewhere? The Moreaus' wood perhaps?'

'No, Madame would get suspicious if she saw, and she sees everything, believe me. Upstairs. Besides, I want to show you something.'

'I've seen it, Patrice.'

'No, not that. In the studio.'

'The studio? But . . .'

'It's the last place he'd look. Come on.'

He'd taken me by the hand, and was pulling. I went, feeling naughty and expectant, but more than a little nervous. The studio was Phillippe's sanctum. If he caught us he would be furious. He would be furious anyway, but more so. Patrice was right though, if he thought we were up to something it was the last place he'd look.

No sooner had the door closed behind us than we were in each other's arms. He was as urgent as ever, and as rough, tugging up my top and bra to spill my boobs out even as we kissed. My jeans and panties followed, pushed rudely down to my thighs even as I fumbled for his fly. His cock came free at the same instant a finger slid into my body. For a moment we were masturbating each other, his cock swelling in my hand even as his finger probed deep inside me. The instant he was erect he pulled out his finger. I was taken under my bottom, lifted, and pushed against the door, his cock filling me as he lowered me onto it. His mouth found one of my breasts and we were fucking.

It was no good. Each push was crashing the door into its frame, and making enough noise to wake the dead, never mind Phillippe. He pulled me off, grinning in lustful delight as he set me on my feet. He held out his cock, the full length slimy with my juice, and pointed to it.

'*Faites une pipe, Natasha.*'

I went down, to suck up the taste of my own pussy, eagerly, thoroughly enjoying the mixed taste of man and girl. It was my third cock of the day, and it would have been easy, to masturbate and let him come in my mouth or over my face, soiling me as I brought myself to a peak. I'd barely had him in me though, and my pussy was badly in need. I pulled back.

'Fuck me from behind, and don't do it in me, over my bum.'

He nodded, and was twisting me around on the instant. I went, round and down, sticking out my bottom for him as I grabbed hold of the sink. He took me by my hips, pushing his cock in, only to have it slide up between my cheeks. For a moment he rutted between them, his balls rubbing on my bumhole, before he took himself in hand and pushed his cock head into my hole. I sighed as my pussy filled, and then he was fucking me, fast and furious, slamming his body into mine, his muscular belly slapping on my bottom.

All I could do was cling on and take it, trying not to be too noisy as we fucked, good and hard, with all the energy I missed out on with Phillippe. I couldn't get to my pussy to frig, for fear of being knocked off balance, but I knew I'd be coming, just as soon as he'd spattered my bottom with hot sperm. I was going to play with it, to rub it in between my cheeks and over my pussy and bumhole as I masturbated, lewd and dirty in front of him, showing him what he'd done to me.

I never got the chance. I don't know why, maybe it's the shape of my bum, or the way my anus winks when I'm excited, but I don't often have to trouble to draw men's attention to my bottom hole. Patrice whipped his cock out and I thought he was going to come, only to have the helmet pressed to my anus even as he tightened his grip and ordered me not to move.

There was no need to force me. I was ready, willing and able, my bumhole sloppy with my own juice. Another minute and I'd have been begging him to do it. I just relaxed, pushing down, and up he went, groaning in pleasure as his knob popped up into my rear passage. I was really moaning as he stuffed it up, my toes wriggling and saliva running from my mouth as my rectum was jammed full of fat, hard penis. He laughed as he realised just how willing I was, and gave me a slap across my bum as he called me a whore.

All I could manage in response was a choking sob. He was up my bottom, deep up, and moving in me, buggering me. He'd slapped my bum too, hard, hard enough to make my skin tingle, and to need more. As he began to ram his cock up and down in my bowels I was begging for a spanking, in English and in French.

He finally got the message, calling me a whore again as he began to slap at my bottom, setting my cheeks jiggling and dancing as he rained blows in, all the while buggering me and calling me names. I had to come, but I was scared I'd collapse if I let go of the sink. I did it anyway, only for his next shove to knock me off balance and send me sprawling.

His cock pulled from my bumhole with a sticky noise, and I groaned in disappointment as I went down onto my knees. I had to come anyway. My hand found my pussy and I was rubbing, even as I pushed up my bottom in the hope of having his cock stuffed back up my gaping, slimy hole.

What I got was his hand twisted into my hair and his dirty cock shoved into my face. I was too high, to close to orgasm, to stop it. My mouth came open. His cock went in. I just came, the orgasm hitting me from nowhere, even as my mouth filled with my own earthy, acrid taste. He grunted, forcing himself deeper in as I struggled to suck him. He came, adding his sperm to the mess in my mouth right at the peak of my orgasm, to send me into a series of ecstatic spasms. I shoved a spare finger into my bumhole at the last instant, to feel it squeeze tight as I gulped down Patrice's sperm.

It took me longer than him, and he let me suck as I came down. When I finally let his cock fall out of my mouth it was halfway to being limp and I had a thick curtain of sperm and saliva hanging from my chin. I managed a weak smile, and got the same in return. Then, to my amazement, he apologised.

'*Tu me* . . . excuse me, if I called you . . . know, a whore. I was, er . . .'

'Don't worry. A lot of men like to do that.'

He nodded again, pleased.

'You are cool, Natasha, you know that?'

'Thanks. Don't you think we should clean up? You granddad might well have heard something.'

'*Oui. Bien sûr.*'

He just put his cock away. I washed my mouth out and sat in the sink to clean my bottom, which he watched with amusement. I was trying to hurry, but there hadn't been a sound from downstairs, while it felt nice with my hot bottom in the cool water. I had to let myself dry too, and so once I'd finished I peeled off my jeans and panties rather than pull them up.

Patrice had been toying with one of Phillippe's brushes, and chatting casually, although always with an eye on my body. It was flattering, considering he'd just buggered me and come in my mouth, so I pulled off my top and bra, to stick out my boobs for his inspection.

'Ready for more?'

'In a while, yes. For the instant, there is something I have wanted to do, and you are perfect.'

'I'm perfect as in ten out of ten or I'm perfect as in dirty enough for whatever perversion you have in mind?'

He laughed and stood up, to take a palette from among Phillippe's things.

'Careful, he'll notice.'

'And so? I may paint. He encourages it. I have no real skill, true, but I get by. Are you dry?'

'Just about.'

'Dry in your back slit, then kneel down and push up your bottom.'

'What are you going to do?'

'Paint you.'

He meant paint on me, probably some piece of graffiti, or a tag, making his mark across my naked bum to show he'd had me. It was a bit childish perhaps, but also humiliating, and I could see the appeal.

I took a clean piece of the rag Phillippe used to clean his brushes and dabbed my pussy and bottom crease dry as he squeezed colours onto his palette: white, a rich orange, red, black, a deep pink. I got down, giggling as I swung my bottom around towards him and pushed it out to give him as broad a canvas as possible. He went on as he began to mix his colours.

'It is something I saw at college, a cunt butterfly.'

'A cunt butterfly?'

'*Exactement!* Hold still.'

I still had no idea what he was doing, except that it involved painting my rear end. I couldn't see at all, but only hold still as he began to mark an outline across the width of my bottom and upper thighs. I wondered if he was going to make a pattern, or some sort of clever scene, using the details of my sex as features, perhaps even an actual butterfly.

Regardless of what he was doing, it felt good. The brush tickled, especially between my cheeks, making it extremely hard to keep still, and impossible not to giggle. It felt cool too, where he'd painted, an odd sensation with my cheeks still a touch warm from the impromptu spanking he'd given me during sex. It got better too, as he began to fill in the outline and the soft, moist sensation of the brush on my skin moved nearer to my crease and more sensitive areas. It tickled more too, and he kept having to tell me not to giggle, which only made it worse. By the time he got to my crease I was having to clutch at the floor to stop myself from going into fits. I was ready too, and when the paint laden brush finally touched my bumhole and slipped a little inside, I was hoping he'd open me up and put his cock back up.

Sadly he didn't, but set to work again, brushing gently to blend the paint in, and to create a slow, agonising tickling which had me shaking my head in anguish. It took longer than the first bit, and all the while I could feel the blob of paint in my bumhole, cool and squashy, at one making me desperate to touch and to have his cock jammed up me. Finally he finished, stopping suddenly to rock back on his heels, laughing.

'Superb! You must see yourself . . . better, I must take a photo!'

He left the studio at a run, leaving me on all fours. I called after him to bring a mirror and he promised he would, just as the door banged shut behind him. Moments later he was back, carrying a compact digital camera and the mirror from his dressing table. He put the mirror down and I crawled into position as he fiddled with the camera.

It was a butterfly, the wings composed of my bottom cheeks and upper thighs, with the groove between them as the dividing line. The body was in my crease, the antennae rising up to the twin dimple above my cheeks, the head well down between them, the wrinkled oval around my anus the thorax. The really clever detail was the abdomen, unpainted, but composed of the furry brown bulge of my pussy.

It was clever, I had to admit, and cute in a way. The colours were good too. He had used the slight pink flush of my spanking as one of the colours on the wings, blending it to a richer hue, a bit like a Painted Lady butterfly, which was appropriate. I badly wanted a photo, and so did he, snapping picture after picture, most with me looking back, smiling happily for the lewd show I was making of my bottom.

I was enjoying myself, and so was he, too much to pay attention. The first we heard of Phillippe was the bang of his bedroom door, then his voice, asking who was upstairs. We were caught, cold. There was no way to escape and I was stark naked with my bottom painted up as a butterfly, a very rude butterfly. The only consolation was that Patrice was fully dressed and so there was no suggestion we'd actually had sex. The was no time to even start getting my own clothes on, but I stood up.

Phillippe had immediately started up the stairs, and to keep quiet was only going to look suspicious. So I called out, trying to keep the guilt out of my voice, as if we hadn't been doing anything out of the ordinary. I couldn't see it working, but after René-Claude he could hardly object to me going nude in front of Patrice.

He did.

Even as he pushed open the door he was looking pretty cross, and when he saw that I was naked his face went dark with anger. Patrice had set his face in a look of stubborn mutiny. Phillippe's eyes flicked between us, hot and angry.

'Patrice? Qu'est-ce que . . .'

'We were just mucking about,' I broke in, still determined to at least try and make light of the whole thing. 'Look.'

I turned, sticking out my bottom to make the best of the cunt-butterfly with a laugh that sounded hollow even to my own ears. Phillippe stared at me, his face going slowly red. When he spoke, it was to Patrice, one of his rapid fire lectures covering Patrice's stupidity, lack of respect, childishness and artistic incompetence. All Patrice could do was mumble a barely audible apology and when his grandfather roared at him to get out, he fled. Some man he was. That left me.

I had no idea what to say, and took my own tirade in silence with my head hung. If he'd had any sense he'd have just spanked me and that would have been that, although it would have made a serious mess. He was angry though, really angry, and his jealousy was showing. By the fifth time I'd denied having sex with Patrice my patience was beginning to wear thin. After René-Claude it was so hypocritical. Finally I snapped.

'For Christ's sake, Phillippe, what are you on? You make me suck René-Claude's cock, and then you lose it because I let Patrice see me naked! We didn't have sex, you know, we were just mucking about, and anyway . . .'

'*Ce n'est pas la même chose! Tu es incroyable . . . sal . . .*'

'I'm dirty! You're one to talk! And yes, it is the same thing. Just because you're old and bitter and Patrice reminds you of the way you were you get jealous, but it's not the same with René-Claude, is it? You can condescend to him, that's it, isn't it, you . . .'

I stopped. I'd really hit a nerve. His face was crimson and he was clenching his fists. I stepped back, wondering if he was going to hit me and whether I should kick him in the balls and run for it. If I did, that would be the end, I knew it, but for all I was prepared to accept, getting beaten up was no part of it. Maybe he saw it in my face, because he finally got himself under control, and spoke again.

'*Non! C'est nul* . . . this is not right, Natasha.'

It was right, and he knew it. I said nothing, but my feelings must have shown in my expression, because when he spoke again it was a shout.

'Get to the bedroom, now!'

I went, hurriedly, snatching up my clothes on the way, only not to the bedroom, to the bathroom. He saw, but said nothing, marching straight past and downstairs. I got into the shower, struggling to calm down and think clearly. He meant to punish me, I was sure of it, and this would be no erotic punishment. I'd hurt his pride, badly, and I had a nasty suspicion he was going to want to prove himself by taking it out on my skin.

It took ages to get the butterfly off my bottom, and I was close to tears as I did it. Okay, Patrice and I had had sex, but what did he expect? Anyway, when he'd caught us we'd just been messing around. Percy would have laughed. Percy wouldn't have minded me having sex with Patrice either. He'd have punished me, yes, but it would have been erotic, deliberately erotic. Then Percy had an inner confidence far beyond that of Phillippe.

By the time I was clean I was thinking clearly again, or at least fairly clearly. I was in no mode for discipline, of any sort, but I wanted those paintings, and I knew that if I didn't accept the punishment, that would be that. I still had to force myself to go to the bedroom, but I went, telling myself that my sexuality would pull me through.

I even tried to tell myself that being sent to my room for punishment was good. Certainly it was something I'd fantasised over often enough, the idea of lying on my bed, perhaps naked or in some humiliating costume, and waiting for the man or woman I was to receive discipline from to come up. It didn't work. The man was an idiot, a brute, with no understanding of me, or of how to handle me. He thought he understood about submissive girls and punishment, but he didn't.

In the bedroom my feelings slowly changed, to self-pity. I felt vulnerable, so I dressed in tight jeans and a sweater, then threw myself down on the bed, trying to tell myself I wasn't scared, or sulking. I knew I was, both, but it was impossible to pull myself out of it. It was my fault too. I'd really stuck myself in it by getting carried away with Patrice. Either I could take what was coming to me, or walk out. If I went, that would be the end. It might be possible to come back, but only at a yet greater cost to my dignity.

Finally I managed to get my feet back on the ground. It was all a ruse, a show, however real it felt. Presently Phillippe was going to come upstairs and punish me, then fuck me or make me suck his wrinkly old cock, that was all. Maybe he'd cane me, or take a belt to me, but what he really wanted to do was prove his masculinity, to himself. He thought he was genuinely putting me in my place too, but he wasn't. I'd taken worse, far worse. Just days ago I'd wet my panties and been spanked on the soggy seat, for fun, not to punish me. I'd been made to eat dirt too, and revelled in it. In the past I'd taken the cane, hot wax between my bum cheeks, been put in nappies and made to mess myself . . .

Phillippe was nothing.

I rolled onto my back, forcing myself to be calm. All I needed to do was let my arousal overcome my anger and I could take anything he could dish out. That had to be simple enough. I undid my jeans, to slip a hand down onto the low bulge of my pubic mound. My pussy felt sensitive under the cotton of my panties, ready to be touched.

Closing my eyes, I began to stroke myself, very gently, focussing on rude thoughts. I was about to get my bottom spanked, my favourite thing. If the spanker was some cantankerous old git, then all the better. It would be more humiliating, more intense. The best sex is not always with someone you like, masochistic sex especially. Phillippe wouldn't have understood why, but he was good. What he thought I should accept as my role I found humiliating, and that assumption of right made the humiliation more intense still. Now he was going to beat me in a fit of righteous indignation, and undoubtedly fuck me afterwards, maybe even bugger me. I could take it, and I'd know what was going on. He wouldn't. I was in charge.

My tension had begun to drain away, slowly but surely. Soon I'd be ready, able to act the part of the brat, fighting as I was forced into position and stripped for spanking . . . howling my heart out as my naked bottom was smacked up to a rosy glow . . . crawling and penitent afterwards, tears streaming down my face as I surrendered my body for the satisfaction of the man who had punished me . . .

I blew my breath out, and with it the last of my bad feelings. I was so clever, to manipulate Phillippe into doing exactly what I wanted, and thinking he was in charge. It was just funny, his understanding of what having my bottom smacked did to me trivial, and for a man of his age and experience.

It was a while since I'd been given a really hard punishment. Percy's clothes brush had bruised, but it hadn't been all that bad. Certainly if Phillippe took a stick to my bottom it would be worse. I didn't know if he had a cane though, and in fact it didn't seem very likely. He wasn't that much of a perve, unlike Percy, who had a whole collection of the things.

If not the cane, the belt seemed most likely. He was sure to be inept, so I'd have to be very meek about it, positioning myself bum-up over the bolster so that my bottom got it and not my hips. The same was true of any flexible implements, in the hands of an angry and unskilled man, and it was a good position even for a hard implement, keeping the girl's bottom chubby and soft instead of taut. Not just that, but if he found me in such a submissive and revealing position it might cool his anger and balance it with lust.

It was only sensible. I rolled over and pulled the bolster down the bed. My jeans came open and I pushed them down, hesitating before my panties followed, just tucked down at the back. It made me feel extremely vulnerable as I laid myself down to let my bottom lift into position, but it made sense.

I still wasn't ready, and went back to massaging my pussy. He would come up soon, I was sure of it. When he did he would find me, bottom high, ready and waiting, in acceptance of his right to beat me. I was completely vulnerable, my bottom naked, my pussy peeping out from between my thighs at the back, my cheeks just far enough apart to hint at my bumhole.

He would have to have sex with me, once he'd given me the belt or whatever he'd chosen. I'd be ready, my pussy juicy and open for his cock. Or he might put it up my bottom, as Patrice had done, opening me up with my own juice and buggering me: Either way I'd be masturbating before the end, and I'd come, in grovelling, submissive ecstasy . . .

I stopped. I'd been on the edge of orgasm. Just a few more touches would have tipped me over. I hadn't realised I'd been so close, but then I had spent about an hour having a butterfly painted onto my bare bottom, and I was waiting for punishment. I did need it, very badly, but I had to wait, or . . .

Maybe Phillippe wasn't as stupid as I thought? Maybe he knew full well the state I was in? No, he'd been really angry. There was no calculation in his actions. Yet he was making me wait a terribly long time. It had to be intentional. Perhaps he had the sense to let himself calm down while my apprehension grew unbearable? That was what Percy would have done, what any skilled dominant male would have done.

If that was true, then it was going to be good. By the time he got to work I'd be trembling with submissive anticipation, utterly servile, ready to take whatever he chose to give. He'd be cool, dominant, in control. I'd be grovelling, vulnerable, near naked. I'd probably cry. I'd probably wet myself, over the bed and into my panties, into my hand as I masturbated, wet, beaten, brought low, rubbing myself in my own urine, utterly humiliated . . .

I cried out as I came. I hadn't been able to stop myself, my sheer physical need too great to be denied, but even as the climax went through me I knew it was a mistake. I'd got carried away, with a vengeance, and now I was going to have to take my spanking on the come down instead of on heat.

For a long time I lay still, my hand still down the front of my jeans. As I adjusted myself into a more comfortable position over the bolster I managed a rueful smile for my own dirty mind, but I was genuinely cross with myself.

I was also cross with Phillippe, for making me wait so long among other things. It was good that he clearly had the sense to get control of his anger before he punished me, and the best thing to do had been to send me to my room to wait. He was taking his time about it though. A girl's erotic apprehension can only grow so strong, to the point where she ends up masturbating. Eventually she'll get bored. Percy would have known that. Unfortunately Phillippe didn't know the rules, or had a hazy idea of them at best.

What had seemed amusing began to be frightening again, but it was only when I heard the back door slam and Madame Vaucopin's voice that I began to think it might be worse than I could cope with. She was angry too, her voice raised in complaint about some woman she'd argued with in Challones. My fears came back with a vengeance.

Maybe he'd waited for her so that she could hold me down? She could handle me, between them they certainly could. Maybe they'd go completely over the top and put me in straps, then birch me bloody, or beat my back and legs as well as my bottom. It explained why he'd waited, and it was not a nice thought at all. Sure, he could call her up to hold my legs while he spanked me, even to sit on me. Unfortunately he didn't seem too concerned with my consent, and I could be certain she wasn't.

I got up, feeling far from secure. I could hear their voices, and caught my name. A door banged, sending a sharp jolt of fear through me. I was tired, hungry, scared and I'd just come, not the best conditions to take a heavy punishment. The sensible thing to do was to go downstairs, to break the tension. He wouldn't beat me in front of Patrice. He wouldn't want to give Patrice the satisfaction of watching. I hoped.

I was buttoning up my jeans when I heard his tread on the stairs. He was alone, Madame Vaucopin's complaints still audible from the kitchen. Again I changed my mind. Biting back my irritation, I sat down on the bed, determined to act the part if I couldn't do it naturally. The door swung open and I managed a sorrowful look as he came in, only for it to change to shock as I realised that he was carrying a cane. No, it wasn't a cane, it was a walking stick, a three foot long, knobbly malacca about as appropriate for erotic punishment as a full grown marrow would be for a dildo.

He looked serious, but he could not possibly expect to beat me with it, it had to be a joke. I smiled.

'Very funny, Phillippe.'

His expression grew sterner still.

'You have earned this, Natasha. Go on your knees, on the bed, and take down your jeans.'

He wasn't joking.

'Don't be silly, Phillippe. Spank me, sure, but . . .'

'On your knees!'

'No! Look . . .'

'Do as I order, or I call Madame Vaucopin to hold you.'

'No, and I mean it, Phillippe . . .'

He grabbed for me. I struck his arm aside and dodged out of the way. The stick came around but I grabbed it, wrenched and sent him sprawling across the bed. He came up red-faced, snatching for the stick even as he bellowed for Madame Vaucopin. I got the stick first and jerked it out of his hand, to send it crashing against the wall.

I fled. I could handle him, no problem. He was getting on and no strongman anyway. I could not handle her. I'd be held down and beaten, with something that could do me a serious injury. It was not going to happen.

She reached the bottom of the stairs at the same moment I did. We collided. She sat down, hard. I was knocked back, but was up again before she could recover, past her and out the door. I kept running, not stopping until I reached the end of the track. Looking back, I found the house bathed gold and rich pink in the evening sunlight, looking beautiful and serene, without a hint of the passions within. Nobody had followed.

Seven

My plan was wrecked. I simply hadn't reckoned he could be such a malicious old bastard. Stern, yes, but what he had intended to do to me went far beyond the bounds of what was acceptable.

It was my fault though, in a sense, at least that I'd failed. I'd known all along that he was a wild card, that he had no concept of how a sadomasochistic relationship should work. From his point of few a submissive woman was simple someone who could be conveniently abused, and if she liked it, that just made matters simpler.

That did not excuse me. I'd known I was playing with fire, but all I'd needed to do was play the obedient little moppet for a couple of weeks and I'd have been home dry. Instead I'd had to flout his precious authority, not to mention shagging his grandson. It was just stupid.

All that went through my mind as my emotions cooled on the walk into Rochefort. Percy was at the hotel, tucking into the *Gastronomique* in the dining room, and I joined him, downing a glass of wine before I spoke. He waited, and listened patiently, nodding at intervals as it all came tumbling out, all except my larcenary intentions. When I'd finished he didn't even lecture me, but signalled the waiter to bring the menu.

By the time I'd eaten my way through all six courses I was feeling a great deal better. I hadn't been beaten, after all, just threatened, and I'd handled Fauçon and even the redoubtable Madame Vaucopin. Being thrown across the bed was going to injure his overblown male pride considerably, while a woman of her weight was sure to have a nasty bruise where I'd sat her on her fat arse.

Percy did his best to encourage me to take a triumphant and humorous view of it all. By the time I had a large glass of old Armagnac in my hand I was giggling over it and describing the expressions on Fauçon's face. He laughed with me, and was clearly overjoyed to have me back, making me feel wanted and safe.

We didn't have sex that night. I slept cuddled onto his shoulder, and he didn't even try it on, which was sweet of him. By the morning I was feeling a great deal better, and promised him a leisurely suck later on. His response was to raise his eyebrows at me and make me do it then and there, on my knees by the bed, his normal self once again.

He had been tasting not just along the Layon Valley, but over the river at Savennières and even further afield. All the while he'd been making notes, and collecting samples for my benefit, basically doing my work for me. It was going to cost me, naturally, but that was cause for nothing worse than pleasant apprehension. He knew the rules.

I might have wrecked my get-rich-quick scheme, but I still wanted to know the truth behind the Helene story. It made a difference, emotionally, as I wanted to know how genuine Fauçon's feelings had been. He certainly been expressive enough, and pretty emotional while he was drunk, swearing a tender and intense devotion to me. That in turn he had used as an excuse for his jealousy, but it didn't entirely square with the way he used me for sex, as if I was a slave.

Percy had heard that an elderly man in Challones owned a tiny parcel of Bonnezeaux and vinified it himself. It was just about the only example he hadn't tasted, and he was eager to investigate. I joined him, adding a tight crop-top and a diminutive pair of jeans shorts to his powers of persuasion, and by mid-morning we were in the man's garden sipping one of the last bottles of his 'seventy-six.

The man's generosity didn't extend to lunch, but the wine had perked up Percy's appetite, leaving him determined to visit the best among the town's restaurants. I had already focussed on the local library, which boasted Internet access, and left him to his search, intent on learning the full and hopefully sordid details of Phillippe Fauçon's early career.

My initial search produced some pretty impressive results, nearly one thousand web pages. Most where minor references to him on sites devoted to art or the history of art, and in everything from his native French to Finnish and Japanese. Other were commercial, galleries offering examples of his work at prices that made me wince consider that I'd just blown my chances of getting hold of some for free. Among the remainder, none gave more information than I already had, so I changed my search, feeding his two names in separately and adding Helene.

I struck gold immediately, the first page of results listing not one but two sites referring to the great scandal. Both were in French, but I didn't need the translation facility. They were clear enough. Fauçon was a liar, but it was not that simple.

He had been born in nineteen thirty-four, which made him sixty-eight, and therefore ten when Paris was liberated, not an age he'd have been having a passionate affair with a resistance fighter. There had been a Helene though, Helene d'Issigeac, and she had been his model and lover, only ten years later than he had claimed. There was no picture, or any mention of the nickname *La Pêche*, but she had apparently been a great beauty, highly rebellious and the daughter of a prominent politician.

Helene being his model had given Fauçon's reputation a healthy boost without creating more than a minor scandal. However, he seemed to have had a self-destructive streak, producing ever more outrageous paintings and reacting with scorn to accusations of sensationalism and being deliberately offensive. A full length canvas of Helene laughing as she peed into the Seine had seriously ruffled her father's feathers and led to a demand that she leave Fauçon. She had stayed, and his response had been to paint another, larger still, of her using a chamber pot, and not just to pee in. That had really been the last straw, and Fauçon had made a hasty departure under threat of a prosecution for obscenity, while Helene had been recalled to her family home.

Neither site showed the two paintings and one implied that they had disappeared immediately after the incident. I couldn't find them on any other sites either, despite knowing what I was looking for, but from what I knew of Fauçon's style, I could just imagine how detailed they would have been. The artist should conceal nothing, as he never tired of saying, and I could bet he hadn't. They wouldn't have been like Picasso's 'Woman Pissing' either. Helene would have been recognisable, more likely unmistakable.

The story was funny, and I could just imagine Fauçon's delight at the pricked pomposity of Helene's parents. Despite that, it seemed a pretty puerile thing to do, until you considered Fauçon. He wouldn't have done it for prurient reasons, but he would have been delighted at the outraged response of the establishment. He saw them as hypocrites and prudes, holding up art as a medium of honest expression while unable to face the fundamentals of life, and they didn't come much more fundamental than crapping in a chamberpot. It also explained his sudden and manic decision to sketch me when I wet myself.

So why had he lied? Perhaps because he thought I would be narrow-minded about it, reacting with a disgust born of a failure to understand. It made sense. I was young, belonging to a generation which took fully operative plumbing for granted. I was also English, a race for which bodily functions are either humorous or unmentionable, according to background. So he had replaced the somewhat earthy truth with an romantic invention, borrowing a few years in the process to get as much sympathy as possible.

Unfortunately it no longer mattered. I'd broken Fauçon's authority and humiliated him physically. He would be too proud to come to me, and I was not going back to him if he expected to hit me with his stick. Nor could I see him as willing to negotiate the boundaries of what he could do to me.

I spent a while more on the net, tormenting myself by looking at the prices his work was fetching. They were impressive, and several sites commented on his growing popularity, especially for his early work. Presumably the knowledge that he smoked like a chimney and drank like a fish had begun to get around.

Percy was waiting in the square when I came out, looking hungry. He had discovered a good restaurant on the waterfront, and we ate there, admiring the Loire and taking our time over oysters and *Crémant*, a highly spiced local sausage and apricot tart. I told Percy about Fauçon's past as we ate, to his immense amusement, and by the time we'd finished I was feeling mellow and a great deal more philosophical about it all. I'd had an interesting experience, some memorable sexual encounters, and if I had no paintings, I did at least have a story I could dine out on. Fauçon, meanwhile, could seduce some other girl, or go back to his studies of Madame Vaucopin.

After sharing three bottles over lunch Percy was in no state to drive anywhere, and also in need of an afternoon nap. I laid out the rug from the car on a gentle slope of smooth cobbles that ran down to the river and sat beside him, but his responses to my efforts at conversation became grunts, then snores. For a while I sat in silence, just watching the river. Bored, I walked back to the library and set up my search again, determined to find out more.

It was not easy, and those sites I did find simply trotted out the same information, or subtly different versions of it. Nor could I find the two pictures, or any by him in which the model was definitely Helene. After an hour I was ready to give up, but tried one more time, feeding her name in, but with his excluded.

There was one site, in Italian, and there was no painting, but there was a photograph. There was no question that it was her. It had been taken some years after their affair, but the dates were right, and more importantly, it was like looking into a mirror. Her hair was different, and her make-up very much period, but otherwise we might have been twins.

I sat back, staring at her image. Fauçon's emotion had been real, for all his lies. She was strikingly like me, more so than my mother, or either grandmother, all of whose pictures I'd seen from their twenties. I pressed the 'translate' icon, and began to read.

It was very mundane. Shortly after her affair with Fauçon, she had married an Italian diplomat. One of her granddaughters had put the photo up on a personal website about her ancestry, which was why it include Helene's maiden name, and that was that. There was no indication that the granddaughter even knew about Fauçon or the scandal.

Resisting the temptation to send Helene's grand-daughter some interesting urls, I left the library. If anything, I had been more deceitful than Fauçon. Certainly my intentions had been less honest. That didn't excuse his behaviour, even had he known, but it still made me feel bad. At the least I could have been a little more open, told him where I stood and asked for a picture or two in return for my services. It wouldn't have worked. He was a romantic and a male chauvinist pig. I'd have got a stony silence at best, at worst a lecture on the crass commercialism of the modern world. With Fauçon there was no com-promise. You could be an admirer, an enemy, or cheat. I had cheated, and I knew I would again in a similar situation. Blind worship is just not me.

I went back to Percy to find that some teenage humorists had surrounded him with empty bottles and beer cans, making him look as if he had passed out after a bender to end all benders. When I woke him up his reaction was mild outrage at the suggestion he might have drunk anything of such low quality.

We returned to the restaurant for coffee, Percy cheering up as he came round properly. I could tell he was hoping for something fairly exotic in the way of sex to make up for the time I'd spent with Fauçon. He deserved it, but finding out about Helene had left me with an odd sense of melancholy, and I wasn't really in the mood. So rather than flirt or tease I suggested that we had time to fit in another tasting before returning to Rochefort.

I'd had a mischievous thought earlier, while he was casually pronouncing on the different vintages of Bonnezeaux, to see if he could detect the adulteration in the Moreau's Cabernet. So I suggested making use of our open invitation and buttering them up in the hope of getting one of the really ancient bottles opened.

Half-an-hour later we were in the modern part of the winery, with Percy rather impatiently considering the rich purple contents of a tasting glass and Alain Moreau waiting respectfully for an opinion. Percy noticed the flavour, but failed to realise its origin, simply pointing out that the wine was surprisingly soft and resembled Chilean as much as French. I gave Alain a wink that caused a flicker of alarm to run across his face. Percy failed to notice and began to ask questions about ripening red grapes.

As we were talking, some of the pickers had begun to come in, walking behind a tractor loaded with hods. Alain gave out a quick dinner invitation and excused himself and walked quickly over, to climb up on the footrest. The tractor moved off in the direction of the older part of the winery, leaving us with a dozen or so of the pickers.

All were male, and they were looking at me. In fact they had been from the moment I came in, first with glances, then with bold, hot stares that were more than a little unnerving. I caught part of a remark, including 'La Pêche' as one nodded in my direction. They started over.

Percy saw, and greeted them in French, grammatically perfect but unashamedly English in style. I managed to nod and smile. They smelt of sweat, male sweat, and there was a raw, hard masculinity about them that spoke to my instincts if not my common sense. I knew sex with one of them would make Phillippe or even Patrice look like a tantric guru, but they set my body tingling.

They knew who I was, obviously, although I had no idea I'd caused such a stir. I was still a little surprised when one asked why I wasn't with Fauçon. It seemed almost an accusation, and I wasn't having that, so I told them the truth, that we'd argued and I'd walked out. That caused a flurry of remarks too rapid and indistinct for me to catch. I caught the sense though, disapproval and a measure of excitement, anticipation almost. They also mentioned Patrice.

That explained a lot, but not their apparent disapproval. It couldn't have been that strong, because they stayed to talk, a difficult conversation requiring a lot of attention. It was focussed on me, unashamedly, and they obviously thought Percy was my father, or an uncle or something, because while they treated him respectfully, there was no hint of jealousy or rivalry.

While some spoke with us, others talked together, making it even harder to follow what was going on. Several times I heard Patrice's name mentioned, and Fauçon's also. Some sort of debate seemed to be going on, and when a decision was reached both of us were invited to join them in a celebration of the end of the vintage. We were already going, as guests of the Moreaus, but we made polite noises and promised to come over and share a glass with them.

My feelings were ambiguous, blended of an instinctive arousal and a resentment of their assumption that as I had left Fauçon, one or another of them was going to end up fucking me. I hate it when men do that, a group just assuming that one of their number is going to 'get' a girl, when she might be completely uninterested. I'd had my fill of rough, animalistic sex too, what with Fauçon and Patrice. If I was going to play, I wanted it slow and kinky. They were clearly not capable.

A second wave of pickers came in, this time mostly female, and our audience drifted away. Alain Moreau was clearly busy sorting out the end of the day's work, so it seemed rude to disturb him. He had repeatedly stressed that we were to treat the place as our own though, so we filled our glasses from the Cabernet tank and went to sit by the river. Several of the pickers were staring as we crossed the yard, making me very aware of the amount of bottom cheek I had showing around the hem of my jeans shorts and strengthening my feelings, both good and bad.

Their behaviour was both puzzling and annoying. I hadn't realised that modelling for Fauçon had given me such local celebrity, although perhaps notoriety was more accurate, least of all among migrant workers. Patrice clearly knew them, and they seemed to have a lot of respect for Fauçon, which might explain their disapproval of my walking out on him, although it was none of their business.

That was irritating, but they seemed to assume it gave them some sort of right to me, who got to fuck me only a question of competition between them. Certainly that was their intention, and several of the younger men were watching us and joking among themselves. I could just imagine the conversation, each boasting of his own prowess and putting the others down, while it was simply assumed that I'd be there, on my back with my legs spread, a prize for the victor. Yes, they were sexy, in their way, but the choice was still mine.

It was more than I was prepared to put up with. Moving closer to Percy, I put my arm around his shoulder, then kissed him. It made no difference, presumably taken as affection rather than anything sexual. I pulled his arm around me, positioning his hand so that it was one the curve of my bottom. Still it made no difference, Percy obviously having been written off as irrelevant.

I could hardly suck him off in front of them, and any less blatant sexual display was sure to be taken as done for their benefit. So was covering up, as they'd just assume I was being deliberately coy, or at the least that their attention had got to me. Men can be very hard to reject.

The afternoon was beginning to lose its heat, so I made Percy give me his jacket anyway. For all his casual attitude to what I do with other people, I knew he would appreciate a show of affection, and some sort of sexual treat. I determined to give it to him, if only to spite the pickers. Not that they'd know, but I would, and that was what mattered.

I suggested a walk to the mill, and he didn't need any further encouragement. We went, and beyond the fence he placed a proprietorial hand on my bottom, which they must have seen. That was just right, not display from me, but from him, to show he could touch me and not be rejected. I took Percy's hand and hooked his thumb into the top of my shorts, making sure it stayed on my bum, and made a point of not looking back as we walked away.

Percy likes comfort for sex, preferably a large armchair with me down between his knees or sat in his lap with his cock in the appropriate hole. The old mill was not especially strong on comfort, and I knew that putting me up against a wall or having me touch my toes to take it from the rear would probably be beyond him. Giving him a show was a better idea, something naughty, while he masturbated. It suited my mood too, and if I wanted him inside me or a suck I could do it at leisure.

I tried to think naughty as we pushed our way through the undergrowth to the mill. It was a matter of pride not to imagine sex with the grape pickers, for all that I could appreciate the fantasy, if not the reality. It wasn't the same anyway. They were too macho. Instead of sharing me so that I got a worthwhile fucking, they'd compete among themselves. Only the Top Dog would get to have me, The Man, which would be inadequate.

Kinky was better, naughty in the English sense, something to express the impropriety Percy enjoyed so much, and which I had come to appreciate more and more. Spanking would be good, as always, but so much of the mental pleasure in it came from outraging modern politically correct ideas. I could easily imagine the pickers considering it entirely appropriate for a girl to get her bottom smacked.

Wet games were better, something they wouldn't even begin to understand. It was also perfect for showing off, Percy would appreciate it, and with the amount we'd drunk over the afternoon there was plenty inside me to play with. Better still, with Percy's jacket to cover me I could go bare underneath and nobody would be any the wiser. It would be a thrill if the pickers saw as we went back, with my bottom and pussy bare under the coat, and them not knowing.

Percy buys my panties, and never begrudges me more, just so long as I wear plain white cotton in an old-fashioned cut. As to my shorts, they could be washed, or discarded. I had plenty more old jeans I could cut down, and the waistband was too high to be fashionable anyway. I had to do it.

We had reached the mill buildings. There was the same air of desertion, now thrilling in view of what I intended to do. My tummy was fluttering as I looked around, Percy waiting patiently with a quiet smile on his face. The best place was an area of flat concrete between the main building and the pond. It made a good striptease stage, there was plenty of stuff Percy could sit on in moderate comfort, and if anyone did come I could jump in the mill pond and pretend I was just going for a dip.

By the time I'd got Percy sat down on a chunk of ancient machinery with his back to the wall my heart had already begun to hammer. I was going to be rude, really rude, maybe worse than I'd ever been in front of him. Whatever I did, I knew he would enjoy it, and understand. No matter how dirty, no matter how humiliating, even if it left me in tears as I masturbated over my own, self-inflicted degradation, he would accept it. There would be no recriminations, no embarrassed silences, and if I needed a cuddle I would get it.

I was still unsure of myself, and it was not something I wanted to hurry. So I began by just posing, showing myself off in the sort of naughty, mildly erotic postures I'd seen in some of the oldest of the dirty magazines in his collection. It was just smut, little stronger than the naughty seaside post-cards of the time, bums stuck out, boobs stuck out, but nothing really showing.

It put an instant smile on Percy's face, encouraging me, boosting the sense of having good, naughty fun, of old-fashioned English sex. I began to get a little ruder, teasing my nipples up to make them show through my top. I'd quickly got them nice and perky, but my bra was spoiling the effect. It came off, tugged down a sleeve to keep Percy in suspense.

I began to pose again, moving now, to make my boobs bounce under my top and jiggling my bottom. Percy had begun to massage his cock through his trousers, and his eyes were fixed on me, enjoying the view with no trace of embarrassment. I made it ruder still, turning my back and bending down to let my bottom cheeks bulge out from the hem of my shorts. My legs came apart, I gripped my ankles and I was showing the shape of my pussy too, with the denim pulled tight over my sex lips.

It was a favourite of his, a position he likes to make me adopt for the cane. The punishment comes panties down, naturally, but it was still more than he could resist. His cock came out, already erect, and he began to stroke himself. I reached back, to pop open the button of my shorts and take hold of the waistband, making as if to ease them down off my bum, showing my taut panty seat to his burning gaze. He began to wank faster, perhaps wanting to come at the moment my panties followed and my bare bottom came on show.

I stopped, and stood, throwing him a coquettish look as I once more began to move, dancing now, moving into a series of lewd poses, sticking my bottom at his face and wiggling, making my cheeks bounce in my shorts, cupping my boobs and running my fingers up and down over my nipples. He just stared, never once trying to touch, but taking it all in as his face grew slowly redder and beads of sweat began to form on his forehead.

Again I changed, strutting and posing, teasing with my clothes, up and down, playing peek-a-bo, first with the undersides of my boobs and my panties. It looked like he was going to explode by the time I gave him the first proper flash of my tits. I was enjoying myself far too much to want him to finish off. I covered my boobs again, and gave him the same treatment with my bum, this time peeling my shorts down, far enough to show my cheeks properly and let him have a good stare at the bulging white cotton seat of my panties.

I knew he wanted them down badly, and it was time he got what he wanted. My thumbs went to my waistband. His hand began to hammer at his cock. I pushed, quickly, providing just a brief peep at my bare bottom before they came up again. I skipped away, laughing as I tugged up my shorts. Percy's face was crimson and beaded with sweat, his cock so engorged that the head was glossy with pressure.

He needed to come, but I was having too much fun to let him. I pulled up my top and began to pose again, boobs out. I knew it would drive him wild, but that he would hold off for a proper show of my bum, by far his favourite part of my anatomy, of any girl's anatomy. Most of all he'd want to see my bumhole, and I could be pretty sure he wouldn't come until it was showing.

So I teased, dancing and posing, first with my boobs bare, then topless altogether. I was being dirty now, getting into lewd, unrestrained postures, many with my shorts pushed down and my panties pulled aside to show off my pussy. He got plenty of my bottom crease too, with my bum stuck right out, wriggling in his face with my panties pulled up tight, or half-down, but never all the way.

I thought he would come anyway, even without my bumhole to lech over, but he didn't. Any other man I knew would have done so, that or fucked me on the spot for being such a tease. Not Percy, he'd held back, to the point where it would soon be me who snapped.

The time had come. I turned, stuck out my bum one more time and pushed my thumbs down the sides of my shorts, my panties too. Percy groaned as I began to push it all down, wanking faster and faster as inch by inch my bum came on show. I bent lower as I pulled, letting my cheeks flare as they came free, and looking back to watch as he jerked at his cock with desperate energy.

I felt the cool air on the rear pouch of my pussy and I knew I was showing, everything, with Percy's eyes fixed on my pouted sex lips and the tiny, wrinkled hole between my cheeks. Again he groaned, I pushed everything down the last few inches, and just let go, my bladder erupting into the crotch of my lowered panties. Percy gasped, and a fountain of thick, yellow-white come erupted from the tip of his cock.

He'd done it, but I couldn't have stopped if I'd wanted to. My pee was gushing, spattering my thighs and bubbling out around the side of my shorts, to run down my legs and into my sandals. I let it come, all of it, until I was standing in a wide pool of my own piddle and my shorts and panties were sodden. It was still dripping from my crotch as I pulled my clothes up.

Percy might have come. I hadn't. It felt glorious, my pussy and bottom encased in warm, soggy cotton, the piddle still running out in rivulets as it squeezed free to the pressure of my flesh. My pussy mound was wet with pee, the dark stain outlining my sex, with the material clinging to my flesh, tighter even than before. My bum was soaked too, the whole seat sodden, as if I'd sat in a puddle. It was easily enough to come over. I'd wet myself in front of him as he masturbated, on purpose, then pulled up my panties and shorts to make sure I got even messier. It could get better though, if only I had the courage.

I was close. Percy had taken out a handkerchief to clean himself up, but I stopped him, squatting down to take him in my mouth and suck the sperm from his cock. He let me, watching as I fed on his mess, and as I opened my mouth to show the pool of sperm on my tongue.

Again I stood up, to spit my dirty mouthful out into my hand so I could play with it. Some went on my boobs, smeared over them to leave my nipples stiff and glistening under a coating of sperm and saliva. I opened my jeans again and more went down my panties, at the front, down into the pouch of pee-soaked cotton around my sex. It wasn't all pee down my panties either. Even without the handful of slimy sperm I was as juicy as I've ever been, and my fingers went up into my hole with ease.

My hand was still slippery, with enough of his come to cream my bumhole for a badly needed finger. I pushed my hand down the back of my shorts, into my panties, feeling in the wet valley between my bum cheeks. My anus felt puffy and sensitive, opening easily to the pressure of my finger. I knew I was quite full, and I could feel what I had inside myself, a hard lump in my rectum.

That touch broke the last of my reserve. I pulled my finger free and stuck it in my mouth, sucking eagerly. Again I fastened my shorts and again I began to show off, dancing slowly, posing my wet clothes, front and back, adopting one lewd position after another, only no longer for Percy's benefit, but for my own. I wanted him to watch though, to be my audience, to bring my humiliation to a peak. It was right that he should watch anyway, my boobs were coated with his sperm, my pussy smeared with it, my bumhole greased with it.

My breathing was deep and even, my fingers were trembling, my tummy fluttering. I could feel the pressure, but I didn't have to give in. Each rude pose made the sensation of strain in my belly worse, yet I knew that when it happened it would be no accident. It would be on purpose, quite clearly on purpose. There would be no excuse.

I took it to the point of pain, to when I was no longer dancing, but wriggling in desperation. An agonising, delicious sense of helplessness built up, higher and higher, into an ecstasy of discomfort and consternation at what I was about to do. Finally the pain was just too much. I had to do it, then and there. With my back to Percy, I bent down, resting my hands on my knees with my back pulled in, flaunting my bottom. I could feel the pressure, enough to set me sobbing as I held it in. The urge was to let go, to give in, to abandon myself to my dirty fate. I had to, and I did, just a little, until my bumhole started to spread. Immediately a wash of panic hit me, and shame, at the thought of doing in my panties what years of training had taught me to do in the toilet. Just the idea was enough to put a lump in my throat, anytime, but now I could really do it. I couldn't not do it. The time was right, the place was right. There was no excuse.

There was every excuse. I had time. I could get into the bushes, get my clothes down, hide my shame. It was an appalling thing to do, unspeakably dirty, impossibly rude, so naughty, so delightful . . .

I just had to. My mouth came wide in an ecstatic gasp as I let my bumhole open, and it was too late. The panic came back, visions of outrage and disgust at my behaviour filling my head as the lump I'd felt up my bottom squeezed out of my hole and into my panties. Now it really was too late. I'd let it happen. I was dirty, so I might as well do it all. With a loud and shame-filled sob I pushed, letting my bumhole spread to the weight in my gut, and out it came, squeezing between my bum cheeks and into my kickers. I felt the tension in my panty seat as they started to bulge, and in my shorts as the lump grew bigger, more dirt squeezing out as I pushed again, and bigger still, wadding into a fat, squashy ball beneath me.

Suddenly I didn't need to push anymore. It was coming out anyway, in a great rush, forcing out my wet panties behind and squeezing up between my bum cheeks, down over my pussy too. I was sobbing, gasping, overcome with emotion at what I was doing. That didn't stop me, and I stayed put, legs braced, bottom well out, revelling in the sensation as my panties filled with shit. I screamed as I felt the mouth of my pussy open to the pressure, but I could no longer stop, the entire contents of my rectum squashing out into my now straining panties until I was shaking my head in an agony of emotion.

My tears started as my bumhole closed, running over my face to drip down and splash in the pool of piddle I was standing in. I felt utterly humiliated and aroused almost to the point of orgasm; my tears blended of shame and delight, of despair and elation, of misery and ecstasy.

There was a little more left, and I pushed it out, sighing as it joined the rest, with my bulge growing fatter and tighter with each piece, until the full bulk of my load was in my panties. It felt hot against my skin, and squashy, truly disgusting and truly wonderful. I had to come, soon, but now I'd done it I was determined not to waste it.

I stood, to stretch high, my hands behind my head, my boobs pushed out, much the same pose in which Fauçon had painted me, only now I had a couple of pounds of my own dung in my panty pouch. I could feel the weight, hanging heavy beneath my bottom, quivering slightly as I moved. That felt good, and I wiggled, making it move again, wobbling beneath me like some sort of obscene jelly. I had to touch.

My hand went down, to feel it, and I let out a fresh sob as I pressed on the soft, round bulge. It was big, and I knew it would be blatantly obvious what I'd done. I took a pinch, my face screwing up into a grimace, half disgust, half delight as I felt it squash between my fingers.

That was the limit of my patience. I had to come. I stepped forward, to the edge of the pond, and sank down into a squat. The motion squeezed more mess up between my bum cheeks and over my pussy, taking my dirty feelings higher still as I jammed my hand down the front of my panties. It was all over my pussy ... no, my cunt, my dirty, soiled cunt, soggy and warm under my fingers as I began to masturbate. My other hand went back, to cup my bulge.

I didn't need fantasy. I was topless outdoors, in nothing but jeans shorts and panties, and those sodden with pee and bulging with mess, my own mess. Just that awful weight and the squashy feeling in my hand was enough, that and the slimy sensation around my clitty as I brought myself up, and up, and up ...

At the last possible moment I squeezed my load, hard, squashing it out of my panties and the legs holes of my shorts, up my cunt hole and over my busy fingers. Immediately I was coming, screaming and shaking in blind, uncontrollable ecstasy as I masturbated in my own filth. I felt my pussy go tight, squashing out what was inside and I hit a new peak, blinding, wild pleasure, my mind burning with erotic humiliation, the tears streaming from my eyes, my fingers working over and over on the fat, obscene bulge in my panties, squashing it, kneading it, until at last I could take no more.

I sank down, to sit in the mess with a wet squelch that gave me one final jolt of ecstatic self-disgust. Then it was over. My body went gradually limp, my breathing slowly returning to normal. When I finally screwed up the courage to look back, it was to find Percy staring at me in astonishment, his cock still in his hand. He began to clap. I managed a grin, rocked forward on my heels and tumbled myself into the water.

The pond was deliciously cool, a wonderful sensation when my whole body was prickling with sweat, and worse, much worse. I ducked under quickly to wet my face and hair, then got down to the dirty bit, blushing and giggling as I struggled off my shorts and panties. I had expected to feel bad, at least a little guilty, but I didn't at all, just wonderfully naughty.

Percy came to stand by the edge of the pool, watching as I cleaned myself up. His fat red face was wreathed in smiles, which I knew was a reaction as much to the intimacy I'd shown with my own masturbation as the effort I'd made for his. If there had been any lingering bad feelings about me going off with Fauçon, they were gone. Once I'd let him inspect me, dried off in the sun and wrapped myself in his coat, we walked back hand in hand.

I was bare underneath, as I'd promised myself I would be, my soiled panties and shorts having gone to the bottom of the pond with a large stone to weigh them down. Nothing showed, although I knew I would have to keep firmly upright or I'd be showing my bum. I didn't care. This time I was ready to cope with any amount of a male attention.

Sure enough, the pickers were still there, lined up in front of a table at which Monique and Marie-Armelle Moreau were handing out bundles of Euros. It was more than I could resist not to smile, and to put a deliberate wiggle into my walk as we passed. The looks I got in return were searing, as before, but my mood had changed. Marie-Armelle had turned too, and that really was more than I could resist. As I reached the far side of the yard I bent, briefly adjusting the buckle of my sandal, just low enough and just long enough to give them a taunting flash of my bare bottom.

Eight

In the morning the entire episode with Fauçon seemed like a bad dream. I had reasserted my sexuality with a vengeance, not just at the mill, but later, with Percy, in a session of spanking and humiliation and anal play that had lasted into the early hours of the morning. I had left him utterly exhausted, and as he was still fast asleep when I'd washed, dressed and made-up, I decided to leave him. He'd buggered me and I'd masturbated with the handle of his clothes brush up my bottom, so I was waddling a bit as I made my way downstairs. I didn't mind. I was happy.

I'd been spanked too, well, and I had to lower myself carefully onto my chair to spare my bruises. When Madame Sinson came with my coffee she gave me a look of deep sympathy and asked if there was anything special I needed. I nearly laughed, as it seemed likely that she had heard something and thought I was being abused, but I held it back, assuring her I was fine. If she was sympathetic, then there was more than a little jealousy in the expressions of both her husband and the two other male guests who shared our floor. I ignored them, save to make it clear by my actions that I was not in distress.

There was still no sign of Percy, so I took another coffee out into the garden to relax and think things over. Most of my things were at Fauçon's, which was a bit of a problem, but I was sure I could prod Percy into going to fetch them. I didn't want to go with him, because it would be too emotional, and not just because I was already beginning to feel nostalgic about my time there.

I had lost a lot, or at least the potential to gain a lot. At the very least Fauçon might have been persuaded to part with one or other of the sketches he'd done of me, but now I had nothing at all. Nor had I realised the full potential of the situation. Now I did. Somewhere among the stacks of canvasses would be the two paintings of Helene, almost certainly. They were important. The others were simply paintings, valuable maybe, but without that special something to grab the public's imagination. Those two alone had the potential to become something more.

They had a story, and the public loves a story. Just think of Van Gogh's ear or the Mona Lisa's smile. Okay, so the details were a touch too dirty for a fairytale, but it was still had all the ingredients of a classic romance. There was the ardent and handsome young lover, Fauçon, struggling with his art. There was the beautiful and strong-willed girl, Helene, rebelling against her tyrannical father. Disney could have done it, only they'd have had to cut out the bit with the chamberpot.

The art world might be less than impressed, but that didn't matter. The public did. It isn't dealers who pay the truly astronomical sums for art, it's wealthy institutions keen to buy into a dream, to glamorise whatever tedious function they perform by association. If Van Gogh had been a sensible, down to earth fellow and laid off the absinthe, his paintings wouldn't fetch a fraction of what they do. Okay, so the two of Helene were a bit strong for the foyer of a Japanese bank, but there would be collectors, no question.

All it needed was good marketing. That I could see to. I had the contacts in London, friends in advertising, PR, product placement. With a little persuasion and perhaps the occasional blow-job, I would be able to build the thing into a legend. Then *voila!* Who has the two paintings, looks like the model and was the final lover of the now conveniently dead artist? Me, Natasha Linnet, what a surprise!

They might even let me play Helene in the film, perhaps opposite Patrice, whose performance while I was stuck up his chimney in the nude suggested no small skill as an actor. That was a daydream. The rest wasn't. It was not easy, but it was practical. Or it would have been, had I not let myself get carried away and shagged Patrice. Now all I had was the story, most of which was unrepeatable to all but my most intimate friends.

Percy eventually rolled out into the garden at nearly ten o'clock, complaining about the French breakfast and running over the virtues of sausages, bacon, eggs, fried bread and even baked beans. He always got like that after a few days in France, and I let him ramble, wondered when would be a good moment to broach the subject of my clothes.

It had to be pretty soon, because other than those I'd escaped in, all I'd had were the jeans shorts, now sunk at the bottom of the mill pond, my bikini and a couple of tops. There were also four three-packs of plain white cotton panties in Percy's luggage, but even he would have to agree they were inadequate for polite company.

The problem didn't seem to have occurred to him, as he immediately began to outline his plans for a series of tastings along the Aubance Valley. I had to speak, before he got completely carried away with his enthusiasm. His response was a deep sigh.

'It is not a task I relish . . .'

'I have paid, in advance, surely?'

'Yes, you have, and yes, I will do it. After all, if I must, I must, and what else could a gentleman do?'

'Thanks, Percy. I'll make it up to you.'

I leant over to kiss his nose, then sat back, glad that I was to be spared one embarrassing scene at least.

'I'm sure you will,' he went on, 'but you are to come up to the house with me, and no nonsense.'

'Percy!'

'No nonsense.'

He wagged one plump finger at me. I opened my mouth to remonstrate, only to close it again. I could see what he was thinking. From his point of view the whole episode was the result of me behaving like a brat, and I could hardly expect him to shoulder the entire responsibility of extricating myself from it. I nodded.

It was barely a day and a half since I'd walked out of Fauçon's house, but it seemed like an age. We drove up the track this time, past the gnarled old Chenin vines and the red and white roses, stopping at the gates. Percy got out, to walk up to the door, entirely confident as I trailed along behind him, trying to keep the hang-dog expression off my face. Fauçon opened the door, glancing to Percy only for an instant before looking past, right at me.

'Natasha, you are back!'

'Just for her clothes, I'm afraid,' Percy put in. 'Perhaps if you could fetch them?'

Fauçon ignored him completely, addressing me.

'This is not true, Natasha. You are back, yes?'

I hesitated. It was a chance, the chance I needed. I had come up beside Percy, and he put a protective arm around my shoulder. Fauçon's eyes went wide in apparent disbelief.

'*Non!* Tell me it is not so? Impossible! You are with this fat old man? I do not believe it, Natasha. You seek to make me jealous? Do you think I am a fool?'

Percy was going to say something, but it really was up to me. I stepped forward even as Fauçon did, leaving us face to face.

'No, Phillippe,' I answered him. 'I am sorry. Please just get my clothes.'

'But why? You left, yes. You were frightened, I understand, but you surely must understand my own anger?'

'No. You broke the rules, Phillippe.'

'Rules? What rules? Who sets these rules?'

'I do.'

'What? This is nonsense! We quarrelled, that is all! Now come in, and stop being foolish. All is forgotten.'

'Not by me. I suppose you think it's fair to beat a girl with a stick just because she ... because she has a little fun?'

He stopped for a moment, his face set in surprise, then spoke again.

'But yes. Naturally.'

'What!?'

'You yourself accepted that I should beat you!'

'Spank, Phillippe, spank, for fun, for sex! Yes?'

'*Non, pas du tout. Tu* ... You asked if I would ... Yes, you said spank ... but you understand, I think ... I thought? It is the way of the world, no, for a man to command?'

'No, it is not, you male chauvinist pig!'

'Why then?'

'For fun, you idiot! Like I said. Why do you think I . . . I liked it so much?'

'Liked it? You cried! You ran to the room, in tears!'

'And the first time?'

'Also you cried, yes, after . . . but this is between us, not, not in front of . . .'

He broke off, making a gesture at Percy, utterly contemptuous, clearly no compliment. Percy's face had been going gradually red, and took on a yet deeper shade. It was up to me to speak.

'Do you mind?'

'Come inside,' he went on, taking no notice whatever. 'We will speak of these things, over a glass of wine. You will understand me, I know.'

'No, Phillippe, sorry.'

'No?'

'No.'

'But you can not mean this, Natasha. We quarrelled, yes, but you were the cause. You can see this, surely?'

'Phillippe, you are a good artist, a great artist maybe, but you are also the most arrogant, stupid, narrow-minded man I have ever met! You have to control everything around you, and . . .'

'You fucked with my grandson, I know . . .'

'Yes, I fucked Patrice, and I sucked René-Claude's cock! Because you told me to, because you made me! So don't give me any of this "you weren't faithful" bullshit!'

'*Ça c'est nul!* You are my lover! I catch you with my grandson, my own flesh and blood, and you think I should not be angry!?'

'I . . . Angry, yes . . . maybe, but you don't have to be a hypocrite, and it doesn't give you the right to beat me up even if I'd fucked Patrice a thousand times, and I wish I had!'

'You, you little whore . . . you . . .'

He started forward, anger blazing in his eyes. Percy put up a finger and took one step towards us, but Fauçon had stopped, and again began to speak.

'This is not right. This is a travesty! I am wronged, and you leave? And what of my work? Does that mean nothing to you?'

'I think we had better be going, Natasha my dear,' Percy stated, his tone absolutely formal. 'Please send her clothes to Monsieur Moreau, Monsieur Fauçon.'

He was right. I didn't answer, but turned on my heel. Percy took my arm, steering me towards the car with Fauçon following, now talking in French, a mixture of threats, pleas and expressions of exasperation. Even when I'd got into the car he came to the window, still talking until Percy let in the clutch and he had to jump back or risk having his foot run over.

'What an unpleasant fellow,' Percy remarked as Fauçon's expostulations and entreaties faded behind us.

'I said I shouldn't have come,' I replied. 'Now I've got nothing to wear until he sends my clothes down, and he might very well not, just out of spite.'

'No matter, we will go shopping, in Angers.'

It was a generous offer, from a man whose idea of Hell came pretty close to spending a day being dragged around women's shops, especially when he could have been wine tasting. I accepted, trying to seem happy.

I continued trying to seem happy for the rest of the day. Percy was incredibly generous, but no amount of clothes shopping was going to make the fact that I'd been given a second chance and turned it down go away. I'd had no choice though, not with Fauçon being so openly rude to Percy. Percy takes a very relaxed attitude to my wanderings, but to go back to a man who had deliberately insulted him would be too much, for me even if not for him. I found myself wishing more than ever that I could tell Percy my true intentions, but it was out of the question.

Despite my best efforts, I could think of little else all day. Percy treated me to a exceptional dinner, with a full *Menu Gastronomique* at a restaurant with a pretty open air pavilion overlooking the Loire. It was dark by the time we left, and on the way back we stopped for me to get a spanking and Percy to have his cock sucked. I made it good, taking my time and using my boobs, but my heart wasn't in it. If he noticed he was too tactful to say anything.

It was much the same the next day, a wine tasting trip I would normally have enjoyed immensely. Even the prospect of the wine festival at the weekend did little to cheer me up, and the fact that Patrice and presumably Fauçon himself would be there just made it worse. Fauçon was almost certain to approach me again, and I would just have to turn him down. What with the respect the pickers had for him, I could see I was going to be really popular.

Percy didn't seem to mind, but then he was never one to let other people's opinions affect him. He was determined to go anyway, pointing out that we could just sit with the Moreaus and enjoy their company, rather than mix with the pickers, who he considered riffraff. He was right, that it didn't matter, really, but then they were neither reproachful of him nor wanted to fuck him. With me it seemed to be both.

We were having dinner with the Moreau's that evening, and with the vintage nearly in they had pushed the boat out. Unlike Fauçon, they had some understanding of what a dinner should be. They produced oysters, a salad made with local goat's cheese, *foie-gras*, duck in a blackcurrant sauce, cheese and a *Tarte Tatin*. Every course was accompanied by their own wines, and we finished with a bottle of the Clos St Aubin 'twenty-one, which was exquisite, and had Percy in raptures.

The conversation was good too. They'd heard about Fauçon and I, and while Alain tried to take a balanced view, the others were firmly on my side. Old Moreau gave the opinion that Fauçon was an idiot who didn't know a good thing when he saw one, and was clearly wishing he'd got into my knickers himself. Monique and Marie-Armelle were more scathing still, both have experienced what it was like to model for Fauçon. They didn't give any details, but I could read between the lines, which was intriguing, especially in Marie-Armelle's case.

She was sitting opposite me, and full of sympathy and friendliness. Her good humour was infectious, with her pretty face bright with laughter. She was cute too, sexy, with her plump boobs quivering in her dress, making me think of being suckled and cosseted, spanked too. It had been too long since I'd played with another girl, never mind someone so curvaceous, and as I grew slowly more drunk and more and more of our attention came to rest on one another, it became impossible not to think of it. There was Fauçon's picture of her and Monique too, which suggested an intimacy beyond friendship.

I was sure she was flirting with me too, repeatedly trying to lead the conversation to what had happened between Fauçon and I. That could only mean two things, that she retained an interest in him, or wanted to hear about me. She thought he was a pig, but that didn't mean he wasn't interesting to her sexually, so I held back, feigning embarrassment. That just made her keener still.

By the time we retired to their living room I was finding her very hard to resist. There were only four comfortable chairs, so I slumped down on a huge bean-bag beside Percy. Marie-Armelle immediately came to sit beside me, nudging my hip with hers to make me move up. The soft feel of her flesh sent a jolt right through me, and as she twisted to reach for a glass of *Crémant* her bottom pressed to my leg, softer and fleshier still.

The temptation to grab her was close to overwhelming. She brought out my dirtiest and most dominant feelings at the same time. Not just that, but after Percy and Fauçon, I needed to be in charge for once, but not with a man. Marie-Armelle was ideal.

I took my own glass as Alain passed it to me and leant sideways, against Percy's chair. Marie-Armelle's hip was still touching mine, a contact of which she could not fail to be unaware. Not that it meant her interest was sexual, not necessarily. Many girls allow intimate contact exactly because it's not sexual. Not me.

She had me trembling, just sitting there, and thinking of full boobs and soft, round bottoms and juicy pussies. It had definitely been too long. She was so cute too, and so tempting. I had to at least try. If she rejected me, then it would be embarrassing, no more. This was not London, with its gossip and my mixed-up friends who want to accept lesbianism because it's terribly PC but can't really handle it at all. This was the Layon Valley, where my reputation was already pretty rude, and if she accepted me . . .

If she accepted me, I was going to ravish her. I leant close, to whisper.

'I need a little fresh air. Do you want to come outside?'

She nodded and smiled. It was a pretty obvious advance, or I thought so, and she seemed keen. Still I hesitated. Outside I took her arm, steering her towards the old winery, which I knew would be deserted. She gave no resistance, and seemed nervous. I was very drunk, and I knew it, but the voice telling me to hold back, to be cautious, was faint and growing fainter. I could smell her, a perfume I didn't recognise, something in her hair, and her. She tripped, staggered and clung on tighter, giggling drunkenly as her arm came around my waist.

I had to be right. It felt right, intimate and open. At last she spoke, her voice soft, her English hesitant, making her more attractive still.

'For Fauçon, I was a model, also.'

'I know, I saw the paintings, some of them anyway.'

'You did?'

'Yes, Marie-Armelle, of you on the swing. Bad girl.'

I had to do it. I gave her bottom a pat. She giggled. I patted again, harder.

'Naughty . . .'

She giggled again. The next instant she was in my arms, my lips pressed to hers. For just an instant there was resistance, and then her soft, full mouth had opened under mine and we were kissing. I gave in to my needs, hugging her to me, my hands going lower. Her bottom felt glorious, full and cheeky and feminine. Her dress was light, her shape natural underneath, her big cheeks free of panties. I needed to feel her, desperately, to spank her too, and I no longer cared what her reaction was, so long as she let me do it.

Her arms were around my shoulders, holding me tight to her body. There was no resistance as I fondled her bottom, her kisses growing more urgent, more passionate. Only when I started to bunch her dress up did she pull away, giggling in protest.

'Natasha! We will be seen!'

She took my hand, pulling, to set me stumbling after her, towards the dark bulk of the old press house. At the door she stopped, to reach up above the lintel. I cam behind, cuddling up to her, kissing her neck as I took one plump boob in each hand. She was huge, each breast maybe three times the size of mine, round and fat and heavy, perfect for suckling, or to rest on my back as she spanked me, or to have hanging under her chest, bare and quivering as I rode on her back or she went down to lick on my pussy . . .

'Stop! Not here! I can't find the key . . .'

I ignored her protests, too drunk to care, except for the feel of her flesh. Her nipples had started to come out, two big, hard bumps, like her boobs, much bigger than mine. I badly wanted to kiss them, to suckle on her, to take birch twigs or nettles to them and leave them red and sore, her nipples angry points of fire . . .

She found the key, dropped it, and at last fumbled it into the lock. It took her ages, and I turned my attention to her bottom, feeling her big, bare cheeks under her dress and wondering if she was really nude, or in a thong. I had to know, and as she struggled with the key I twitched up her dress, exposing her fat, pink bottom to the pale glow of the security light. She squeaked in alarm, snatching back at her dress to cover herself. I laughed, and gave her bottom a good, firm smack, to make her squeal again.

'Not here! Inside.'

The lock groaned. The door swung open and we were inside, tumbling through, both giggling in guilty delight. For a moment we cuddled, and this time her hands went to my breasts, stroking very gently, to perk my nipples up and set me trembling. At last she broke away, and I let her do the door, steadying myself against the handle of a pallet truck as she shut and locked it.

It was hard to see, the security light outside casting some areas into bright white light, others into dense shadow. I could smell the fermenting wine though, and grape pulp, and the rich, decaying scent of what had been rejected from the *triage*. I could see the spoil too, a great wooden vat half full of golden brown pulp and whole grapes.

Marie-Armelle stepped away from the door, into a patch of light. Her pale hair was a mess, her face rosy pink, her eyes half-lidded. She was smiling drunkenly as she lifted a finger to beckon me to her. I came into her arms, my hands going straight to her bottom. Her giggle was cut off abruptly as our mouths met, and I was pulling up her dress.

This time there was no resistance at all. It came high, and off, Marie-Armelle stepping back just long enough to let me strip her. She did her bra herself, reaching back to tug the heavy catch wide and spill out her huge boobs. They were lovely, pink and round and fat, wonderfully feminine. I cupped one, to take a nipple into my mouth, suckling on her as she sighed in pleasure. As I sucked I began to feel her bottom again, her fat pink cheeks spilling out to either side of a tiny thong. She was so big, and firm too, breasts and bottom heavy above and below, her little tummy firm and round, her tightly curved waist soft and fleshy.

I pulled down her thong, eager to get her nude. She let me, stepping out of it as soon as it hit the floor and kicking her shoes away with the same motion. I went back to kissing her boobs, but she had already began to tug at my dress, and for a moment we were in a tangle of cloth and flesh, both giggling stupidly. I had to stop to get my dress over my head, and had my panties pulled down as I shrugged it away. She held onto them, for a moment, kneeling at my feet, and I felt her lips pressed to my pussy mound, warm and soft. Her tongue came out, burrowing between my sex lips, and she was licking me. I dropped the dress, closing my eyes in bliss and taking her gently by the head, to hold her in.

She was no innocent, no straight girl carried away in a drunken moment. She knew how to lick pussy, and well, her tongue flicking at my clit, teasing me, until I was whimpering with pleasure. When she finally came up it was slow, kissing my tummy, wriggling her tongue into my bellybutton, licking the undersides of my boobs, and letting a nipple briefly between her lips before our mouths met again.

I'd wanted her before, now I was desperate. So was she. Our hands were everywhere, groping at each other without the slightest inhibition. Her body was so full, so feminine, and I just couldn't get enough of it fast enough. I wanted her huge breasts, her fat, wobbly bottom, her plump, juicy pussy, all at once, to smell her, to taste her, to smother myself in her. She was no less eager, her hands stroking and kneading my flesh, one moment pulling my bottom cheeks wide to stretch out my bumhole behind, the next cupping my boobs to rub at my nipples.

Soon we were rubbing our bodies together, each greedy for orgasm. She was trying to do it on my leg, like a dog, rubbing on me in raw passion, and smearing the wet of her pussy onto my skin. I was little better, wriggling against her hand as she tried to frig me, with one finger pushed deep and her palm on my sex. It was working though, little jolts of ecstasy shooting through me, taking me right to the edge.

My hands were on her bum, feeling her gorgeous, meaty cheeks as they bounced to the motion of her rubbing, and pulling her tighter still to my leg. She was going to come on me, and I wasn't far behind, my pleasure pushing higher still as I found the wet dimple of her bumhole and pushed in a finger. She grunted, I felt her muscles twitch and she was coming, her whole body jiggling against me, her hands clutching at me as she brought herself off on my leg.

It didn't stop her, and she was still frigging me as she came down, rubbing my clitty as she nestled into me in bliss. I held onto her, enjoying the feel of her in my arms and the intimacy of what she'd done, all the while with my own pussy sending little sharp thrills through me. I was going to come, and it felt so good, held in her arms, masturbated to orgasm as I caressed her beautiful bottom . . .

I came, the orgasm hitting me even as I imagined how it would feel to bury my face between her plump cheeks and lick her from behind. My body tightened against hers, both holding the other as she brought me off and I found myself mumbling her name over and over, in ecstasy, yet even at that moment knowing I had not done enough.

We held together long after my orgasm was over, just snuggling into each other. Our skin was flushed hot and wet with sweat, the scent of our bodies strong in my nose, mixed with that of grapes and perfume. I didn't want to let go, but to draw out the moment until I had the energy to start again, and this time to really take my fill of her delicious body.

In the end it was her who pulled away. Her face was set in a drowsy, satisfied smile. Her make-up was a mess, her lips reddened from the passion of our kissing. I knew I looked as bad, and she giggled as she focussed on my face, took a step back to get a clearer view and stumbled against the edge of the *triage* vat.

She went over, squeaking in shock as she lost her balance. I was already laughing as she sat down in the pulp with a splash, spraying juice and bits of skin to every side. She was laughing too, an instant later, too hard to get up. I took her by the ankles and lifted, tipping her back into the pulp. She squealed, failing with her arms to save her hair as she went over, but too late. I hauled her up and her head went under. She looked so funny, almost upside down, with her legs waving in the air, her boobs and tummy sticking up out of the pulp, and her plump little pussy on plain view, struggling to keep her face above the mess.

I let go, to step back, laughing so hard I could barely stand. She tried to get up, slipped and landed back in the mess with a squashy sound, dissolving into giggles immediately. I just doubled up, my eyes streaming tears as I watched her frantic efforts to get out of the vat. Again she tried, rolling onto her knees to present me with her big pink bottom, both cheeks smeared with pulp and only the deep valley between still clean. An image of a pig wallowing in mud came to me and I was laughing harder still, so much I could barely see, which was when a handful of grape pulp caught me full in the face.

That shut me up, and I stood up blind, my eyes tight closed with the muck dripping down my forehead and off my nose. My mouth was wide in shock and disgust, and I caught the second handful full on, leaving me coughing and spluttering as I tried to spit out bits of stalk and rotten grapes and wipe my eyes at the same time.

Marie-Armelle showed no mercy at all, laughing as she caught me across my boobs with a third handful and gave me a fourth right in the face again. I gave up trying to get it off, clutching for her as I staggered

181

forward, to trip over the edge of the vat and go down headlong.

I might have hurt myself, but it never even occurred to me. I was just too drunk and too high on Marie-Armelle to care. She gave another of her high-pitched, piggy squeals as I came down on top of her. For a moment we were just laughing, but as I pulled myself up onto one elbow she gave me another handful in my face, not pulp this time, but half a bunch of decaying grapes. I caught the taste of mould as they burst against my lips and squashed up into my nose, and for an instant I was too shocked to respond, simply letting her smear them over my face and into my hair as she laughed gleefully over what she'd done.

Not that it took me long to recover, and she was still rubbing the grapes in when I got my hand to her face and pushed it under, to hold her down in the mess. She went wild, kicking and flailing with her arms, until I lost my grip. She came up gasping, just in time to catch the really big, mouldy bunch I'd picked up in her face, her mouth too. It went right in, to leave her coughing and blowing bits of grape skin and mould out of her nose.

That had me laughing too hard to control myself again, and the moment she'd got her airways clear she grabbed at me. I fought back, and then we were grappling in the pulp, slipping and sliding, each trying to get on top of the other, and to squash more of the mess into each other's faces. I was covered in no time, and half under, my mouth full of mouldy pulp and hard, under-ripe grapes. Her flesh was so slippery it was impossible to get a grip on her, but she was having the same problem with me, worse if anything.

I was going to spank her. I had to. I had never, ever had such a good excuse to dish out a spanking

without having to bother to ask. She deserved it too.
I got her hair, ignoring the sudden pained note in her
squeaks as I dragged her off me and scrambled
around in the muck. It was not easy, with my knees
slipping on the wooden base of the vat and her
struggling like mad to stop me as I dragged her body
across my knees. I think she wanted to lose though,
because she could have bitten or scratched if she'd
had to, but she just kicked and writhed and squealed
in helpless protest, until as last I'd got her in position,
across my lap with her fat bum stuck up in the air
above the surface of the pulp and her head held
securely by the hair. She was still kicking, but I
pushed her face under the pulp and told her to stop
it, which she did. As her head came up she spat out
a mouthful of muck to speak, panting the words out.

'Okay . . . *paluches-moi le con* . . . hand my cunt,
Natasha.'

'Hand your cunt? Frig you off?'

'*Oui.*'

I realised why she'd given in. I chuckled.

'Oh, no, Marie-Armelle, that's not what I had in
mind! It's your bottom I'm after, my girl.'

She started to say something, a question, but her
voice broke to a squeal of shock as my hand landed
hard across her bottom. Her cheeks bounced, juice
spattered my chest and the spanking her begun. She
went wild, and I had to grab at her waist to keep her
across my legs, holding on for dear life as she thrashed
wildly from side to side. It was just funny. She was
squealing like a pig. Her fists were thumping up and
down in the grape pulp. Her little fat legs were going
up and down like pistons, splashing mess everywhere.
I clung on, laughing at her plight and spanking
furiously at her wet, quivering bottom, to send more
juice and bits of pulp flying with each smack.

It must have been totally unexpected, which was just wonderful. It must have hurt too, because she was squeaking like anything, in real pain, but she was giggling too which just encouraged me, so she had no chance whatsoever of escaping her punishment. She was lovely to spank too, her big bottom a treat, soft and fleshy and wobbly, to give me plenty of target. It didn't sting my hand either, or else I was too drunk to notice, but it stung her all right, sending her into an absolute frenzy long before she had even begun to pink up properly.

I just kept going, it was too good to stop. She was perfect spanking material, so cute, and a real screamer, small enough to hold down too. All the while I was laughing, and getting more and more turned on, until when I finally did stop, it was only because I wanted my pussy licked and felt it was about time she did it.

Her bum was red, really glowing, shiny with grape juice and covered in goose-pimples, a well-smacked bottom if ever there was one. She had given in too, completely, not even trying to get away, but with her bum raised of her own accord, the big cheeks wide, her anus showing between, a little fleshy ring, pink and ever so slightly pouting, the central hole deep and moist. My pussy was tingling with need, my head full of sadistic thoughts. Pussy could wait. I tightened my grip on her waist, took a big handful of pulp and squashed it between her cheeks. She gave a delighted squeal and started to kick again. I took another handful, ignoring her giggling protests as I squashed it up between her legs, over her pussy. Some must have gone up her hole, because she gave a single shrill squeal, louder and longer than before, and began to kick and struggle with renewed energy. It just made me worse. I took a third handful, making sure I got plenty of unbroken grapes, and pressed it to her, pushing my hand against her hole to force it up. She squealed again, and burst into a fit of uncontrollable giggles.

I was really enjoying myself, having her helpless as I soiled her pussy and bum crease, and the rude view I had of her as well. She was still protesting in broken, mumbling French, but it was fake, just a sop to save herself from having to admit she enjoyed being molested. She was going to get done anyway, thoroughly.

There were unripe grapes among the overripe ones, little hard green balls, just right to pop up into her pretty bumhole. I took one, pressing it to the wet pink hole. She gasped in shock as her anus opened to the pressure, but said nothing, and sighed as my finger slid in to push the grape up into her rectum.

She had given in, surrendered to me completely. When I'm drunk and horny and in a dirty mood, that is a very foolish thing to do. I tightened my grip still further, locking my arm into the plump flesh of her waist. She let her legs come fully apart, showing off her pussy, with golden pulp oozing from the hole. I took another handful and squashing it up, filling her until she had began to whimper and the mouth of her vagina showed as a wide pink hole, plugged with the mess I'd stuffed up her.

I slapped her as she began to wriggle again, ordering her to keep still. She promised she would, her voice quiet and soft, which really sealed her fate. I began to pick unripe grapes from the pulp, the biggest I could find, until I had a good handful. A slight movement of my knee brought her bottom up, spreading the fat cheeks wide to make her bumhole fully available. My hand went between her cheeks, a grape to her anus. This time, as her bumhole swallowed the grape she only gave out a little whimper. I began to feed them up her, grinning maniacally as one after another popped up the soppy little hole.

She was open, her bumhole moist and receptive, the grapes slippery with juice. They went in easily, each one pushed well up, my finger burrowing again and again into the hot, slimy interior of her rectum. I could feel them inside, hard and round against my finger tip as I pushed each one in among the growing clump. Soon I'd begun to laugh again, revelling in her utter submission and my own dirty behaviour. She'd given in, making herself my plaything, seemingly ripe for any dirty amusement I decided on.

Had I been just a little more sober I'd have taken it slow, maybe made her squirt the mess out into her panties, or seeing if she'd eat it from my hand, willingly, then laugh at her for being such a slut. I didn't know if she could handle anything so calculatingly dirty, but that wasn't why I didn't do it. I was just too drunk to think, and too horny to hold back. I wanted to come over her, over the state she was in, and to make her come too.

I pushed her off my legs and climbed onto hers, ordering her to keep her bottom up out of the muck. She did it, kneeling with her boobs hanging in the pulp and her face only just above the surface, her big bottom facing me. Pulp was oozing out of her pussy hole, and her anus was a little open, and sloppy wet. Once more the image of a pig wallowing in swill came back to me.

'Frig yourself,' I ordered. 'I'm going to watch. '*Te planches ton con, Marie-Armelle . . .* or whatever it is.'

Her hand came back, in instant obedience. Two fingers spread her sex lips to show off the neat, pearly bud of her clitty and she was frigging, and making a fine display of it as well. I slapped her bottom, hard, but she only grunted and began to rub harder still. It looked great, really dirty, masturbating herself in dirty ecstasy as grape pulp oozed from her hole and down over her pussy. It gave her plenty to rub in, and me too.

I moved back, spreading my thighs to get at myself. I was cleaner than her, but only just, and there was pulp squashing under my fingers as I began to tease my pussy. It wasn't going to take much. My head was swimming with dirty thoughts, some dominant, some not, my sadistic feelings slipping as my pleasure rose.

She was close too, her pussy already contracting. A fat wad of grape pulp came free, to roll down her sex, thick and sticky. My efforts to keep her the submissive one just snapped. I buried my face in her sex, lapping up the sweet, decaying mess, swallowing, and bursting into fits of giggles as more of the golden pulp squeezed out of her pussy. It went straight into my mouth and I swallowed it down. My head went down again, to suck more pulp out of her hole, once more filling my mouth. I could taste grapes and mould and girl, all together, then I had swallowed once more. My dirty instincts were coming to the front, and I was thinking of it balling in my stomach, making me want to be more dirty still, to pee over her bottom and lick it up.

I was kneeling up again immediately. My bladder was tense. I knew I could do it. I had to. I didn't care what she thought, and I was moaning in ecstasy as I released a stream of pee full into the her gaping hole of her sex. She gasped as her hole filled, but kept on frigging, with my pee bubbling out of her body. She knew, she had to, but she obviously didn't care. In fact she was coming, her muscles contracting to squirt piddle out backwards over my belly and legs even as my stream splashed over her.

She needed licking, but her bumhole had started to wink. A grape squeezed out, to drop into the wet muck below her with a plop, and for an instant leave her anus a dark hole into her body. My pee caught her ring as it closed, splashing out across her bottom and back onto me. She was in orgasm now, gasping and snatching at her sex, too far gone to care as once more her anus opened, this time to immediately fill with my piddle.

I went down, still pissing, over my hand as my fingers found my pussy again. A golden-brown mixture of piddle and grape juice spurted out of her bumhole, full in my face, and a second, into my open mouth. I had to lick her. She gave a groan as my tongue found her sloppy little hole, and her bottom tightened in my face. My mouth filled with grapes and pee and mess and I was in orgasm, in mindless ecstasy as I fed on her pulsing bumhole, with my mouth full of her taste, coming and coming until I could stand no more.

Both of us collapsed, to lie gasping in the mess, Marie-Armelle with soiled pulp dribbling from her vagina and bottom hole, me with the same sticky mixture running out of the corners of my mouth. I'd stopped peeing as my climax started, but there was more to come, and I let it, pattering into the puddle of liquid under my pussy until at last my bladder was empty.

It had gone far, far further than I'd intended it too, and I found myself blushing in hot shame as Marie-Armelle finally turned to look at me. Her face was red too, or what I could see of it was, through the mask of pulp smeared over her features, but she was smiling. I smiled back, and took her hand to help her out of the vat. We came up with a sticky, pulling sound, to stand, dripping with muck, and immediately both of us burst into giggles.

We were filthy. Every inch of my body was dirty with grape pulp, from my toes to my hair. Marie-Armelle was the same, while the area around the vat was spattered with it and even some of the nearby barrels and bits of machinery had not escaped. I took it in open mouthed, wondering how we were going to clean up, or explain the mess. Finally Marie-Armelle found her voice.

'You are a bad girl, Natasha!'

'I know.'

'To *pipi* on my bottom!'

I just gave her a big grin. I was the bad girl. She'd just surrendered, or at least, she could tell herself she had, or even tell herself I'd made her do it. That was fine, so long as she didn't go off on a guilt trip over what we'd done.

She didn't, but turned the lights on long enough to locate a hose and the drain at the centre of the press room floor. We were in hysterics as we cleaned up, giggling over what the others would think if they knew what we'd been up to. With the floor clean, I stood on the drain as she hosed me down, trying to concentrate and not giggle too much. The water was cold, which was lovely at first, but left me shivering by the time I'd got all the pulp out off myself. Marie-Armelle took her turn, throwing me looks of mock accusation as she used the hose to get pulp out of the deeper crevices, which had me laughing more than ever. Only when she was clean did I realise just how red her bottom was. So did she, craning back to inspect her smacked cheeks and coming up with an accusing look.

'My bottom ... she's so red, and so hot! You smacked me hard!'

'It was nice though, wasn't it, and don't tell me you've never been spanked before.'

189

'No! Not . . . not that way.'

'Seriously? That was your first proper spanking?'

'Yes! What do . . . how . . .'

'Oh beautiful! A virgin! I'm privileged, Marie-Armelle, honestly.'

'And I could have said no?'

'Of course.'

She didn't believe me, or she didn't want to, making a face in response to my claim. We were both stark naked and dripping wet, cold too, but with no way to get dry properly all we could do was wait, and check that there was nothing to give away our dirty little secret. The contents of the vat looked a bit squashed, but a good stir helped, leaving just one question in my mind as we sat down on a barrel to dry.

'Er . . . what do you do with the pulp?'

'It is to the government . . . for to be distilled.'

'Oh, that's all right then. Industrial alcohol, I hope, not cheap brandy?'

She laughed and reached out to smack at my bottom, catching me well above the target as most of me was on the barrel. I gave a squeak, half-pretend.

'If you're going to spank me, Marie-Armelle, put me across your knee and do it properly, on my bum cheeks.'

'I could not . . . dare not. You are bigger, stronger too.'

'Oh I'd go willingly, or maybe you'd like to see me get it?'

She said nothing, but with her sudden little smile said all that was needed. Being spanked in front of her was an appealing thought, but not so appealing as being done side by side, which had my mischievous mind working.

'Percy would do it, and if you ever want to be spanked properly, just ask Percy.'

'Is he a good bottom smacker?'

'A spanker. And yes, the best. He'd love to spank you too.'

'He enjoys bottoms fat?'

'He'd enjoy yours. So do I. You've got a lovely bottom.'

'No. Your bottom is lovely. Mine is just . . . gross.'

'You mean fat.'

'Sorry . . . fat. Mine is fat.'

'You have a gorgeous bottom, and never let anyone tell you otherwise.'

'No, she is too fat.'

'There's no such thing, in Percy's book, so long as a girl's bottom is nice and round, womanly, and believe me, yours is. Offer him the chance to spank you and you'll see.'

'Would he . . . wish to?'

'Would want to. Yes, one hint and you'd be over his knee with your knickers around your ankles.'

She laughed.

'But he . . . he make himself, so . . . so pompous.'

'Pompous? He'd love you! I think you mean proper, and that's a fine joke. He's genteel, that's all, and very English. In fact, he makes a bit of an act of being English, especially when he's abroad. Underneath all that, he's . . . well, a dirty old man, I suppose.'

'And you like this?'

'Yes. He's gentle, generous, polite, he lets me do as I please, and he knows exactly how to handle me sexually.'

She nodded, apparently in comprehension, although I wasn't even sure how much she had understood. I went on extolling his virtues.

'He won't try and push you into anything else either. If you say just spanking, he'll stick to that, or if you say he can make you come but you won't touch, or if you say you'll suck his cock but he can't fuck you, whatever.'

Again she nodded, and made a face which I took to mean that she was impressed.

'There aren't many men you can trust that way, especially during a heavy session, if you're tied up or something.'

'No.'

'Fauçon for one. He'd just take what he wanted.'

'I know.'

'I suppose you do. You modelled for him, didn't you?'

'Yes. He is a beast . . . a goat.'

'Why do it then?'

'I had . . . I was sixteen. Fauçon, all the world respects him . . . his art. In our place . . . *chez nous* . . .'

'Locally?'

'Yes. He is well known, very well known.'

'A local hero, and you were flattered?'

'Yes, absolutely.'

'And then after you'd stood there stark naked for half the day he made you suck his cock?'

'Yes. And after . . . when me found another model, he . . . sent me away. He is a goat.'

'He kicked you out? He's a goat, yes, a pig. It was the same with me, only I walked out on him. Did he spank you?'

'No.'

'He did me. He had Madame Vaucopin hold me down, and it was in front of that René-Claude. How did Madame Vaucopin treat you? She hated me from the moment I walked in the door.'

'Madame Vaucopin? *Non, pas du* . . . not at all. All the days . . . always she was kind. She held you . . . to be smacked . . . spanked?'

192

'Yes, by my panties! Bitch!'

'She is always kind.'

'Not to me she isn't! Look, I'm freezing, we'd better get dressed and start back.'

Nine

Sex with Marie-Armelle had done me a lot of good. Sometimes, after a lot of submissive sex, particular the sort Fauçon liked, it can get to me in a way, making me subdued, without me being aware of it, or not fully aware. I'd been like that, even after walking out on him. She had picked me up, and the next day I was in a much better mood.

I was also sore behind, the result of a session across Percy's lap with his clothes brush once we'd got back to the hotel. He'd guessed I'd been up to something, and I'd given him the whole story. That had left him with two excuses to punish me, my behaviour and the state of his cock. I'd got to him so much that he came on my tummy while I was across his knee, which is rare.

We'd come back by cab, leaving Percy's car at the Moreaus', and it had been close to three in the morning by the time we'd finally got to sleep. When I woke up it was close to noon, and Percy was still snoring. I felt weak, but surprisingly clear headed, presumably having worked most of the alcohol out of my system during sex with Marie-Armelle and then Percy.

It was going to have to be an easy day in any case, and a sober one. The following evening was the wine festival, which undoubtedly meant another drunken night. Marie-Armelle was going to be there, so I was no longer so worried by the pickers' attitude, or by the prospect of a show of artistic temperament from Fauçon. In fact, if I played my cards right it might be possible to get off with both Marie-Armelle and Percy, and let Fauçon know it, which would be immensely satisfying.

For a while I just lay in bed, staring at the ceiling and fantasising over increasingly complicated and impractical revenges, both on Fauçon, and on Madame Vaucopin. In ways she deserved it more than he did. After all, I'd done nothing to her, and as she had been nice to Marie-Armelle, it seemed that rather than simply being a bitter old harridan, she had something against me personally. Considering she had taken against me the instant she set eyes on me, that was really unfair. So was holding me down for a spanking. Unfortunately, while it was easy to imagine ways to revenge myself on Fauçon, from offending his over-precious sensibilities to simple theft, it was not so easy with her.

When I finally got bored and dragged myself out of bed to open the shutters, it was to discover that the weather had turned. It was raining, hard, a steady fall from ash grey clouds, with the leaves in the hotel garden whipping back and forth. It was a piece of timing that was going to make the Moreaus and every other grower in the area extremely relieved. A week earlier and the late vintage might have been written off. As it was, it looked like being an excellent year. That was going to make the festival something special, assuming it had stopped raining by then.

I dressed, putting on a jumper, which was a must. Percy was still asleep, and it seemed pointless to wake him, so I went downstairs. It was just about time for lunch, but I was feeling a little queasy and stuck to coffee, sipping it as I stared out of the window at the rain. A few twigs had come down in the garden, and it was threatening to turn into a full blown storm.

Going out was not a good idea, and with the car at the Moreaus' we were pretty well stuck. I was getting bored though, and from the haughty looks Madame Sinson was giving me I was sure she had heard me getting my spanking the night before, and figured out I enjoy it. In other circumstances that would have been a turn on. Alone, with the rain running down the windows and the room cold and dank, it was just embarrassing.

In the end I decided to call a cab and fetch the car, if only for something to do. That also meant a chance to see Marie-Armelle, and while mornings after a first sexual encounter can be difficult, its always better to talk than not. I didn't want the first time to be the only time either, and wanted to reassure myself that she felt the same way.

So I went, feeling pretty confident. After all, our session had got very dirty indeed and she'd been no more than mildly shocked. I was sure she had a fair bit of experience of sex with other women, and of sex in general, and that she had been as keen to seduce me as I had been to seduce her.

I was right. They were at lunch, and greeted me with enthusiasm, especially Marie-Armelle, who even gave me a pat on my bottom as she ushered me through the door and into the kitchen. Old Moreau was there, and favoured me with a gap-toothed grin as I came in, also Monique and Alain. So was Madame Vaucopin, with my bags beside her chair.

It was completely unexpected, and very awkward indeed. I really didn't know what to say, but I could have managed had it not been for the accusing glare she gave me as I walked in. All I could do was to make small talk, and to accept some lunch despite my stomach, just to give me something to do.

The Moreaus did their best to dispel the bad atmosphere, Monique in particular, but their embarrassed efforts only made me feel worse. Madame Vaucopin was entirely tactless as well, even commenting openly on my ill grace in leaving Fauçon, which was the last straw. I asked coldly if she could leave it to a more appropriate moment. Her response was to ask me for a word in private, as, so she said, she had something important to tell me. I could hardly refuse.

The weather was beginning to clear, with the clouds breaking up overhead and the wind sending ripples across huge puddles in the Moreaus' yard. I got the speech out by Percy's car, in sharp, assertive French, which I had considerable difficulty following. The essence was clear enough though, and hardly flattering. Fauçon, in her book, was a great man. I by contrast was a selfish, manipulative little slut, or words to that effect. According to her I should have been deeply honoured at Fauçon's attention, and subordinated everything to his artistic needs, rather than 'disturbing him with my dirty behaviour, high temper and petulance'.

It was pretty rich, considering the facts, and I gave her back my opinion in no uncertain terms, adding a few choice remarks on her own behaviour. I got it back in spades, a real torrent of abuse. Apparently from the moment I'd brought the two roses to the door she had decided that I was bad news. Since then my behaviour had gone from bad to worse, upsetting René-Claude, fucking with Patrice, wandering off without telling anyone where I was going, and generally playing the brat. Then there was the enormity of my crime in leaving him, which she claimed was beyond her powers of expression, although she had a pretty good try. Last came the real bombshell. She had devoted her life to him, both as model and later by looking after him in his old age, all of which she considered an honour beyond value. Then I had turned up, with my capricious behaviour and lack of respect, taking his attention and even her nickname. It took a moment to sink in, with her spluttering in my face, but it did. Helene d'Issigeac was not *La Pêche*, she never had been, that title had belonged to another model, Madame Vaucopin.

It left me speechless, although far from repentant. She seemed satisfied anyway, finishing with the suggestion that I come back and beg Fauçon's forgiveness and that I would never have hers. She then stormed off, not back to the house, and so rapidly that I couldn't help wondering if she was trying to hide tears.

I went though, to accept the Moreaus' sympathy and shocked apologies, also a very large glass of Alain's farmhouse marc. I drank it, my hand trembling with reaction so hard that Marie-Armelle had to help me at first. She came to sit with me too, on a sofa in a different room, and put her arm around my shoulder as I struggled to tell myself that being hectored by Madame Vaucopin was no big deal. It was, unfortunately, and that wasn't all.

Fauçon's lie had been more complicated than I'd realised. He hadn't just altered a story, he'd combined two, to create a romantic picture that was almost entirely phoney. I could understand Madame Vaucopin's feelings as well, although it seemed a bit unfair to take them out on me rather than him. After all, he had been an utter bastard to her, for years, ever sine he'd returned from England. Yet she worshipped him, and obviously expected me to treat him with the same blind reverence. Clearly Marie-Armelle had done, as a naïve sixteen year-old, but nobody gets that from me, especially some abusive old git.

I actually felt sorry for her, for all her venom. It also made me realise just how far submission can go beyond my own brand of playful, dirty erotica. She had devoted her entire life to him, and in return been thoroughly abused. Not just that, but she accepted it. It was impossible not to wonder if it went deeper still. Obviously they had been lovers. Maybe they still were. Maybe her pleasure came from his abuse, as mine had. If not, maybe his rejection of her represented a level of masochistic pleasure beyond anything of my experience, of my comprehension.

Maybe it did, but it was not somewhere I wanted to go. Taking something to its extreme conclusion is not necessarily the way to get the most out of it, and anyone who claims otherwise is a fool. That's like saying because I enjoy a good spanking my ultimate erotic experience would be getting beaten to death. Anyone who thinks that deserves what they get – life.

Fauçon might not have been an actual psycho, but he was pretty bad. Looking back, I realised that he must have concocted his story as he sat watching me, judging the best way to appeal to my sympathy and so get my knickers down. I could see how it went, with his own obsessions combined with my chance resemblance to Helene, so that it seemed genuine. He was an utter bastard.

There was a good side though. He thought I'd fallen for his patter, but I hadn't. I'd never entirely believed him, and my true motives had been very different, and not something calculated to put a smile on his face. That was satisfying, only far less so than the prospect of telling him, which of course I could never do. The idea was funny though, of walking up to Fauçon and pointing out to him that far from being yet another pathetic little waif in awe of his reputation and style, I was in fact a potential sneak thief. Thinking about it even made me laugh, which earned me a hug and another glass of marc from Marie-Armelle.

By the time I left I was thoroughly drunk again, and in no condition to drive Percy's lumbering great hulk of a car back to Rochefort, or anything else for that matter. Monique gave me a lift, dropping me outside the hotel with my bags. I felt slightly sick, very dizzy and in no mood for conversation, let alone explaining to Percy. He wasn't there anyway, but had left a note he'd walked down to the Loire to take some photos of the Savennières vineyards while the sky was so spectacular. I was in no mood for anything of the sort, and collapsed on the bed, falling asleep in seconds.

The rest of the day barely happened for me. I was woken by Percy at dinner time, with a horrible taste in my mouth and a headache. Eating was more than I could possibly face, and he put me to bed with a couple of painkillers before going down to make the best of the hotel menu. I don't even remember him coming up.

Sunday was very lazy indeed. It rained off and on all morning, clearing in the early afternoon to leave everything shiny wet and the road outside the hotel a string of great glassy puddles, each running into the next. I'd managed a salad for lunch, and we took a walk afterwards, down to the Loire to admire the view and drink in the cool fresh air. That left Percy eager for tea, and I left him trying to explain his exact requirements to Madame Sinson as I went back to our room.

When I woke up again it was time to go to the festival. It had actually been going on most of the afternoon, but neither Percy nor I had been in any mood for paying polite attention to French folk revelry. A huge dinner was much more his thing, and being Percy, he insisted on putting on evening dress, assuring me that we would be sitting down at tables and that it was therefore appropriate. I knew full well he was just playing up to his image as the English eccentric, but humoured him by putting on a short black cocktail dress, along with proper stockings and lacy black silk panties. Having gone that far I could hardly wear sensible shoes, so ended up in black court shoes with three-inch heels. I took a coat, as although there was supposed to be a huge fire it was getting chilly at night, and a bag I'd bought in Angers with some emergency make-up and Percy's spare car keys in case I needed somewhere private.

I was hoping I would, preferably along with Percy and Marie-Armelle. I adore seeing another girl get it from him, spanking especially, and I was fairly sure she would be up for it. I also owed him a lot of favours, and I knew how impressed he was by her figure. My suggestion that we might try had him beaming like a schoolboy – well, like Billy Bunter anyway.

The evening was bright, and almost completely clear, with just a few wisps of dark cloud to mark the rain that had passed. Everything was still wet, but the wind had dropped, leaving the air pleasantly fresh. We took a cab in, to find the open area beneath the Clos St Aubin set out with tables and bunting in a huge square. There was a bonfire at the centre, a great pile of vine cuttings and broken pallets and cardboard. There were also two spits, each with a whole goat turning over an ancient cast-iron brazier, which would have been wonderfully rustic had it not been for the clutter of modern barbecue equipment beyond.

Everyone else seemed to be already there, and already drunk. They were also sensibly dressed, in warm, practical clothes and boots. That included Marie-Armelle, looking deliciously cuddly in jeans and a thick woolly jumper. She greeted me with a kiss so passionate it made my heart jump, and the hug she gave Percy suggested considerably more than polite greeting. She was as keen as we were.

She took us to sit with her too, beside the Moreaus, who seemed to have plenty of prestige among the village families. They had one of the best tables anyway, in the front rank and next to what was obviously the top table, with the mayor, the local remnants of nobility, a couple of ancients I didn't recognise, and Phillippe Fauçon.

I ignored him, refusing to meet the accusing glance he threw me and keeping my attention firmly on the others at my table. His face was already flushed with drink, and I was sure he was going to make a scene, but to my relief he stayed put, and as I took my own place I found he was obscured from view by the reassuring bulk of Percy.

We were very much at the polite end. All the tables around us were occupied by growers and other landowners, or local businessmen, with a fair sprinkling of guests. Beyond, at the sides of the square, where the other villagers and those who worked among the vines, while at the far side the tables were banked three deep and occupied by a great, rowdy gang of pickers. I remembered our promise to share a glass with them, which brought me the same ambiguous feelings as before.

The light was beginning to fade from the sky as we settled down to drink and talk. There was a brief ceremony as one of the young girls from the village lit the bonfire, Alain explaining to me that it was a genuine pre-Christian tradition and joking that she was the only one they'd been able to find who was still a virgin. That took me aback a little, as he was normally quite reserved, but it seemed to be the mood of the evening, which was just fine by me.

Sure enough, by the time we been served out plates of roast meat, local sausages and other goodies, couples from the less genteel tables had already begun to steal off into the shadows. Nobody seemed to mind, generally ignoring them as they left, and greeting them with laughter and coarse jokes when they came back flushed and dishevelled.

Nobody from the better tables had done it, but all it needed was a bit of courage, although I could see a few eyebrows might be lifted if we took Marie-Armelle with us. All the activity I'd seen had been strictly hetero, no gay guys, no pairs of girls. It was tempting anyway, just with Percy, because Phillippe Fauçon could hardly fail to notice. I wasn't going to be first though, and Percy was enjoying himself hugely, red-faced and laughing as he stuffed himself with food and downed glass after glass of wine. So I waited, and concentrated on chatting up Marie-Armelle.

She was drunk and giggling, her eyes full of mischief, making arch remarks about who was having sex with who, and who would like to. There were ripe grapes on the table, Chenin, the rich apple taste not so very different from the ones we made each other eat in the vat. I popped one in my mouth, holding it between my lips, which made it pretty clear who I wanted to have sex with. She immediately began teasing me and telling me I was bad girl. I told her to mind her language or Percy and I would take her into the bushes for a spanking. She burst into giggles and my last doubts dissolved. She was game, there was no question about it. Before I'd finished eating I was as excited and horny as her, waiting only for the right moment.

The sensible thing to do was to arrange it first, and one of us to go to the car in advance. More than one of the local boys was showing an interest in Marie-Armelle, and I was sure that if she went alone she'd be followed. I might be followed too, if I went without Percy. He had to go first, as if off for a pee, and we could then follow together on the same excuse.

I put my dirty little scheme to Marie-Armelle and it was accepted with giggling delight. Percy was just as enthusiastic, agreeing to meet us at his car, which was comfortable, dry and close enough to be convenient. It could also be moved into the shadows where we were unlikely to be disturbed. I confirmed what was happening to Marie-Armelle, and had leant close to whisper a filthy suggestion into her ear when everything went suddenly quiet.

We turned to the front, surprised, to find Fauçon standing in the open area between the tables and the spits, his arms raised for silence. He was drunk, maudlin drunk, one cheek showing the trace of a tear, and there was already an uneasy feeling in my stomach as he began to make a speech. Sure enough, I came into it pretty soon, not as Natasha, not even as *La Pêche*, but as *ma Pêche*, his peach. It got worse, louder, more rambling and less distinct. He talked about his art and his masculinity. He waved his arms and exhorted God and the spirit of the vines. He quoted Zola.

He drew closer to our table as he spoke, and more emotional, until the tears were streaming down his face. He was making a complete idiot of himself, and I was absolutely cringing in embarrassment, but not one person told him to shut up and sit down. They listened, respectfully, as if he was making some great and moving oration, not jabbering drunkenly over a girl who'd walked out on him with perfectly good reason. He was seriously arrogant as well, making me out as weak and emotional, without so much as a hint of guilt for his own behaviour. The final sentence was an offer to take me back as he extended his hand.

That left me with a simple choice, go, or publicly humiliate him. Every single person there was staring at us, in absolute silence, me looking shocked, Fauçon in his pose of noble forgiveness, his emotion plain on his face. He was emotional, yes, but the whole thing was carefully contrived, a set-up, to leave me with no choice but to accept. If I didn't, I was going to look a complete bitch, to everyone, except Percy, and Marie-Armelle. He had his arm right across her face, so that she had to lean back. He was indifferent to her, the girl he had seduced at sixteen and then dumped when he'd grown tired of her.

I had no choice, not that I wanted one. I stood up, slowly, looking right at him, smiled, and slapped him full in the face. A gasp went up as he staggered back, taken completely by surprise. He was cursing in French, clutching at his cheek and calling me some choice names, but I ignored him, instead reaching out for Percy's hand. He looked pretty embarrassed, but he took it, and as I helped him up I ducked quickly down to whisper to Marie-Armelle. She nodded, her eyes bright with gratitude, worship almost, and I left, with Percy in tow.

He didn't say a word until we were well clear of the tables. When he did it was to tell me off for slapping Fauçon, briefly, and then to thank me for not going.

Percy rarely shows much emotion, but there was real gratitude and affection in his voice, and it meant all the more to me because it was so rare. I squeezed his hand and glanced back as we reached the entrance to the Moreaus' winery. Nobody was following.

We didn't even need to move the car. It was in deep shadow, with no more than a dull gleam of distant light to illuminate it, while the Moreaus' house had the shutters closed. No one knew we were there anyway, except Marie-Armelle.

I was still shaking with reaction for what I'd done to Fauçon, but Percy took his time, helping me into the back and stroking my hair to calm me down. My adrenaline was really pumping, and I was shaking hard, but before long my arousal had begun to come back, along with feelings of triumph and satisfaction.

By the time I was ready Percy had his cock out. I took it in my hand, stroking at the little hard shaft and running my fingers over the bulging sack of his balls. For all the aggression of my act I was feeling very submissive, and eager to show Percy that I was his. I went down on him, sucking and licking at his balls before I took his erection into my mouth. His arm came around me, his podgy fingers caressing the flesh of one breast, to tease my nipple up to erection.

I'd only been sucking a moment when there was a tap on the window. It was Marie-Armelle. She slipped quickly in beside us and I pulled up to make room. As the light came on she got a fine view of Percy's shiny wet erection. She just giggled, and kissed me. I returned the kiss and hugged her too me, even as she slammed the door shut.

Once more in darkness, there was a moment of giggling adjustment before we got in place, Marie-Armelle and I on either side of Percy. She showed no reluctance at all, but joined me as I went back down on his cock, taking it in her mouth as I sucked on his balls. He was already groaning, and I knew I'd get what I wanted even if he'd come, so I sucked harder, taking the full bulk of his ball sack into my mouth and rolling them over my tongue as Marie-Armelle sucked him deep into her throat.

He grunted in ecstasy, and wet sperm splashed on my cheek as it erupted from around Marie-Armelle's lips. I felt her swallow her load, and then she was pulling off and opening her mouth for me. I let Percy's balls free and met her kiss, pushing my tongue into the pool of sperm still in her mouth, to share, and swallow.

We came apart when Percy took us both firmly by the scruffs of our necks. I'd told him what I wanted, and I knew he'd be good to his word. Sure enough, we were hauled up onto our knees, and pulled over the seat, both giggling as our bottoms came up for his attention. I had to press myself tight to the window to let him get proper access to my bum, but I didn't care. I wanted to be spanked more than anything, and to feel Marie-Armelle's reaction as she got the same treatment.

Percy didn't seem to mind either, chuckling as he knelt between us and his hands found our bottoms. I could only purr in pleasure as he began to grope me, his fingers pushing my dress into the crease of my bottom. Marie-Armelle's hand found my hair, pulling me in, and our mouths met once again in a sticky kiss, all saliva and sperm. Behind, Percy started to strip us, fumbling at our clothes. I held on the Marie-Armelle, letting wave after wave of the most delicious submissive pleasure wash over me as I was molested.

My skirt was inched up, to my waist. A fat, warm hand settled in the waistband of my panties. They came down, slowly, baring me, only to stop halfway, with most of my bottom crease on show, but no more. I gave a disappointed wiggle and got a slap across my thighs for it, then his hands had found my dress once more. It was pushed high, to my shoulders, leaving my boobs hanging from my chest, against the cool leather of the car seat. His fingers brushed my rock hard nipples briefly and returned to my panties.

Down they came, eased off my bum, all the way this time, to my knees, leaving me to all intents and purposes nude, my bottom framed in lowered panties and stocking tops and suspender straps, and with that delightful sensation of having been interfered with. He began to stroke my bottom, across my cheeks, then between them, one finger tracing a slow line to my anus, loitering briefly in the little wet hole and on, to tickle my pussy and make me jump.

He let go, leaving me high. I felt Marie-Armelle tense and knew he was touching her. Soft noises came as she too was exposed, her jeans taken down and her jumper pushed high, her huge breasts flopped out of bra and her panties taken down, to leave her as bare and vulnerable as I.

Once more Percy's hand found my bottom, cupping my sex with the ball of his thumb right on my bumhole. He began to masturbate me, and Marie-Armelle, the sloppy sounds of our pussies being handled loud in the quiet of the car as we kissed with ever mounting passion. I really thought I was going to come when he stopped, suddenly. I knew it was spanking time even as the first slap caught my bottom.

Marie-Armelle gasped she was given the same treatment. I clung on tighter, holding her and kissing her as Percy set to work. I could hear the slaps, hers and my own, with my bum flesh quivering to each blow, and the stinging sensation already warm and arousing. I opened my knees until my panties were stretched taut between them, eager for more and to be groped as I was punished. Again a finger slid up into my vagina, probing briefly before the spanking started once again.

I had to come, and soon. I could feel Marie-Armelle trembling as I held her, and we were kissing at each others faces, our lips, noses and chins joined with sticky tendrils of Percy's come. The spanking was getting harder too, until my boobs had begun to swing against the seat with a fleshy slapping sound.

Once more Percy fingered me, this time pulling his juice soaked finger out to trail it up over my anus, and briefly invade the little hole. A moment later Marie-Armelle let out a sob, and I knew her bumhole had been given the same dirty treatment. The spanking started again, and I stuck my bottom out, now urgent, to get my bottom warmed, and to have a finger stuck in properly, right up my bottom.

Percy obliged, spanking harder still, until I begun to gasp in pain, then to cry out. He just got harder, now puffing as he belaboured our bottoms, both of us squealing in time to the fleshy slaps. I'd held off as long as I could, but it was now too much. As my hand went back to my pussy I was begging Percy to spank me harder, to really make me scream, and to finger my bumhole as he did it.

I was told not to be selfish, and groaned in despair as he turned his full attention to Marie-Armelle. She gasped and her grip grew tighter still as she was penetrated, mumbling a half-hearted protest about her bumhole being used even as his finger must have been going up. She didn't try to stop him though, and the smacks grew louder as he set to work on her bottom with all his force.

Her arm came away, I heard new, wet noises and I knew she was masturbating. Percy chuckled, her body went tense and she was there, babbling in French as her muscles went tight, begging to be smacked and kissed and fucked and fingered all at once as the shocks went through her, again and again, until at last her muscles began to go slowly slack.

I was still rubbing my pussy, holding myself just short of orgasm. There was a sticky sound as Percy's fingers left Marie-Armelle's body, and suddenly his hand was at my face. I gaped wide, and two slimy fingers were fed into my mouth. I sucked, eager for her taste as he began to spank me once more, hard, to set my bum bouncing and my boobs slapping on the seat again. Marie-Armelle cuddled me close, huge boobs squashed to my side, holding me as I sucked up the taste of her pussy and bumhole from Percy's fingers. I was rubbing frantically, right on the edge, as not Percy, but Marie-Armelle, beautiful, sweet, curvy little Marie-Armelle, stuck a finger firmly up my bottom.

I just screamed, my bumhole locking tight on her finger as I started to come, with Percy spanking away for all he was worth and my mouth agape on his dirty fingers. Two more fingers went up my pussy, Marie-Armelle pushing hard into me at exactly the right time. At that instant I wanted every hole filled, every square inch of my body stimulated, stroked or scratched or smacked, anything to add to the wonderful sensations as they brought me through my orgasm, with Percy planting smack after smack across my bottom and Marie-Armelle's fingers wriggling deep up my bumhole and pussy.

They kept going until I asked them to stop, my voice weak and faltering. My bottom was glowing with heat, my bumhole sore, my pussy aching, but I was well satisfied, and sorry only that we hadn't had more time and more space to play. It would come later though, I was sure. Marie-Armelle was too eager, too uninhibited to go coy on me.

I was all for going back to the hotel, but both of them agreed that we should return to the festival. After a bit of half-hearted argument I let them convince me, Marie-Armelle pointing out that it would look as if I'd run off in tears and lacked the courage to face Fauçon again if I didn't. So I cleaned up as best I could and went back, feeling distinctly uneasy, but determined to hold my own.

Fortunately Fauçon had gone, while most of the others were too drunk or otherwise engaged to pay me any attention. One or two among the pickers gave me hard looks, but most didn't even notice I'd come back, and as I sat down old man Moreau laughed and cracked a joke, at Fauçon's expense. Suddenly I was okay, and I gave him a big grin in return. His response was to wink and push a bottle of wine towards me, then give Percy a slap on the back and whisper into his ear, doubtless something obscene.

I was soon laughing and joking with the others, untroubled by what bad atmosphere there might have been. Cheeses had been put out on the table, and there were still plenty of grapes, so I began to nibble, and to drink steadily, until at last I reached the point when I knew I was going to regret it in the morning if I kept on. Some fresh air seemed like a good idea, so I excused myself. Percy was deep in conversation with old Moreau, and barely noticed. Marie-Armelle gave my bottom a pat.

The festival was beginning to break up, with people standing and chatting in twos and small groups and moving away long the road. I needed a moment of privacy, to pee, so quickly pushed across the road and up the side of the wall of the Clos St Aubin. The rows of vines ran up the hill, making each one an aisle of light, so I had to go halfway up, to where an old gate opened into the Clos before I could get any privacy.

I looked back, half expecting to find a gang of pickers following me. Nobody was there, giving me the familiar pangs of relief and disappointment. I still felt horny, and could have done with a good fucking, but the idea scared me too. Certain I was alone, I took my coat off and squatted down between the wall and a particularly luxurious Chenin vine. The dim light from the distant street lamps and the bonfire let me see what I was doing, but it was so muddy I didn't dare try and take my panties right off. I was urgent though, and just took them down to knee level and clutched them in my hand as I let go.

There was a wonderful sense of relief as the tension went and my pee splashed out in a glittering arc, the droplets shining orange and yellow in the light. It felt rude too, rude enough to set me giggling as I watched it squirt out onto the wet soil. There was plenty of it too, enough to have fun with, and I giggled again, imagining doing it in Marie-Armelle's pretty mouth, or over her glorious boobs.

A shadow fell over me. My heart jumped, only to still as I recognised Patrice's voice. Instinctively I tried to cut off my flow, but it only hurt. I couldn't stop.

'Natasha?'

'Patrice! You bastard!'

He laughed. I could do nothing, only stay in position as he watched my pee gush out of my pussy. It was seriously embarrassing, and I wishing I'd gone into the full shade and risked wetting my panties. I was a little scared too, after what I'd done to his grandfather, for all that a hundred people would hear me if I screamed. He was enjoying the view though, his face showing only amusement, with his eyes fixed to my pussy as he squeezed at his cock through his jeans. I gave him back a dirty look, but his grin only grew broader. As I was dabbing my pussy with a tissue from my bag he finally spoke.

'You want to fuck then?'

'You little . . . Oh, okay.'

I did want it, and a last fuck wasn't going to hurt. If he was on his usual form, it wouldn't take long either. He just stepped forward as he opened his fly, to stand right in the puddle I'd made as he stuck out his half-stiff cock. I was going to make a snappy remark about getting hard over watching girls pee, but choked it back and instead rocked forward to take his cock in my mouth.

He gave a happy moan and called me a slut as I began to suck. I put my arms behind him, to squeeze his hard, muscular bottom as his penis grew in my mouth. Soon it was going to be in me, and I slipped a hand under my body to get my pussy ready. I needn't have bothered. I was still wet from before, my pussy sloppy and open, my bum crease slimy with my own juice. I began to tease myself, wondering if he'd give me time to come while he was fucking me, or if he was going to want to put it up my bottom.

I'd quickly got him rock hard. He pulled my head from his cock, calling me a slut again and not to make him waste it in my mouth, even as he tried to push me back. I resisted, not wanting my dress ruined, as I'd have been on my back in a pool of mud and my own piddle. I rose instead, and was about to take hold of my ankles when I realised there was a better way.

The gate was perfect. His hands found my hips even as I took a firm grip on the bars. My dress was yanked up, to my waist, then higher, spilling my boobs out into the cool air. I stuck my bum out. He closed with me, his hands coming around me, to take one breast in each, teasing my nipples as he rubbed his crotch against my bottom. I could feel his erection, a hard rod in my bum crease, making me think of the way he'd used me up my bottom, and made me suck his dirty cock.

He was muttering, in French, calling me a slut and a whore and a dirty bitch. I didn't bother to contradict him, wishing only that he'd make the best of his insults and fuck me, bugger me even. He didn't bother, but went on rubbing, letting his cock slip lower as he grew more urgent, until his helmet pushed between, right on my anus.

I cried out as my ring pushed in, a completely pointless permission to bugger me, as I knew he'd have done it anyway. His cock had already slipped lower, to the mouth of my pussy and in. My eyes shut in ecstasy as my hole filled with big, firm cock, and then we were fucking, my body jerking with each push, to press forward, against the gate, my boobs squashing out between the bars. I just clung on, panting and gasping as he slammed into my body, harder and harder, until I was sure he would come up me at any second.

It was all I could do to hold onto the gate, never mind to frig myself, but I wanted to come, badly. I was mumbling brokenly and begging him to take his time as his hard, muscular belly slapped on my bottom, over and over, as if I was being spanked and fucked at the same time. It had driven me right to the edge, but I still needed that final touch to make it.

The first I knew of anyone else being there was when rough hands took hold of my boobs. I screamed, by eyes flew open, and I found myself looking through the bars at an ugly, grinning face, side-lit dull orange from the distant light of the bonfire. I tried to tug back even as I recognised one of the pickers, but Patrice hadn't stopped, and was jamming me into the gate harder than ever. The man had me firmly by the boobs too moulding them in his hands, then his mouth had found a nipple and he was sucking.

My pride and fear just dissolved. I was still calling him a bastard as his tongue began to lap at my nipple. He was going to have me, I knew it, make me suck his cock or fuck me. I could stop him, if I screamed my lungs out, but that was not what my body wanted. I could handle it, I knew, or more, just so long as they let me come.

Patrice grunted and I realised he'd come up me. Hot sperm spurted out onto my inner thighs and over my bumhole as he jammed himself back up, and he had finished. He pulled back, to leave my pussy gaping wide and running sperm. His orgasm had brought me as close as I could possible get to my own without my clitty being touched, to leave me dizzy, urgent, and far from resentful of the man at my chest.

I was going to frig, as he fondled my boobs, in front of him, in front of Patrice. He had them so tight they were bulging out through the bars of the gate, his hands trapping my blood, to make them fat and hard, my nipples fit to burst. I wanted that, and more, as I reached down for my pussy. He got rougher, pulling me hard against the gate by my boobs and biting at my nipples. I didn't care. I'd started to masturbate and there was only pleasure, the abandoned bliss of complete submission and the heady thrill of being touched by a stranger.

He laughed as he realised what I was doing, a harsh, grating sound. Patrice said I was a slut, even as the man in front of me started doing something new and wonderful to my boobs, twisting something around them, tight, to bring the pressure in them to a glorious, agonising peak as I started to come. I cried out, begging to be fucked, to be buggered, to be made to suck my tormentor's cock . . . and someone had taken my hands, pulling them away from my sex and onto cocks, big cocks, already swelling with blood.

Voices sounded, harsh, French; pleased, amused, insulting, demanding that I wank them . . . *c'est La Pêche! . . . . . branle, pouffiasse . . . oui, comme ça, salope*. I protested, telling them to fuck off, that there were too many of them, but I didn't mean it, and they knew it. They scared me, but I was too high on sex and my own submission to stop it, or even really try. Then I was begging to be allowed to come, but I was already doing as I'd been told, jerking at the two cocks and wishing I had more hands.

My panties were jerked down to my ankles. Someone took me by the hips, prodding a stiff cock between my cheeks. I tried to stick my bottom out properly, to let him get in, just by instinct, only to find I couldn't. I was trapped, my boobs stuck, and as I glanced down in surprise I saw them, fat, bloated orbs, tense with blood, deep red in the distant fire light, and not just roped, but roped together. My squeak of protest broke off in a grunt as a cock was pushed firmly up into my pussy.

I was grunting complaints as the man started to fuck me, truly frightened, and calling them all the names I could think of, in between begging for him to go faster, and deeper. Others moved in, shadows in the half darkness, around me and beyond the gate. The man at my chest grunted, and a moment later he was wiping his sperm over my straining titty skin. He moved, and the next instant was replaced, another man scrambling up onto the central bar of the gate, monkey like, to thrust his already hard cock at my mouth. I took it in, sucking, now penetrated front and back, with men readying their cocks all around me.

They were talking, boasting and arguing, over who was going to do what, and who was going first. No one asked me. I had no choice. I was bound, their helpless toy, to fuck and suck and wank as I was ordered. Fresh sperm erupted from the mouth of my pussy and the man in me had come, without me ever knowing who he was, or even seeing him. It didn't matter, I was just their fuck toy.

I was stripped, my dress jerked up over my head and thrown aside, my panties pulled off and left in the mud at my feet. One, rougher or bigger than the others, got behind me and a third cock was stuffed up my slippery hole. He growled something as he pushed in, complaining that I was too sloppy, that my cunt was full of sperm, as if it was my fault. It didn't stop him though, and an instant later my bottom was wobbling to his thrusts. Again I tried to get my hands to my pussy, but they wouldn't let me, two holding my wrists to force me to wank them.

The man inside me called me a slimy whore and pulled out, jamming his erection between my buttocks to rub in my crease, and come, spraying sperm up my back. Immediately he stepped back they came in closer, jostling for position, groping me, muttering coarse compliments and dirty words as they fondled my body, callused, hard fingers running over my skin and probing into the sloppy hole of my vagina. Someone touched my bumhole, my sperm-slick ring giving easily to his finger. I was going to be buggered, I was sure, and all I could do was make muffled noises on the cock stuck so deep in my throat I could barely breathe. Then the man came, and suddenly my throat was full of sperm and I couldn't breathe at all.

It came out, a great gout of it as I went into a coughing fit, then more, erupting from my nose, mixed with mucus. Most of it went over my breasts, a man who'd been groping them exclaiming in disgust as the mess caught his hand. Not that he cared too much, wiping it in my hair and across my face before replacing his friend on the gate, and soon I was sucking again.

The man's finger was still in my bumhole, deep, moving inside me to set me dancing on my toes and wiggling my bottom. They laughed at that, someone slapped my bottom, another called me a dirty bitch. The finger came out of my bumhole. I farted, more laughed, and a man's cock was being pressed to my sloppy, slimy anus. I forced myself to relax, to take him in, and up he went, grunting as his prick head popped my ring. Rough thumbs prised my cheeks open, showing off my buggered hole as he began to force himself up into my rectum.

I could barely breathe, the cock in my mouth pushing deep as more and more was jammed into my bottom. I struggled to pull back, straining my boobs against their binding. The man's cock came free of my mouth, jerked, and erupted sperm across my face and into my eye. I cried out, but only got another inch of penis stuffed into my rectum for my trouble. Another man climbed up to fill my mouth, and I was left wriggling on their cocks, my needs ignored as I was used.

Men were pressing in on all sides, demanding, urgent, each wanting his fill of my body. I could do nothing, dizzy with sex, half-blinded, my arms held, my boobs two aching balls of flesh, my bumhole straining to the thick cock shaft inside. My control was going, my senses slipping into a world of stretched flesh and eager cocks. I felt the man come up my bottom, his balls slapping my empty cunt as he did it in me. He pulled out, his spunk bubbling and farting from my anus the instant his cock head left the hole. A new cock slid up the same dirty hole, a big one, going in with a wet squelch. As he began to bugger me the man started to make weird hooting noises. It was René-Claude.

That René-Claude's cock was up my bum was my last rational thought before everything just dissolved in a welter of cocks and sperm and pain and ecstasy. He buggered me well. So did others. I was fucked again, over and over, and made to suck cock after cock. Man after man grunted his way to orgasm in one or another of my holes. My breasts were sucked sore, my bottom slapped red, my arms pulled and twisted onto cocks until both seemed to be on fire and my hands were too slimy with spunk and mud to grip the shafts I was being made to hold.

At some point the twine binding my boobs was cut, or just rubbed through on the bar. I went down, into the mud where I'd pissed, as my exhausted body slid off the cocks in my mouth and pussy. Another man was in my mouth immediately, a moment later I'd had my bumhole invaded once more, a big prick pushing deep until his balls met my empty, sperm-smeared cunt.

Never once was I allowed to get to my sex long enough to reach orgasm, and the point came when I couldn't have anyway. I'd collapsed, totally, but they held me up, keeping me kneeling. Not one licked me, or helped me with a well-placed cock head on my clit. They just used me, cock after cock thrust into my body, until I was close to fainting, the world spinning around me, the only reality the men, their erections and my body.

I never did faint. Slowly they became less urgent, and more rude as they took more time with me for their second orgasms. Cocks were stuck in my mouth that had been up my pussy or bumhole, the men laughing and clapping to see me sucking up my own mess. I was held by the hair to take it in my face, over both eyes, leaving me blind and soiled. I was beaten, thick belts taken to my bottom and legs and back.

Even when they'd finished, every one of them drained into or over my body, they still amused themselves with me. They had found my bag, and one rouged my cunt lips, nipples and anus. Another wrote something obscene across my buttocks, drawing a gale of laughter from the rest. Finally I was pissed on by René-Claude, the others cackling with mirth and yelling their encouragement as he sprayed his urine all over my bottom and back and in my hair, finishing up my cunt until the hot fluid was bubbling from the open hole.

That was it. I was left, kneeling in a puddle of mud and urine. Eventually I managed to open my eyes. I was plastered in spunk, my hair a filthy, matted mess, my face a mask of sticky white, my breasts coated, my tummy spattered, my pussy dripping, my bumhole oozing. Bits were hanging from my nose, my nipples, my pubic hair, my sex lips. It was coming out of my nose, in bubbles, and my mouth, the white froth running out over my lower lip to hang from my chin like an obscene beard.

There was mud too, my boobs and belly covered in filthy brown handprints where they'd groped me, my bottom too, my stockings filthy, bits caked into my hair. I couldn't stand anyway, and just collapsed into the muck beneath me, even as my fingers went back to my cunt.

I was barely aware of what I was doing as I started to masturbate. They saw, gasping in surprise, calling me more names. I didn't care. All that mattered was the feeling inside me, that I had to come, no matter what. As I came up towards orgasm they started to close in. Some still had their cocks hanging from their trousers. One was hard, and he stuck it in my mouth. I sucked. René-Claude mounted my bottom, to rut his balls and cock in my slimy crease, and as I started to come I was wishing he was hard, so that he could bugger me ... jam his cock up my sticky, slimy bumhole ... spunk in my gut ... fuck my bottom and then stick his dirty cock in my mouth ...

I screamed as I came, writhing and squirming myself in the mud, sucking on the cock in my mouth with demented urgency, wiggling my bottom on René-Claude's balls and penis, out of my mind with pleasure, utterly wanton, revelling in what they'd done to me, and wanting far, far more. The man in my mouth came, giving me a last mouthful of spunk right at the peak of my orgasm, and filling me with utter gratitude as I swallowed down the salty, slimy mess. As he pulled out I was still rubbing, but my orgasm had begun to fade.

When it finally finished the world was spinning around my head, a whirl of shadows and red-orange light, bits of leg and vine leaf and wall and soil. I must have passed out, and I think René-Claude came in my bottom crease while I was unconscious. In any case the next thing I remember is Patrice pulling him up and chiding him for what he'd done, which even at that moment seemed an absurd thing to say.

Someone pressed a bottle to my lips and I drank, swallowing down the cool, sweet wine and washing the foul tastes from my mouth until it was pulled away. I couldn't get up, and I was far too far gone to even care about being nude. My dress was gone anyway, my pretty black silk panties had been under me and were now nothing more than a filthy, mud smeared rag. I'd lost my suspender belt, and my stockings were ruined, foul with mud and badly torn. By some miracle one shoe had stayed on. The other was lying in the puddle, half full of mud.

The bonfire had begun to die down, leaving everything in gloom, with only dull orange highlights thrown up by the distant street lamp. Slowly my senses came back. I realised I could still hear voices from the festival, and wondered what had become of Percy, who had no idea were I was, let alone what had happened to me. he was going to be worried, but I simply couldn't face trying to get up.

I started to unbind my boobs instead, trying to pick open the tightly knotted twine with trembling fingers. The men had started to argue, their speech fast and aggressive, mostly in slang. I could barely understand, but I caught their meaning. They were arguing over what to do with me. Some wanted to just leave, saying I was soiled, others to take me somewhere.

One was particularly insistent, and seemed to seemed to have some authority, finally drowning out the others, who went quiet. He spoke to Patrice, urgently, and I caught enough to realise that he was saying I ought to be taken to Fauçon. Patrice's response was doubtful, but the answer came back more urgent than before, and aggressive. This time Patrice responded with a shrug and turned to me.

'He says you should be with my grandfather.'

The man repeated what he had said before, only to me. I barely caught the meaning, but I didn't need to. There was something in the way he said it, as if there was no possible question of me being in the right, or even of having the right to challenge his opinion. My anger was bubbling up on the instant, and I on the point of giving him my opinion of him, Fauçon and men in general, especially French ones, when I realised I was making a big mistake. I let out the breath I'd taken to start my little tantrum and hung my head.

'I'm sorry. You're right, of course.'

The man gave a satisfied grunt. Patrice nodded and leant down, to help me with the knots, which came open immediately under his fingers. I hissed in pain as the circulation came back into my boobs, and took hold of one in each hand, to massage them back to life. Someone laughed, and asked if I was going to masturbate again. I could find no answer.

Patrice helped me to my feet, but it was the other man who took me by the arm, not gently, and began to lead me through the vines, uphill. I trailed after him, my head still hung, the very picture of miserable repentance. The others followed, laughing and joking. Many had wine bottles, including Patrice, who let me drink from his. Others were less sympathetic, one using a piece of vine cutting as a goad across my bottom, others swapping obscene suggestions, such as leaving me for Fauçon bound and gagged with vegetables stuffed in my holes.

After that they began to swap worse suggestions, but I never realised some had run back down the hill, until they caught up again. We'd reached the top, by the Moreau's wood, which was in utter darkness, but they brought a lantern back, and something else, one of the spits, the carcass still on it, a mess of bones and grease and bloody meat. A quick question was put to the man they seemed to look up to. He just shrugged. They advanced on me, grinning.

I never once thought the spike was going up my arse, but I guessed I was going to be hung from the pole, and was immediately backing away, straight into the arms of Patrice. He held me tight, my legs kicking as the other came up, even as I babbled out my protests. Patrice just laughed and gave me some advice.

'They do not understand, Natasha, and they are only having a bit of fun. Lie down and make it easy on yourself.'

'A bit of fun! No ... Hey, come on, no ... this is going beyond a joke! *Non!* Stop! *Arrêtez* ... At least take the bloody carcass off, you bastards! *Retranchez la chèvre ... retranchez la* fucking *chèvre!*'

They took not the slightest bit of notice, just laughing together as they grabbed me, to holding on so that I couldn't possibly struggle free. I was pushed to the ground, my stockings peeled off, to leave me at last completely nude. My wrists were held, and lashed together, my ankles too, the nylon pulled tight enough to hurt. I was squeaking in pain and frustration as I was rolled onto my back in the mud, tied and ready. My knees were forced apart, held wide, and the spit was pushed through, the goat carcass rubbing on my sex and belly to leave a greasy smear. I cried out in disgust, and immediately had my filthy panties crammed into my mouth, filling my head with the taste of clay and piddle. For a moment I was struggling to spit them out, only to have them wadded tighter in with a dirty hand, making it even worse. I gave in, utterly, parting my arms quickly to avoid being spiked as the spit was pushed between. Then I was on, trussed and gagged and spitted, with still warm goat fat dripping down onto my boobs and belly as they took the strain.

I came up, my weight going onto the spit, which hurt like hell. A muffled scream forced its way from my throat, and someone among them must have had some decency, as a moment later strong arms were lifting me under my bottom and shoulders and the agony had begun to subside. I hung my head, a trickle of goat grease immediately running down my neck from where it had pooled between my breasts and into my hair, to drip down from the lank strands to the soil beneath.

They were making jokes as they carried me, about roasting me and how I'd taste, what sort of wine would go well with me, and what stuffing they should use. At the last one somebody pointed out that I'd already been stuffed, with spunk. He was right, and it was still oozing from both my pussy and my bumhole. Fauçon was going to see, and I didn't know if he'd laugh, or lose his temper, or just bugger me in it.

I was tied anyway, helpless for him, to do with as he pleased, to fuck or sodomise or beat. He'd said he loved me, in public. He'd called me a wayward angel, his peach, his glory, and more. I'd slapped his face for him, and now I was being delivered, on a spit, nude and filthy, ready basted in spunk and mud and his demented grandson's urine.

We'd got there, almost before we seemed to have started. There was a hurried conversation, Patrice wanting to untie me and let me wash, the others arguing that I was better the way I was. He gave in quickly enough, and went to the door, but before he could turn his key in the lock the light came on in the kitchen. A moment later the door swung open, to reveal the massive form of Madame Vaucopin outlined against the light.

I could see her face, harsh, angry, totally unsympathetic, to them, and to me. They held their ground, the man demanding that she fetch Fauçon. She ignored him, and looked down at me. I managed a pleading look. She spat, full in my face and snapped out a sentence.

'*Qu'est-ce que tu fais ici, salope . . . morue?*'

'*Je suis pour le maître, Madame.*'

Her answer was a snort of contempt, then a nod. The men put me down, not gently, and I rolled over as I landed, onto my side, half on top of the goat carcass. I must have looked truly appalling, with my entire body filthy with mud and sperm and piddle and goat fat. Madame Vaucopin was looking down on me, her big red hands on her hips, to stare for a moment in utter disgust before she stamped back into the house muttering to herself, about the state I was, as if it was my fault.

I waited, the muck dribbling slowly down my body, only for her to come back in moments, not with Fauçon, but with a bucket and a big, bristly scrubbing brush. I tried to spit my filthy panties out to protest and got the full contents of the bucket in my face for my trouble. It was freezing cold, and soapy, leaving me with my eyes tight shut and stinging, gasping for breath through my nose, too distressed to realise that all of them had gone quiet.

At last it sank in. I risked opening my eyes and looked up. Fauçon was there, standing straight and still in the doorway, his lean body covered by a silk robe. He was looking right at me, emotions flickering across his lined and sun-browned face. Fresh fear filled me, my stomach fluttering and a spurt of urine escaping my sex, to trickle down across one soiled buttock and onto the ground. He was sure to beat me, he had to, in public, maybe in front of them all, reducing me to snivelling, miserable tears as they laughed at jeered and my pathetic protests and useless struggles. He spoke.

'*C'est juste. C'est la terre.*'

He let his robe fall open. Underneath he was naked, his cock hanging down, flaccid but stirring. He took hold of it, tugging, left handed. His right hand came out, palm up. There was a murmur of approval. The man stepped forward, already tugging a thick leather belt from his trousers. Fauçon took it, hefting it in his hand as I began to squirm, and to chew on my filthy panties in fear and in abject, grovelling submission.

The belt came up, and down, hard across my naked buttocks, to spatter out mud and sperm as I screamed wordlessly into my gag. Again the men murmured their approval, as the pain of my welt settled to a raw sting. Again Fauçon struck, harder, to make my body jerk on the spit and fresh urine to burst from my peehole. His face was set, hard, merciless, but he was still wanking, tugging at his cock as he beat me, and he was growing erect.

Once more the belt lashed down. Once more I jerked and once more piddle sprayed from my sex. His teeth set into a mad grin as he gave me my fourth, and fifth, and sixth, lashing the belt down on my squirming buttocks as I bucked and writhed on the ground at his feet. At the cuts rose to a frantic lashing I lost control completely, wriggling and kicking my knees against the goat carcass, grunting and gulping on my mud-soiled panties, farting repeatedly, piss bursting out from my aching cunt as my bottom flesh distorted to every blow.

Nobody stopped it. Not one even spoke up for me. They left me writhing in my own urine, just calmly watching as he thrashed me, until my whole bottom was a burning mess of red-hot welts, my legs and hip too. When he did finally stop it was only because his cock was hard, ready for my body. I was broken, sobbing and gulping on my gag, the tears streaming down my face, gone beyond any thought of resistance as he sank down to press the fat helmet of his erection to my filthy cunt.

I was still pissing, hot urine dribbling down my buttock, but he didn't seem to care, pushing up me with one long, hard shove. A new mutter of approval ran through the men as Fauçon began to fuck me. Every one was watching, eyes riveted to my filthy, beaten body as I was fucked, fucked as they'd left me, strapped to the spit with my belly and boobs squashing out on the bloody goat skeleton with every push. He was going to finish in me too. He had to, for his own pride, to show what a big man he was, fucking a bound and helpless girl on the ground, after belting her until she cried.

It got faster, his belly slapping on my hot bottom, my juice squelching in my over-lubricated cunt hole, my boobs and belly squashing and sliding against the goat's bones in a mess of sweat and sperm and grease. I thought I was going to faint again, or choke on my filthy panties, but then he'd come, whipping his cock out at the last second to show them he'd done it as he sprayed hot sperm across my bottom and leg.

I lay still, exhausted, utterly broken. The man stepped forward, pulling something from his pocket. It was a flick knife, the edge glittering in the light as he snapped out the blade, to send a shock of raw fear through me before he casually cut the twine binding me to the stake with two quick motions. I rolled over onto my back, into the little puddle I'd made on the ground, unable to rise, barely able to find the strength to pull my panty gag from my mouth.

Fauçon snapped out an order. I barely heard, but a moment later I was deluged with freezing water as Madame Vaucopin emptied a bucket over my head. She threw a scrubbing brush to me, and a bar of hard, green soap, telling me to clean up. Forcing myself to move up onto one elbow, I picked them up and began to scrub at my filthy body as she went back to the outside tap for more water. Nobody said a word, just watching me scrub down, even Madame Vaucopin.

By the time I had finished I was shivering, my skin bright pink save for the scarlet and crimson of my welts, and covered in goose bumps. The cold had brought me round though, and finally I managed to pull myself up to stand, unsteadily, one leg shaking uncontrollably as I finished my ablutions.

One person came forward, to my amazement, René-Claude, stepping from among the others as I rinsed out my hair. He had my coat, my dress, my bag, my shoes. He held them out, grinning as he offered them to me. It was impossible not to smile, in truly pathetic gratitude at the act of kindness. I didn't take them though. I was nude, as I should be nude.

Fauçon was standing near the door, still naked, his arms folded across his chest. I walked forward, my head hung down. As I reached him I went to my knees, down before him in open submission, to press my lips to his foot.

Ten

I woke with a start. It was pitch black, and deathly quiet, but my heart was hammering, my adrenaline pumping. I had to do it.

Fauçon was asleep, and would be for hours. He had had me once more, up my bottom, before passing out in a drunken stupor. My welts hurt, and so did just about every other square inch of my body, protesting as I forced myself to stretch, and my hands were shaking as I gently pulled the bed covers from my body. The gentle pad of my feet as I crossed the room sounded horribly loud. I found my dress, my coat, my shoes, and pulled each on in turn. My bag was to one side, and the contents had spilt out, leaving me cursing under my breath as I gathered them up. Fauçon's door creaked as I pulled it wide, and I was on the landing.

The shoes were a mistake. They came off. I made for the stairs and up, each creak sending my heart into my mouth. The studio door came open to my push, revealing the big window as a rectangle deepest grey on black. There was no hint of dawn.

I closed the door and flicked on the light. For one precious moment I stood blinking in the glare, and I had began to search. As I pulled up a huge canvas I revealed a beautiful sketch of Marie-Armelle, naked and pensive as she toyed with her hair. I had to have it, and quickly pulled it out.

Now there was no excuse. I took another, a work in oil of two men working a vineyard in the dawn light. My third was another oil, larger, an exquisitely executed portrait of Madame Vaucopin. To take it was the least she deserved.

I dug deeper, near to panic but determined to find Helene. Again and again I pulled up canvasses, discovering works of every type, and every one worth having. Only at the wall did I find what I wanted, Helene d'Issigeac, naked and beautiful as she leant on a window ledge to look out over Paris.

Even as I pulled it carefully free I realised that there was more. One edge had caught under another painting, and I could see Fauçon's signature and the date – nineteen fifty-four. It was big, and what I could see showed water. I put the other down and tilted it forward, and there, full length, her neat skirt rucked high and her knickers pulled aside, was Helene, pissing into the Seine.

I had to take it. It was risky, but I had to. Fauçon never paid attention to his old work, ever. If he knew where it was, if he cared, surely he would have shown me? No, he wouldn't because it would have given the lie to his romantic tale . . .

For a moment I paused, holding the painting, my fear warring with my greed. Greed won, and I was telling myself I could pretend he'd promised it to make up for what he'd done to me, and that I'd been determined to take it before he changed his mind. It was a thin story, but there was a lot of money at stake.

If I had one, I needed the other, and there it was, against the wall, a picture of a naked Helene squatting on a chamberpot, a picture at once so like me and so utterly intrusive that it had me blushing to look. I'd expected detail, I'd expecting it to be calculated to outrage. I'd expected every detail of her anus to be showing, and perhaps what she'd done in the pot. What I hadn't expected was for him to show the little pink ring stretched wide as she squeezed out a large, glossy turd. I took it anyway.

That was six, all I could possibly carry. When I finally managed to pick them up, I wasn't sure even of that. I did it though, agonisingly slowly, in utter blackness, inching my way down the stairs and to the back door, three trips, then returning to tidy up as the paintings rested in an outhouse. By the time I was satisfied the sky outside had turned to a leaden grey.

I was running out of time. There was maybe half-an-hour to get to the Moreaus', then I had to blackmail Alain over his little adulteration scam, get the paintings hidden, and so back, into Fauçon's bed before he, or Madame Vaucopin, awoke.

It was an insane plan. The soil in the vineyards was like glue, I was freezing in my dress and my arms were in agony before I'd got fifty yards. It was getting light too, leaving me in full view of the house, and the road. I staggered on, holding the paintings above my head and wishing I'd worn something more sensible. Twice I slipped, smearing my coat and legs with mud, before I was even halfway down the field.

Finally I made it, panting and running sweat, but still cold. There was no sign of life, and at the thought of blackmailing Alain Moreau my courage failed me completely. I couldn't do it, not possibly. It was easy to imagine it, but a very different thing to wake him up first thing in the morning and demand that he conceal stolen goods for me. I could no more do it than fly.

There was another option though. I still had Percy's car keys in my bag. That was better, far better. He was used to my tantrums. I could explain what had happened with the pickers, and even about Fauçon. He'd believe that I'd been upset in the morning, that I'd wanted to go for a drive. He probably wouldn't even expect to cane me, especially when so far as I knew he'd spent the night with Marie-Armelle.

To think was to act, and I had the boot open on the instant. The four small paintings went in, but the others wouldn't fit, or go through the door. I had to get them out of their support frames, and fast. Fortunately Percy's picnic basket was in the back. There was a sharp knife, and I spent a frantic few minutes carving the two canvasses free, in the full view of the house, all the while growing closer and closer to blind panic.

I made it, and jumped on the frames to break them. The whole lot went in the back, and as I slammed the boot shut I finally began to believe I was going to make it. Still nobody stirred as I started the engine, every window in the house a blank face of white shutters, one French habit I was very, very grateful for.

Real triumph welled up inside me as I let the clutch in, and I was gone.

It had to work. Even if the theft was discovered I could claim Fauçon had given the paintings to me, and now I was sure to be believed. I had witnesses, Percy, the Moreaus, any number of others. They had all seen his impassioned plea at the festival, and he'd been so drunk he wouldn't even be able to remember what he'd said or hadn't said. Then there was what he'd done to me, beating me and fucking me on the ground as I lay strapped to a greasy goat's skeleton. Surely that was an excuse for remorse, even from him? I didn't have to worry about Madame Vaucopin either. From what she'd said, demanding valuable pictures in return for a few hours' work was just the sort of behaviour she expect of me. Not that the theft was likely to be discovered, and then all I had to do was wait for Fauçon to drink himself to death.

For now, all I had to do was get to Angers and a large, anonymous post-office. I could cut the remaining paintings out of their frames, and simply send them home in nice thick cardboard tubes. I'd be back by eleven o'clock, maybe earlier. If I wanted I could go back to Fauçon's and say I'd taken an early morning stroll. He'd probably beat me again, which just seem funny. I laughed out loud, at the way he thought he had broken me, at how pleased with himself he'd been about it, at how he would react if he only knew . . .

I'd reached Challonnes, and I put my foot down as I came out onto the bridge, touching eighty on the long straight road beyond. One car flashed me, then another, and I slowed, expecting a speed trap, only to open her up again on the N23.

I was high on adrenaline, singing to myself as I floored the accelerator. The car may have been ancient, but there was still a lot of power, three and a half litres worth. I was laughing as the needle reached the one hundred mark and crept past. I was free, away, my only risk an over zealous policeman. I took my foot off the pedal, glancing in the mirror in a sudden fit of guilt, which was when I realised that there was black smoke pouring out of the back of the car, and flame.

At the same instant the oil light came on. I slammed my foot on the brake. The tyres screamed. There was an appalling bang. Something metal appeared through the bonnet and it was me who was screaming. For one long, horrible moment the car was still moving, with smoke and steam erupting out from around the bonnet, and we had stopped, sideways across the gravel verge.

There were little flames coming out around the dashboard, and I just hurled myself out of the car and ran. I didn't even glance back, not until I was half-way across a field. By then the car was burning well, with a column of black smoke rising above it. All I could do was stare, until the petrol tank went up with a roar, taking my precious paintings with it.

I sank down, heedless of the thick mud I was kneeling in, my jaw dropping as I watched the wreck burn.